I0563241

A Deadly Craft

by

Sydney Abrams

An Arts and Crafts Mystery

Copyright Notice

This is a work of fiction. Names, characters, places, and incidents are either the product of the author's imagination or are used fictitiously, and any resemblance to actual persons living or dead, business establishments, events, or locales, is entirely coincidental.

A Deadly Craft

COPYRIGHT © 2024 by Sydney Abrams

All rights reserved. No part of this book may be used or reproduced in any manner whatsoever including the purpose of training artificial intelligence technologies in accordance with Article 4(3) of the Digital Single Market Directive 2019/790, The Wild Rose Press expressly reserves this work from the text and data mining exception. Only brief quotations embodied in critical articles or reviews may be allowed.

Contact Information: info@thewildrosepress.com

Cover Art by *Tina Lynn Stout*

The Wild Rose Press, Inc.
PO Box 708
Adams Basin, NY 14410-0708
Visit us at www.thewildrosepress.com

Publishing History
First Edition, 2025
Trade Paperback ISBN 978-1-5092-6030-0
Digital ISBN 978-1-5092-6031-7

An Arts and Crafts Mystery
Published in the United States of America

Dedication

This series would not have been possible without my partners in crime—the friends, family, and my art group, who propelled me into this journey. In particular, I thank my husband, whose wit, good humor, and support make me believe I can keep doing this. I continue to extend my gratitude to Bryn Donovan, whose editing and coaching skills evolved into a crash course in writing, and to Eilidh MacKenzie, my incredible editor at The Wild Rose Press, who has furthered my education and is, at the same time, a joy to work with.

Flat Rock Falls is a fictional town, and The Creative Workshop and all the characters in this book are derived from my overactive imagination. Any mistakes with procedures or techniques are mine, and mine alone.

Chapter 1

Thursday Morning

I looked at my watch and blew out a soft sigh of exasperation. After an hour listening to Clive go on and on, I felt myself losing the will to live. I had slumped down in my chair to the extent my next step would be lying on the floor, so I slid back upright and looked around to see how the others were faring. I could only see the backs of most people's heads as they discreetly looked at their phones or stared, unseeing, at the floor, but I could feel the quiet desperation in the room.

Okay, maybe I was exaggerating the situation to be more dire than it actually was. It was just a meeting, and eventually, it would be over. My eyes drifted up to the ceiling, and I distracted myself by taking a moment to appreciate the crown molding and tall windows that lent grandeur to the Bennet House mansion, now an event venue within the grounds of Bennet Park. I was pulled out of my reverie when I recognized a shift in the drone coming from Clive, indicating we might be wrapping this up.

"So, to recap," Clive said, with an inflated self-importance, "as the Bennet House manager, I ask you to read through your welcome packets carefully and strictly adhere to all of the guidelines I've outlined today. Our beloved Bennet Library appreciates that their newly opened children's wing will be the beneficiary of this annual Flat Rock Falls fundraiser, and your compliance will ensure we have another successful Winter Arts and Crafts Festival." He paused during the half-hearted applause, then begrudgingly added, "And we must extend our thanks to Alex, and the Creative Workshop, for helping facilitate the festival this year."

With a slight nod and a smile, I acknowledged those who had turned to look at me.

Clive looked up from his notes, preparing to pontificate further, but when his beady black eyes took in the distinct lack of attention in the room, he finished with a lackluster "Thank you. You're dismissed."

His bluster transitioned to fluster as he shuffled his notes together before quickly and awkwardly departing from the podium. Penny, his tireless secretary, hustled over to his side. I wanted to make a quick exit, so I grabbed my coat, gloves, and hat and made my way toward the front entry of the mansion.

The massive oak front door stood open, and the glistening white snow and fresh air breathed life into the group. I weaved my way around the lobby and found Ryan and Maggie, my two part-time staffers, chatting with some of the Workshop artists. There was a welcome feeling of camaraderie and excitement about the approaching festival until Clive entered the lobby and pulled Ryan aside. Knowing these two were like oil and water, I kept my eye on the situation, and when Ryan put his hands on his hips in a defiant manner, I had no choice but to approach.

"Everything okay here?" I asked.

"I'm trying to explain to Ryan that I need a

detailed schedule for when he and Elliott will be moving the ice sculptures," Clive said tersely.

Ryan was a sculptor by trade, and his youthful exuberance was great, but he hadn't quite gotten the hang of conflict resolution.

"I don't see why it matters," he said, sounding like a truculent teenager.

In an attempt to juggle these two personalities, I said, "Clive, like me, prefers to work in a methodical fashion, so let's sort this out together. How much time do you and Elliott need to load in?"

"Three hours should do it," Ryan answered.

"Okay, Clive, with that in mind, what time would you prefer them to do the work?"

"Early morning. I want the pathway clear as soon as possible."

"Can you guys get here early tomorrow?" I asked Ryan.

"Sure."

"Okay. Everybody happy?" They both reluctantly nodded. "Perfect."

After Clive walked away, I said to Ryan, "That wasn't so hard, was it?"

"No. He just really bugs me."

"Look, you're going to encounter difficult personalities throughout your life, so you might as well learn how to handle them. Don't dig in and fight back. Just figure out how you can both get what you want."

He grinned at me and said, "Right, that's clever."

We returned to the group, and looping my scarf around my neck, I said, "I'm heading back to the Workshop. Anyone coming now?"

After a round of discussion, a handful of us made

our way down the front steps to the walking path. Maggie, Spencer, JJ, and Bitsy took the lead, and I could hear the excitement in their voices as they discussed the upcoming festival, with the cold air creating swirls of vapor as they talked. Annie and I followed a few feet behind, and we commiserated about the colossal waste of time we had just endured and our lengthy to-do list before the festival's opening. These were my closest friends here in Flat Rock Falls.

A little over three years ago, I left my frenetic career as a political strategist and resettled here to start a new chapter. I purchased and renovated an old brick school building, and six months later the Creative Workshop, a collective for artists, opened its doors. We now had over a dozen artists who rented studio space, and we'd become a community center for classes in every art and craft imaginable.

Some might think this was a haphazard transition, but I had grown up immersed in the arts and I minored in art history in college, so to me, although a totally different lifestyle, it felt like I had come home.

Our small, quaint town, surrounded by an abundance of natural beauty, was a magnet for creative people. But I also had family here. My aunt Claudia owned the Main Street Café, and my cousin, Jack, was the top cop in our little hamlet. He also happened to be married to Annie.

Winter was my second favorite season, after fall, and I happily breathed in the crisp cold air as the snow crunched under our feet. The sky was a brilliant blue, with just a few high cotton-ball clouds, and the ice on the pond sparkled in the sunshine. This weather made me feel alive, but I couldn't say everyone else felt the same way.

"Geez, it's cold!" said Annie, her voice muffled behind the scarf she had pulled up above her nose. "It's beautiful, but dang, it must still be in the twenties!" She was bundled up in a big white puffy coat, quilted winter boots, and a matching hat with faux-fur earflaps. Only her bright blue eyes and wisps of blonde hair were visible.

I laughed. "I know! Isn't it great?"

A few minutes later, we arrived at the Workshop. We stomped our feet to dislodge the packed snow, then climbed the steps to enter the building, where the warmth of the lobby enveloped us like a blanket as we unfurled scarves and removed coats, hats, and gloves. I went around the front desk to dump my stuff in the office while the others dispersed to their art studios.

I had a little time before the next meeting to go over our end of the festival, so I jogged up the wide central staircase and went down a short hall to my private apartment. As soon as I opened the door, Baxter, the Bernese mountain dog mix I adopted last fall, thunked down from the leather sofa to the floor, his collar jingling as he shook himself out before bounding over to greet me.

"Hey, buddy, how's my big boy?" I cooed.

He responded with a head nudge to my hip and a rapid tail wag.

We ambled to the kitchen, and once I punched the programmed button for a cup of coffee, I took the lid off the jar decorated with paw prints and handed Baxter a treat. He promptly took it to the well-worn Persian rug in front of the couch to crunch, scatter, and snarf. After grabbing a treat from the people cookie jar, I joined Baxter—in the living room, that is, not to snarf it off the floor—and told him about my morning. I then suggested we might go for a walk later, and he hung on my every word as I discussed our route options. When his big, scruffy face nudged my hand for a pet, I wondered how I had possibly lived without him.

A little bit later I walked into the lounge, where most of the gang had already assembled. Maggie, a professional photographer and my assistant manager, was sitting with Ryan, and they were mock-bickering like siblings. Ryan had stretched out and tipped the chair back with his hands clasped behind his head. He then brought the front legs back to the floor with a clunk and laughed when Maggie thwacked him in the ribs. Yes, I often felt like their den mother.

Ethan and Hannah, professional potters, leaned toward each other, quietly talking. Bitsy let out a joyous laugh with JJ and Annie, as Spencer relayed a story from his early days as a painter, his face full of expression. And Shelby, our crafts leader, was talking with Ari, one of younger painters.

"Alex," Maggie called out, "Lena just texted. She's on her way."

"Okay, but let's go ahead and get started," I said, "and don't worry, I'll keep it short!"

While the Bennet House hosted the festival, the Workshop helped with planning and logistics. It would be an arts and crafts bonanza, where people could buy anything from handmade soaps to high-end paintings, and this year, Lena would be in charge of the book sale table and a reading circle for the kids.

As everyone shuffled their chairs, I dove right in. "Let's start with ticket sales. Maggie? How's it shaping up?"

"We've already surpassed last year's final numbers! I bet it's because this year the festival is falling over Valentine's Day—"

"I'm here!" Lena bustled into the room with much fanfare. "Sorry! I had to go over a few things with Clive, and the clock kept ticking! You know how he is." Her cheeks were rosy from the cold, and the pom-pom on top of her white knit hat bobbed with each step.

Lena was our liaison with the Bennet House library. She joined the staff in January as the author in residence and director of the newly opened children's wing. Lena's personality and laugh could light up a room, and she was totally unaware people were drawn to her like bees to honey.

She hastily tossed her coat on one of the couches, where it promptly slid to the floor, and plopped herself down in a chair. In her haste to get settled, she knocked over her coffee and then rooted around in her backpack to find some tissues to sop it up. She eventually got herself settled, sat back, and looked happily around the group. "Sorry, please continue. Where are we?"

I stifled a laugh before saying, "We're just getting to the load in."

We quickly ironed out the final bits on our end, and I finished with, "As most of you know, with out-of-town artists here, we often meet in the lounge at the Thunderbird Lodge at the end of the day, so please reach out to the newcomers to make them feel welcome."

Lena, being new to Flat Rock, said, "Oooo, sounds great. I generally like to hermit in the winter, but I'm getting a little tired of my own company!"

****

Friday

The next morning was clear and cold, and the walk to Bennet Park was invigorating. I rounded the corner to the pathway around the pond and saw Ryan and Elliott placing an ice sculpture, so I stood to the side until they were done. Elliott was manning the pallet lifter as Ryan guided him like an aircraft marshaller. The sculpture of an owl spreading its wings had been positioned on a three-foot-tall pedestal, at a viewable height for both adults and kids.

Elliott was a gentle giant, his shy manner an unexpected contrast to his burly size. He towered over me and already had a rough five o'clock shadow this morning, but his dark eyes were warm and friendly. He had shoved his sleeves, both coat and shirt, up on his muscular forearms, which were blanketed in dark hair, and his forehead had a light sheen of sweat from the effort of maneuvering the heavy sculpture into place.

"Take a look!" Ryan said enthusiastically. Standing next to Elliott, he looked like a gangly teenager who had not yet grown into his lanky frame. "Pretty awesome, aren't they?"

"Just remarkable," I said, reaching out to stroke the wing of the owl.

"We have two more to unload, then we'll be moving inside," Elliott said.

We ambled down the path to inspect the other sculptures. There was an adorable penguin with a hockey stick, a duck with ducklings, a figure of an ice skater, and an intricately carved rendering of the Bennet House mansion.

"They're beautiful, Elliott," I said in awe.

"Thanks," he replied shyly.

"He's the best," Ryan said, then shifted back into action. "Okay, let's get these last ones placed before Clive comes out here and yells at me again. I tell ya, Alex, my patience is wearing thin with him."

"Wait, what happened now? I thought everything was fine between you two."

"He was out here bright and early barking orders. 'Don't step off the path. Don't leave the truck idling. Don't mark up the floors inside. Don't put anything there.' It was like being with a drill sergeant."

I pinched the bridge of my nose to stave off the headache I felt coming on. "Okay, clearly what I suggested to you yesterday didn't sink in, so let me explain things another way. The Bennet House is his baby, and essentially, we are guests here. Therefore, we must be patient and address his requests with professionalism."

"Well, all I can say is he's skating on thin ice. He really shouldn't talk to us like that."

Ryan was normally an affable guy, and I was surprised by his reaction. "Did you say anything to alleviate his concerns or did you just argue with him?"

"Elliott handled it," he snapped.

Elliott said, "I told him we would move any of the sculptures inside on moving blankets to protect the floors, and they would be set on pieces of felt so there would be no risk of scratching the marble. And we would make sure everything was placed where no one could trip over them."

Ryan interjected, "See? What a no-brainer. Of course we would be careful."

I said, "It's a no-brainer to you, but not to Clive.

He's not asking for anything unreasonable, it's the *way* he's asking that's problematic. Do you know how much it would cost to replace or repair the marble floor? And there are liability issues if someone trips. These are things you have to worry about when you're in charge."

"I hadn't thought about that."

Elliott clapped him on the shoulder and said, "And like I told you, he's not worth getting worked up over. C'mon. Let's get these finished up."

I watched them work for a few more minutes, then continued on the path to the front steps of the mansion. From the lobby, voices came from all directions, and people were crisscrossing from one side of the main hall to the other.

I went to the right and found Annie, Spencer, Hannah, and Ethan setting up in the drawing room. The tall windows let in an abundance of natural light, and the cream silk damask draperies and intricate plaster ceiling medallion surrounding the drop chandelier let you know this had been a grand room in its day. Annie's detailed photorealism paintings and Spencer's meticulous trompe l'oeil and florals flanked the tables full of Ethan and Hannah's pottery. It created a colorful feast for the eyes.

Spencer and Annie were teasing each other across the room. Like Elliott, Spencer was proof you can't judge a book by its cover. He looked more like a rugby player than a painter who did incredibly detailed and delicate work. I opened my arms to give them both a wave as I approached the pottery display in the center of the room.

Ethan and Hannah used acrylic boxes of varying heights on their tables to create dimension, and to highlight some of their more unique vases and decorative bowls. I couldn't help myself from running my hands around the smooth contours of one of the large bowls glazed in a deep green and brown, with delicate etching in the clay.

Hannah stood up from where she had been unwrapping pieces from a box. "Hi Alex, how's it going?"

"Great! And speaking of great, your pieces are simply beautiful."

"Thank you," she said, modestly.

Hannah and Ethan were a perfect match. They were both calm, cool, and collected. Hannah had a healthy, athletic look, and a fresh clean complexion as if she spent a lot of time outdoors. Ethan, by contrast, had dark hair curling around his ears, black framed glasses, and a thin face and frame. What they had in common was their calm disposition. Everything was carefully thought out and executed according to plan. Slow and methodical, staying on task until each thing was done.

I sometimes found myself wishing I could be more like them, but the truth was, the limited range of emotion and motion would probably drive me nuts, and I'd explode. So, in the end, I was content with who I was. And frankly, life would be incredibly dull if we were all the same.

I was considering having them put my name on the bowl to mark it as sold and asked, "How much is this going for?"

Ethan circled around the table to stand next to me. "Hmm, I think we'll be marking it at three fifty. It's high because of the time involved."

"That's understandable. I can tell how much work went into it. I'll have a think on it." It would be perfect on my coffee table, unless Baxter knocked it off.

I then crossed the lobby to the parlor, which was decorated in a soft blush-pink wallpaper, with cream-colored drapery, and an ornate creamy white fireplace mantel. The color scheme provided a soothing backdrop for Ari's still life paintings, and the glass Twila and Hank had brought from Allegheny Glassworks. They had just driven in from a town a couple hours away, and I couldn't wait to see them.

I waved to Ari and went straight over to Twila and Hank's side of the room. Twila's flaming red hair perfectly matched her boisterous personality and defied her march into her mid-sixties. She was big-boned and tall but moved with ease and grace, and she knew how to pick colors best suited for her complexion. Today she wore a flowing periwinkle blue top over jeans and a pair of blue canvas slip-ons.

She opened her arms wide and said, "You come on over here and give me a hug!"

I obliged, then stood back and smiled. "It's so good to see you. How've you guys been?"

"Good, good. Hank...where is he? He was just here. Oh well, I'm sure he'll be right back. Anyway, Hank's been playing around with some new techniques, and we've brought a few samples of them. Otherwise, we're just keeping busy with our usual glass work. It's been a good year."

Hank sauntered in, and his face broke into a wide smile. He was a big guy, and his personality matched Twila's. He was wearing jeans with bright green suspenders over a plaid button-down shirt. "Well, look at you, little bird! Adorable as always," he said, coming toward me for a bear hug.

Hank's hug lifted me a foot off the floor, and when he put me back down, I said, "Twila's been telling me you're working on some new stuff. I can't wait to see it."

"If you have a minute, I'll show you." He went over to the boxes yet to be unpacked, and pulled out a beautiful abstract glass piece with three smooth flowing lines, almost like leaves, wrapped around a perfect sphere, with a swirl of colors inside it. I felt like I could lose myself in the deep hues.

"Wow, Hank. This is incredible. I love it. You must have so much fun experimenting with new things. Clearly, you have the golden touch."

"Thanks, Alex, you are always so sweet to us."

I was reluctant to leave their company, but I wanted to introduce myself to Declan and Preston. "I need to go find the guys from Wild Mountain Woodcarvers. Have you met them yet?" I asked.

They both shook their heads, and Twila said, "No, not yet. I saw a couple of guys I didn't recognize going back and forth to the next room. That's probably them."

"Okay, I'm off. See you guys later!"

I went down the hall to what had been the library of the mansion. It was softly lit, with floor to ceiling bookshelves, rich dark wood paneling, a coffered ceiling, and french doors leading out to a small patio. Maggie was struggling to put one of her large-format photographs on an easel, so I quick-stepped over to grab one end of the frame.

"Oh, thank you. Perfect timing!" Maggie breathed out in relief. Today, her plum-colored hair had a streak of blue framing the left side of her face, and her multi-colored glasses pulled the whole look together.

"Sure! No problem," I said, turning to look at some of the pieces she brought for the festival. Her display of landscape photography was stunning, but I was glad to see she had also included a few examples of her artistic portraiture. Good photographers could create an entire narrative with a single shot.

While Maggie and I chatted, two men entered the library talking to each other in hushed tones. One was quite tall, with warm, brown eyes and a ball cap covering his sandy close-cropped hair. The other was of average height and stocky, with a trendy, shaggy hair style and chunky black glasses in front of hooded, but piercing gray-blue eyes. They reached their destination at the tables with the Wild Mountain Woodcarvers sign. My incredible powers of deduction told me this must be Declan and Preston.

I went over to them and held out my hand. "Hello, I'm Alex Montgomery, from the Creative Workshop."

The tall one responded first. "I'm Preston. Nice to meet you."

"And I'm Declan," the other said, extending his hand in a business-like handshake.

"I'm so glad you're joining us this year."

Preston had an open and affable face, and he gave me a breezy smile as he said, "Us, too. What an awesome venue, and I don't know who thought to put us in this room with all the woodwork, but it was a brilliant idea."

"Thank you. We all worked on the layout."

Declan had become absorbed with something on his phone, softly whistling a tune I couldn't quite decipher. Preston was darting glances his way, but Declan clearly wasn't inclined to participate in any further social niceties. That was fine with me. My duty was done, and I had the second floor to scope out.

"Well, I'll leave you to it," I said.

"Thank you, Alex," Preston said, elbowing Declan to get his attention.

"Uh, yeah…oh, I'm so sorry to be rude. I'm juggling some emails." He put his phone down and turned his full attention back to me. "We're both looking forward to opening day tomorrow," he said, with a sudden expansive grin.

As I left the room, I made a mental note to swing by later to meet Oscar from O&C Lamps, who had not yet arrived, and then I made my ascent to the second floor via the grand staircase. The upstairs artists were setting up later, and after checking the craft rooms, the lounge, and the sale tables on the landing, it appeared everything was ready for their arrival.

After making my rounds, I stopped in the office at the back of the mansion. Penny was sitting at her desk outside of Clive's office. She always looked tidy, with a work wardrobe of modest skirt suits, low-heeled pumps, and blouses buttoned just below her neck.

If I were to guess, I'd say Penny was in her fifties, and if you didn't know her, prim-with-a-powdered-nose would come to mind. But she had a good sense of humor under her uber professionalism, and she easily handled Clive's personality, which made her the perfect secretary for him. Sadly, he didn't realize this place would fall apart without her.

"How's it going, Penny?" I asked.

"Fine," she responded, looking over her shoulder to

see if Clive was in earshot. "I'm just knee-deep in work. His lordship is in a full snit this morning, so I'm trying to put out fires before he has a chance to throw gasoline on them, if you know what I mean."

"Sheesh. What else is he being cranky about today?"

"Oh, you know, the usual. But it's fine, I can deal with it."

"Better you than me," I said, with a laugh. "Anything I need to know?"

Penny held up a finger. "Oh, yes. One of the school groups had to cancel." She handed me a slip of paper with the transcribed message. "Do you want me to try and find another group to come in?"

The groups had been lined up for weeks, and it would be tough for a school to organize something so quickly with all the red-tape they had to deal with, so I said, "You have enough on your plate. I'll handle it. I can probably find another non-school-sponsored group, and if nothing pans out, I can get one of our class leaders to organize a class field trip."

"Okay, thanks," she said, relieved.

"I'm going back to the Workshop, but I'll be here later for a final walk-through before we open up for business tomorrow."

"Okay. Clive or I will be here until we lock up tonight."

As I made my way out of the mansion, I stopped to look at the sculptures Ryan and Elliott had placed since I had been inside. I recognized one of Ryan's near the front steps, a rustically carved stone birdbath with a heating element in it to keep the water moving in freezing temperatures. Light steam was rising where the warm water met the cold air. It felt Zen-like.

"Nice," I said, to no one in particular, since I was alone. I hoped this serenity would wrap its arms around the entire festival.

Chapter 2

I spent the rest of the morning in the office behind the front desk at the Workshop. After multiple calls, I managed to find a replacement for the cancelled school group, and with that task done, I went to my studio for a little one-on-one time with my current art project.

My studio was my idea of arts and crafts heaven. Three large tables held multiple projects, two walls of shelves and drawers stored everything from stained glass materials to small bits for making jewelry, and a long workbench ran under the windows with various power tools.

I was currently working on an abstract piece: a large white panel with three-dimensional wooden cubes and rectangles of varying sizes. Theoretically, it would create an interesting play of shadows from the pieces extending out from the panel. It was a departure from my normal haphazard approach to art, and I was amazed at the patience I was exhibiting and wondered how long it would last.

Later, Annie stuck her head in to say hello. I put my glasses up on my head and straightened my back as she came over to look at what I was working on.

"Hey! That's going to be great. I like how you're covering these." She ran a finger along a smooth laminate piece in brilliant red.

"Thanks! So what are you up to?"

"Just finishing up for the day and thought I'd stop in. You do know you have two pairs of glasses on your head," she said with a laugh.

"Oh, oops." I reached up and flung the extra pair from my head to the table, which was when I caught a glimpse of the wall clock. "Oh my gosh, it's almost five! I'm glad you popped in, or I might have lost all track of time. I want to get back over to the Bennet House to check everything before they close up."

"What are ya doing afterward? Going to the Thunderbird tonight?"

I mulled over the lack of options upstairs in my kitchen, then said, "That's not a bad idea. I can head there after the walk-through. What about you?"

"Jack won't be home till later, so why not? How long do you think you'll need at the Bennet House?"

"I should be able to meet you around six. Sound good?" I unplugged the power tools, then flipped off the lights.

"Yup," she said agreeably. "See you there."

****

Back at the Bennet House, I stopped in the library first to see if Oscar had arrived. He had, and was on his hands and knees, plugging one of his lamp creations into a power strip snaked under the table. I cleared my throat so I wouldn't startle him, but he still jerked up and banged his shoulder. Oscar peered at me over the table with a surprised look, his round tortoiseshell glasses askew.

"Oh my, you startled me! I thought I was the only one left here," he said, a slight blush emerging through his mocha skin.

"I am *so* sorry! I didn't mean to," I said

apologetically. "I'm Alex Montgomery, from the Creative Workshop. I've just stopped by to do a walk-through before we open up tomorrow. I was hoping I might meet you."

He was on his feet now. "My fault, it's totally my fault. I tend to get in my own little world and don't notice what's going on around me." He straightened the lamp in front of him, then extended his hand and said, "I'm Oscar. Of course, I think you already figured that out."

As we shook hands, my eye was drawn to the superb craftsmanship of the array of lamps displayed on the three tables. "These are lovely, Oscar. I'm so glad you've joined the festival this year."

He pushed his glasses up with his finger and raised his dark brown eyes to meet mine. "Thank you so much. I'm looking forward to it," he said, and then fidgeted, moving a lamp this way and that, and then back to where it started; his hands and arms in constant motion.

"So who is the *C*, in O & C Lamps?" I asked, "Assuming you're the *O*."

"I am, I am," he stammered. "The C stands for Charlotte, my wife. We usually travel to festivals together, but she went to help her mother after her hip surgery."

"Oh, I'm so sorry."

"Nothing to worry about. She just needed the extra set of hands."

"That's a relief. And you can let her know we'll take good care of you in her absence."

I found Oscar an interesting character study. He was shy and a little awkward, but I didn't find it uncomfortable. Instead, I found myself drawn to him. Just as with some people, any silences were awkward, while with others, it was comfortable. With Oscar, it seemed to be the latter.

After said moment of silence, I said, "Okay, I'll leave you to it. I'll see you tomorrow. Or, if you're staying at the Thunderbird Lodge, some of us will be hanging out in the lounge this evening if you'd like to stop by and visit."

"Thank you, that might be nice," he said softly.

I jogged up the stairs to see how the second floor was shaping up. Shelby and her crew had done a great job divvying things up across the four craft rooms, with the artwork done by the teen classes hanging in the hallway. They'd also placed tables outside the rooms for the Valentine's bonus buys, which I thought was a great idea.

On the landing, the book sale table was full of enticing books, and the bake sale table held delectable-looking boxed pies and bags of cookies and brownies. I slapped my hand as I reached for the chocolate chip cookies and moved to the lounge where Lena had set up the reading circle. She had placed a large colorful circular rag rug on the floor, with a few brightly colored child-sized beanbag chairs and throw pillows.

It took me back to my own memories of story time. I could still visualize the classroom, sitting cross-legged on the floor, fully engrossed in the book the teacher read to us while my best friend, Kimmy, braided my hair. Kindergarten through third grade was my golden age. Probably because, at that age, life was full of imagination, playing with abandon, naps, and pudding cups. Man, those were the days.

I went back downstairs and found Clive in the parlor. He was scrutinizing things a little more than necessary and had picked up one of Twila and Hank's glass pieces.

"Whatcha' doing, Clive?" I asked.

He whipped around, putting down the heavy glass paperweight. "Just looking things over. What are you doing skulking around?"

"I'm hardly skulking. I'm doing a walk-through."

"Yes, well, everything's in order. Although, people left boxes in the hallway, which went against my explicit instructions, and I spent all day closing the back door, from people being lazy when they went in and out. We must talk to everyone about this tomorrow."

"Clive, everything's going to be fine. Everyone was going in and out getting set up today, and I know you don't like the upheaval, but it's done now. I've found everybody has been respectful of the building, so don't worry."

Clive puffed up and said, "Easy for you to say. I'm in charge, so I have to take charge. I can't just come and go, like you do."

"All you have to do is ask, Clive. I'm happy to be here for whatever you need." I was trying to practice what I had preached to Ryan and made the effort to keep things even-keeled.

Clive started toward the door, but stopped. "Well, I think you've done enough. Ryan and Elliott left that truck out front over the agreed-upon three hours. You just have no control over your people."

Now my patience had run out. "Okay, Clive, I really didn't want to get into this right now, but you need to calm the hell down. I know this is your first year here, but if you didn't want to host the festival, you should have spoken up and said so. These people do not need controlling. That's your whole problem."

"What do you mean, *my* problem?"

"Your need to control. People will rebel if you constantly try to control them. If you want to be respected, you have to treat people with respect. Without the artists, there is no festival. And if the artists don't find this a pleasant experience, they may not come back."

Oscar peeked out around the doorframe of the library with wide eyes. I discreetly patted the air with my hand to let him know I was fine.

I looked back at Clive, who was nonplussed by my outburst, so I dropped it down a notch. "Look, Clive, we all want the same thing, and if we work together it's going to be a great week. Tomorrow will be a new day when the public arrives. You're good with the public, so try and enjoy it."

He stared at me with his beady eyes and then, without a word, turned and stalked off toward his office.

I smiled at Oscar and shrugged. "I'm heading out. How about you?"

He shuffled into the doorway and said, "Um, yes. I think I'm ready to go. I'll just grab my briefcase."

I waited for him, and then we walked to the parking lot together. He was too much of a gentleman to ask what had gone on with Clive, and I didn't feel it was necessary to explain. Instead, I stewed in my own head, wondering what drama Clive would create tomorrow when the public arrived, and if I could keep three steps ahead and, like Penny, put out fires before they started.

****

Saturday

It was opening day, and since I was scheduled to stay at the festival until closing, I got to the mansion at a little after nine thirty and felt a surge of adrenaline at the good number of cars already in the parking lot. A small group of patrons talked and laughed as they shuffled their way through the short queue, while the volunteer checked the tickets clutched in their cold hands. I stood to the side and gave a cheery "Good morning" as they passed, then followed in their wake into the warm lobby.

The clutter of yesterday had transitioned to polished displays, with the glow from the exquisite lighting in the mansion reflecting off all the artwork. A gentle waft of coffee came from the second floor, which created an atmosphere inviting you to linger.

I trotted upstairs. A few people were sifting through the books, but the real action was over at the bake sale table. Those with prior experience knew the pies would be gone if you waited too long. I poked my head into the lounge and saw Lena talking with parents as the kids gathered for the reading circle. I gave her a quick wave, then crossed the landing to the craft rooms. In the first room, Bitsy and JJ were having an animated conversation with a customer, so I checked out their displays while waiting.

These two were both in the enviable position of being retired in their fifties, which allowed them the freedom to let their imaginations run wild. JJ had an interesting blend of super intelligence combined with a healthy dose of free-spiritedness. There was a link between her art and her world of auras, chakras, and meditation, resulting in a well-balanced color story. For the festival, she had an assortment of hand-marbled wrapping papers, watercolor notecards, resin jewelry, and abstract paintings, including some new miniatures I hadn't seen before.

Bitsy had given up her therapy practice when she and her husband, Jim, moved to Flat Rock Falls. He was our town's sole attorney. Bitsy had an infectious personality and was always ready for a laugh. A few years ago, she'd started a line of hats and fascinators with a focus on birds, and I barely looked twice now when she had a bird perched somewhere on her head. But her work was meticulous, and in recent months, she had developed quite a following around the country. Along with a new nature-themed jewelry line, she had some of these spectacular bird hats and fascinators on display at the festival.

"How's it going this morning?" I asked, after the customer moved on.

"We've been pretty busy, so it's a good start!" Bitsy said, gleefully.

I picked up one of her elaborate fascinators but put it back down, saying, "I think I would look kind of ridiculous in this."

She tilted her head. "Possibly. You really have to dress the part to wear those. Maybe this would be better." She extended her hand, holding a hair clip crafted from scrap metal with a small enameled bird.

I clipped it in my hair, which was already coming loose from my pony tail. I knew Bitsy wasn't being judgmental. My regular attire usually consisted of paint-stained jeans and an oversized men's button-down shirt. Avant-garde? Not part of my repertoire.

"How does it look?" I asked.

"Perfect!" she replied.

"Okay, I'll take it." I rooted around in my big leather tote bag for my wallet. "How about you, JJ?

"Good! I've already sold a few things. Can I tempt you with anything?"

I looked at her resin pendant necklaces and picked one out with natural elements of stone and moss enveloped in the resin. "Oooh, I like this, and I'm buying it before it gets snapped up," I said, handing her two twenties.

A crash and a shout of "Johnny!" grabbed my attention, and I quick-stepped into the lounge to see what had happened. Lena was standing, with hands on hips, looking at an upturned table. It had held all the coffee and tea service paraphernalia.

She looked at me in exasperation, and said under her breath, "A group of kids playing tag knocked the table over, and the parents were standing right there when it happened, totally ignoring the havoc they were wreaking."

The parent who had shouted "Johnny" had the child by the hand and was leading him away from the area.

"It's okay, folks! Accidents happen," I said loudly, so no one would feel badly about what had happened.

Lena and I dropped to our knees to gather the sugar packs and the little creamer tubs scattered on the floor. I said, under my breath, "It really is okay. The stirrers hit the floor, so they'll have to be trashed, but most of this is salvageable."

"And at least the coffee and hot water urns are on

the permanent counter."

I said, "Believe me, the Bennet House takes safety precautions seriously. Look, you need to get the reading circle started, so I'll take care of the rest of this."

"Thanks," she said gratefully and pushed herself up.

After a few more minutes of clean up, I headed back downstairs. The mansion's kitchen was in the back of the house, near the office, and during the festival it was serving as the break room, so I parked myself and my laptop at the long wooden table and spent the rest of the morning alternating between festival and Workshop duties. I couldn't believe it was already one o'clock when my phone dinged with a text from Annie, seeing if I wanted to meet her out at the food trucks for lunch.

****

We looked back and forth between the Chick-On-A-Stick and Cheesy Grillers food trucks. The aroma coming from both was enough to make me swoon.

"Which are you going for?" Annie asked, her voice muffled behind her scarf.

"Grilled cheese. How about you?"

"Chick-On-A-Stick. I've been thinking about this all morning! I'll meet ya back here," she said, and quickly attached herself to the Chick line.

A few minutes later, we had our paper boats of food and were looking for a seat in the adjacent tent. It was outfitted with outdoor heaters, which meant it was warm enough to unbutton coats and remove gloves and scarves. Lena was sitting at a table with Maggie and waved us over.

Once we got ourselves settled, I asked Lena,

"Other than the little table mishap, how's the reading circle been going?"

"Ugh, thanks again for your help." Then her eyes twinkled as she smiled. "The kids are so cute, and aside from the occasional nose-picker-while-staring-off-into-space, they've all been captivated by the stories."

I laughed at the image, and said, "That's awesome."

Lena asked, "How about you, Annie? How's it going downstairs?"

"We've had a steady stream of people all day. I've even had a deposit put down on one of my big paintings, which thrills me to no end since my online shopping habit seems to be in full swing this winter!" Annie was an unapologetic shopaholic and was on a first name basis with the UPS man.

"Have you guys met the newbies—Declan, Preston, and Oscar?" I asked.

They all nodded, and Annie said, "Oscar is so nice, and, boy, he's talented. I have my eye on one of his lamps."

"Declan is too handsome," Lena said coyly. "He has those boyish dimples when he smiles. I'm a sucker for that type, so it's a good thing he's a little young for me. Preston is a really nice guy. He's the type I *should* be going for."

"Both those boys are cute," Maggie said, with relish. "They could be trouble with a capital T." She looked at me with mischief in her eyes, and added, "Of course, Alex wouldn't be interested, she's got Walter."

"What?" I sputtered. "Walter is a friend and a business associate, nothing more."

Maggie laughed. "I know. Geez, you're such an

easy target."

"Who is Walter?" Lena asked.

I answered, before Maggie could. "I met Walter during the retreat we hosted in the fall, and since then we've developed a nice long-distance friendship. We're currently ironing out plans for his role as silent benefactor of the Workshop." In truth, sometimes our friendship felt more like a relationship, but I'd avoided examining it too closely, and I certainly didn't want to talk about it over lunch.

Luckily, I didn't have to, because Penny came over and whispered in my ear. "I think I need your help."

"Be right back," I said to my tablemates.

Penny and I rushed back inside to the kitchen, where Shelby was trying to calm Clara, one of the craft artists who had come in from Woodbury, a nearby town.

"What can I do for you, Clara?" I asked.

"I just can't work like this. It's bad enough I'm way down the hall in one of the craft rooms, but there's a draft in there, and I'm freezing all the time."

Shelby gave me a knowing look. This was not about the draft. This was about wanting to be in a higher visibility location.

I said, "Shelby, come with me and let's see what we can do."

We stepped down the hall, out of earshot, and she said, "I'm so sorry, Alex. She didn't say anything yesterday."

"Yeah, it would have been helpful if she had mentioned it before we opened for business." My brain was twirling to find a solution. "Her product is good, right?"

"Yeah, she's quite talented."

"Okay, can she be moved opposite the bake sale table on the landing, just before the craft rooms?"

Shelby mulled it over. "Her work is small, so I think there's enough room. I'll get a couple of people to help me shift two tables, and we should be good to go."

"Great."

We went back to the kitchen, and I outlined the plan for Clara. "Does that sound good to you?"

"Yes, thank you. I'll assume it will be fine, and will let you know if it's not," she said, haughtily.

I went back to the table to finish my now-cold grilled cheese, and we passed the rest of the lunch break laughing as Lena and Maggie tried to one-up each other with stories of their tumultuous dating escapades.

****

Sunday evening

The remainder of the weekend went seamlessly, and on Sunday, a few of the artists from out of town made the commute home, but the rest of us gathered at the Lodge to unwind. The Thunderbird Lodge had a woodsy theme, with a post and beam A-frame entrance and two wings of rooms. There was a restaurant and lounge off the lobby, with a wall of windows offering a view of the outdoor patio and the surrounding forest. The lounge was a great place for visitors and locals to hang out in the winter. The enormous fireplace was perpetually lit all season, with sofas, lounge chairs, and cocktail tables surrounding it.

There was a convivial atmosphere, with multiple conversations taking place at once, as everyone relayed different stories about the weekend. But when the topic came to Clive, everyone seemed to have something to say.

"He's just so pushy," Spencer said.

Bitsy leaned forward and asked, "I don't like to be unkind, but have you noticed he's always nosing around?"

Maggie nodded and answered, "Yes! He came into our room and just hovered."

Annie added, "And he always finds something to complain about. Why can't he just relax?"

Even though I had my issues with Clive, I didn't like it when there was a gang-like snark-fest about anyone, so after a few minutes, I put a stop to it. "I know he gets on everyone's nerves, but I think Clive just doesn't have the social skills to know how to interact well with others, so don't take it personally, and maybe try and be nice to him."

This seemed to shut down any further discussion, and everyone returned to having fun. A little later, as the plates of food arrived, Annie's phone rang with the distinct old car horn ringtone she had assigned to Jack. She caught my eye, and said, "Yeah, sure, just a minute."

She held her phone out to me. "It's Jack. He says he wants to talk to you."

I gave her a questioning look, but took her phone and said, "Hey, Jack, where are you? I thought you were going to meet us here?"

"I just tried to call you," he said impatiently.

"Sorry, I finally felt like I didn't need to be tethered to my phone, and it's buried in my bag. What's up?"

"I won't be making it over there tonight. We just found a body."

Chapter 3

What? He couldn't have said what I thought he just said. "I don't think I heard you correctly."

"Travis took a call from Ben Perkins. He was out walking his dog on the service road past the junction. The dog went nose-to-ground and found a dead body."

I felt like the wind was just knocked out of my sails. There was a whoop of laughter at the table, so I got up from my chair and walked to the edge of the lounge where it was quieter and I could talk in a normal voice.

"Oh my gosh. Who is it? What happened?"

"Don't know, and don't know. I just wanted to check with you and make sure all your festival people are accounted for. I know everyone at the Workshop, so I'm meaning the folks from out of town who I wouldn't know. The victim is a male."

"Oh, let me think. Some did go back home for the night, so I'll touch base with them all. If I can't reach anyone, I'll let you know."

"Okay, I gotta run. Hand me back to Annie. I want to let her know I won't be home for a while."

I walked back toward the group and motioned to Annie. When she approached, I handed her the phone. "He wants to talk to you."

She listened for a few moments, looked at me, then said, "All right. I'll see you at home later." She swiped the phone to disconnect the call. "How horrible," she said, with concern in her voice. "I sure hope it's not someone we know."

"Me too."

"Why did he want to talk to you?"

I grabbed my phone out of my bag. "I need to text those who left town for the night and make sure everyone is accounted for. I'm already worrying, so I hope I reach everyone quickly."

"Do you want to come back to the house with me when we're done here and hang out till Jack gets home? He might have something to tell us by then."

"Sure. I'll pick up Baxter and we'll meet you there," I said.

I walked back to the edge of the lounge to text the out-of-towners, and anyone else I could think of. I stared at my phone, willing it to ding with texts confirming everyone was safe and sound, and my mind whirred trying to think if I had missed anyone. Most of the locals were here, so who else? And who would be out walking on a remote road without identification?

Over the next hour, one by one I received texts confirming all were accounted for, and I let Jack know the festival people were all safe and sound. With my mind free of worry, I picked up Baxter and we headed to Jack and Annie's.

Their house was a short five-minute drive from the Workshop. I knocked as I opened the front door, then walked through the living room to the open kitchen and den, where Annie already had a fire going.

"Hey, grab a seat, and I'll be right in."

I parked myself on the deep cushioned love seat, and Baxter plunked himself down in front of the fire.

"Any word from Jack?"

"Not yet." She joined me, putting two steaming mugs of spiced tea on the coffee table. "Have you been doing much work for him lately? I wonder if he'll need the extra set of hands for this."

"I haven't since the fall," I replied. "And I tell you, I would have lost my mind if another death was connected to us in some way."

"Me, too."

This past fall there had been a murder during the artist retreat at the Workshop, and it was only in the last couple of months that we had all gotten past the ordeal.

Since moving to Flat Rock, I occasionally helped Jack by doing research or data collection. He had a tiny police force, and sometimes they got spread pretty thin. Jack called it tapping into my old skills. Depending on the situation, it actually meant I was a temp secretary, a research consultant, or sometimes just a come-along-and-be-a-sounding-board buddy.

Essentially, once he cleared me through official channels, I was the unpaid help. My previous job involved wearing many hats, and now I was able to use parts of my brain at risk of becoming dormant, so I kind of liked helping out now and then.

During the investigation in the fall, I hadn't admitted it to Jack—or anyone—but while the whole thing was dreadful, I'd actually found the investigative aspect intriguing. I guess it was a family thing, since both our dads had been in law enforcement.

We heard the garage door open, and a moment later, Jack came in through the kitchen.

"Hi, honey," Annie called out. "Are you hungry?"

"I'm starving," he growled but then leaned down to

give Annie a kiss on her forehead. "I'll just make a quick sandwich."

"You sit down, I'll do it," she said, unfolding herself from the couch. Jack gratefully nodded and sank into the recliner, letting out a deep sigh.

"So, what's the word?" I asked.

"Here's what we know so far. Fairly well-dressed male, probably early forties, no ID. Like I told you, he was found on the side of the access road. He was partially covered by the snowbank."

"I hate to say it, but it's a relief it's not someone we know. How did he die? Exposure?" I asked.

"The medical examiner will have to take a closer look, but it was probably a case of hit-and-run. Now, whether he died on impact or, later, from a combination of his injuries and exposure, we don't know yet. And the temperature will make determining the time of death a little difficult."

"I wonder where he was walking to, or from?" I mused.

"That's a good question. You know the area; around the junction there are a couple of fast-food joints, the gas station and truck stop, and three motels, with a few homes farther down the access road. Besides the main intersection, it's not heavily traveled. Maybe we'll get lucky and someone will report him missing. Then we can start to put a timeline together."

Annie brought Jack a plate with a sandwich, a mound of chips, and a tall glass of beer, and I decided this was a good time to leave so they could have some peace and quiet.

"Come on, Baxter, let's go," I called out, waking him from his doggy nap. "See ya tomorrow, Annie.

35

And Jack, I hope you get some rest tonight. Please let me know when you find out who he is."

"Will do," he said, through a mouthful of turkey sandwich.

Baxter and I hustled out to the car, and there was barely time to get the heat going before we were back at the Workshop. We wasted no time getting inside and up to the apartment, where I made quick work of getting snug in bed under the quilt, with an additional layer of an electric blanket tonight. I couldn't help but think about the poor soul whose life had come to an end in a snow drift, and my imagination created the tragic image when I closed my eyes.

****

Monday

The next morning, I cradled my cup of coffee and looked out the kitchen window to the light snow blanketing the Workshop grounds. Cold weather and snow seemed to give everyday things, like toast and coffee, an intoxicating aroma. It triggered a sense of cozy well-being. I had to imagine the smell of toast, though, because I had no bread, but I did linger over a second cup of coffee.

Then I thought about the stark juxtaposition of my feeling warm and cozy when someone else had lost their life in a snowbank. This made me angry. A hit-and-run was such a cowardly crime. Accidents happen. It's tragic, but it happens. But to flee the scene and leave someone on the side of the road is a heinous act. Unforgiveable. I just hoped Jack would have some news soon.

I put my mug in the sink and went downstairs. The festival hours during the week were shorter, from noon to seven p.m., so I didn't need to go to the Bennet House until after lunch.

There was a hum of activity as artists got studio time in before the festival opened. Maggie and Ari's voices drifted down the hall, so I headed in their direction first. Their studios were across the hall from each other, and they had their doors open so they could visit while working.

"Mornin', you two," I said as I approached.

They chorused back, "Morning!"

Ari was seated behind her easel, working on a still life painting. Her overhead light was off, and the glow of the task light created a theatrical atmosphere, like a single spotlight on an actor with the rest of the stage in darkness.

Maggie was hovering by the large format printer, closely monitoring the progress as it ticked its way across a piece of custom-sized photo paper. By contrast, her studio was ablaze with light so she could better scrutinize every pixel of the print. I became mesmerized as the image revealed itself: a snow-covered field with horses in motion, vapor swirling around their noses, and a weathered barn in the background. The way she took the photo made the image appear black and white, except for one small pop of red on the barn.

"That's gorgeous, Maggie."

She carefully took the photo from the printer and laid it on the work table. "Thanks! But I can hardly take credit for the scene. It was a perfect moment just begging for someone to take a picture."

"Well, you have the eye to see those kinds of moments and then capture them. That's what makes you the professional." I moved to where I could talk to both Maggie and Ari. "I just wanted to touch base and see how the festival is going for you guys?"

"I think it's going great," Ari called out. "I've been having such a good time sharing the room with Hank and Twila."

"I bet. Those two instantly become like family," I said.

She continued. "We had good crowds on Saturday and Sunday, and the artists all seem to get along. I really like the new guys, too."

Maggie tilted her head, which gave her an exotic bird look, with the plumes of green-colored hair interspersed with the plum. "Don't tell anyone, but I think Declan might ask me out."

"Oh good Lord, here we go." I laughed.

"Yup," Ari added, good-naturedly.

Maggie defended herself. "Hey now, he's way better than the losers I've come across lately."

"Well, just watch yourself, and don't fall too hard. They're only here for the week."

"Yes, Mother," she teased, then winked at me. She lowered her voice to ask, "So, what were you and Annie huddled about last night at the Lodge?"

I walked over to stand next to Maggie. "Jack called because there was a fatal hit-and-run on the service road by the junction. He wanted to make sure our people were all accounted for."

"Oh no, how horrible."

"I know. They'll have to wait for the medical examiner's report to know exactly what happened."

"Not to be selfish, but at least this time it doesn't involve us," she said.

"That's exactly what I thought. I'm hoping Jack will get the victim's name soon, though. Someone has to be missing whomever it is, and they deserve to know what happened." I pushed myself up from where I had been leaning on the work table and went back into the hall. "Okay, I'm off. I'll see you guys later over at the Bennet House."

I walked back toward the front desk but stopped short when I heard laughter coming from the large craft room, where Shelby, Maura, Eliza, and Becca were huddled around the work table. Maura and Shelby were two of our studio craft artists, and Eliza and Becca were from Brigg's Mill, a small town about an hour away. They were all giggling uncontrollably as Maura demonstrated something, so I ventured farther into the room.

"What are you guys up to? You're clearly having too much fun." They looked up as if caught in the act, and then waved me in.

"Maura is showing us some of her hilarious pop-up cards," Shelby said, jovially.

Eliza tapped Maura's hand. "You are too damned funny. Are you going to sell these at the festival?"

"Yeah. I finished up a batch to take over today."

Becca tilted her head. "I just don't get it, Maura. How is it you were married to Clive? You guys are like night and day."

Maura was dressed to the nines, as always, and she tapped the table with her manicured nails, the shiny dark-red nail color reflecting the light. "He wasn't always this way, you know. When we met after college, he had a great sense of humor and he liked to have fun."

"That's hard to imagine, but I'm glad to hear he's got some fun somewhere in him," I said.

"He was cute, too. Not frat-boy cute, but sort of in a George Constanza from *Seinfeld* kind of way. He lost a couple of jobs—neither his fault, just downsizing—and he became more and more bitter. I could *not* believe it when he came here to interview for the Bennet House job. I mean really, what are the odds we would end up in the same place? I have an excuse to be here. I'm from here!" She shook her head in bewilderment.

"Is it awkward, running into him?" Eliza asked.

"Nah, not really. It's been long enough that we're past any unpleasantness. It's kind of sad, though. I don't recognize who he's become. Maybe someday he'll find himself again." She lightly tapped her palm on the table. "Okay, enough time talking about him."

Shelby nodded and gave a conspiratorial look to the others. "Yeah, let's get back to you showing us how you do these pop-ups so we can steal your method."

I was making my way back to the office when Jack called. "Hey, how're things this morning? Any news?" I asked.

"Still waiting for the ME report, but I did get a hit on the victim's prints. He had a petty theft charge when he was eighteen, so he's in the system. I'm calling to see if you recognize his name. Eddie or Edward Marks."

"Eddie Marks." I rolled the name around in my head and breathed a sigh of relief. "That doesn't sound familiar. Where's he from?"

"Still working on that. The charges were from Ohio, and we did a quick internet search, but without a city or even a state to narrow it down, it's not a reliable way to get information at this point. The Ohio photo is too out of date for me to use, so the ME managed to send me an image where he doesn't look like he got hit by a car. I'm going to be heading over to canvas the motels, restaurants, and gas stations to see if anyone recognizes him. What are you doing? Want to ride along?"

I checked my watch. "I still have a couple of hours before I need to go to the festival, so sure, I'm game. Pick me up?"

Ten minutes later, after I climbed into his tricked-out police vehicle and buckled up, Jack thrust a piece of paper and pen at me.

"Sign this," he said. "This allows you to be present for certain aspects of the investigation. You can accompany me, like today, you can look at evidence, and I can tap you as a research assistant or consultant if need be. Basically, the same deal as earlier this fall."

I used my knee as a desk and scrawled my name on the paper and asked, "Any pay this time?"

He gave me a cheeky smile. "Your payment is the pride that comes from doing a public-service good deed."

"Yeah, right. I thought as much. Okay, what's the plan? Can't you just call the motels?"

"We tried that. No luck. So we have to tick all the boxes and check in person. Sometimes the clerk might not actually look it up when we ask, or Eddie might have registered under a different name or a company name. Let's take the motels first. If we can find out where he was staying, we can find out more about who this guy was, and maybe, why he was here."

"Okay."

He shifted in the seat to look at me, all serious and cop-like. "Now, in the fall, you ignored me and started doing your own questioning and nosing around, and—"

"Hold on, I…"

"Wait, let me finish."

I squinted at him but let him continue.

"As I was saying, you took it upon yourself to step out from the background work you were supposed to be doing. While you haven't said as much, I think you started to like the investigative side. Am I right?"

"Maybe," I said reluctantly.

"Okay, at least you're being honest. Now, you have a tendency to leap before you look, and you could have been seriously hurt last time. So, I want you to pay attention to how I do things, talk to me when you get some hare-brained idea, and don't go off half-cocked and get yourself in trouble. Deal?"

I feigned indignance "Hare-brained? Half-cocked? I don't know what you're talking about. Woof-woof, you're barking up the wrong tree, buddy."

Chapter 4

Jack just stared me down. "You know I'm right."

He wasn't joking around, so I said in earnest, "Deal. You're right, and I promise to be more careful."

"Good," he said, before hightailing it out of the parking lot.

"Take it easy," I said. "Where's the fire?"

"Now talk about calling the kettle black. You're the one who drives like a bat out of hell. I wasn't even going the speed limit." We spent the next few minutes reviving our childhood behaviors, but as we approached the intersection at the junction, we became more serious.

"Let's start with the Pines," Jack said, and pulled into the sparsely populated one-story motel.

It had a vintage vibe, with the original neon sign and a stenciled pine tree above each room number. As we walked under the boomerang portico to the front door, I could hear the hum of the vending machines. I made a mental note to acquaint myself with those vending machines when we were done here.

We approached the reception desk, and a perky girl, who looked fresh out of high school, greeted us with enthusiasm.

"Hi! I'm Tammi, with an I," she said, pointing to her name tag. "Are you checking in?"

Jack pulled out the photo he had printed of Eddie,

put his card on the counter, and showed her his badge. "Hi, Tammi," Jack said amicably. "I'm Chief Maddox. Do you recognize this man? He might have checked in here recently."

Her eyes grew wide, and she looked at the photo. "Um, I don't think so. Should I? Is there a problem?"

"His name is Edward Marks, but he may have gone by Eddie. Could you please check the guest register and tell me if he has a room here?

"Uh, I'm not sure I'm allowed to give out that information," she said, looking around. Her face registered relief when she saw an older woman in the office to her right. "Mary?" she called out. "Could you please come help…" She looked down at the card. "Chief Maddox?"

"What do I pay you for?" Mary chided, as she lumbered out of the office.

Her almost black, bowl-shaped hair was flattened on one side, probably from sleeping on too much hairspray. No wonder she was in a bad mood.

Tammi handed her Jack's card. "What can I do for ya," she said, in only a slightly more pleasant tone than she used with Tammi.

"Good morning. Do you recognize this man?" Jack asked.

"No," she said, after only a cursory glance.

"Could you please check your register for an Edward Marks?"

"Why? What's he done?"

"He's done nothing, that I'm aware of. I'm afraid he's deceased, and I'm trying to track down where he was staying. Now, if you will please check the register. I would also like to know if you currently have any corporate bookings, and if someone else works the front desk who might have checked him in."

She nudged Tammi out of the way and started clicking on the computer keyboard. "Marks, you said?"

"Yes," Jack said, with restrained patience.

"Nope. Nobody by that name. Dennis works nights, so he's not here. And we don't have any corporate bookings, just folks off the highway. Is that all? I have work to do."

"Yes, thank you for your time," Jack said to her retreating back as she walked away. "Let's go," he said to me. "I'll circle back around and talk to Dennis if I have to."

Out under the portico I stopped short. "Just a sec."

I jogged back to the desk and asked Tammi for change for a ten-dollar bill. "For the vending machine," I said, with a sheepish grin.

Back outside, I gave Jack the just-a-minute sign and hightailed it down to the machines. A few minutes later, with an armload of tasty snacks and two cans of iced tea, I climbed back into the truck.

"Look! Best vending machine ever! I haven't eaten yet, and I'm starving. What do you want?"

"Man, how can you still eat like a college student?" But after five seconds of looking at my bounty, he said, "I'll take a candy bar."

We happily munched our way to the next motel. This one was a budget chain motel, so while the visitor got exactly what they expected, it didn't have much personality. Neither did the man behind the desk. He was helpful in a milquetoast, efficient way, but we once again came up empty-handed. I noted on the way out this establishment didn't have visible vending machines and commented to Jack how fortunate we were I hadn't passed up on the opportunity at the Pines.

Our last hope was a few minutes past the intersection at the Whispering Falls Motel, which offered weekly rates and cable TV on their signage. We walked across the slushy parking lot to the office door. The outside of the building looked like a work in progress, but inside, the atmosphere was warm and inviting. A large Lab got up to greet us and then curled back up on his dog bed. There were pretty potted plants, and a TV in the corner with a cooking show playing at a low volume.

The woman behind the desk greeted us. "Good morning. How can I help you?" She pulled her glasses from her friendly face to hang on the chain around her neck.

Jack went through his routine and showed her the photo.

"Why yes, I recognize him, but he checked in with the name John Middleton. Is everything all right?"

"I'm afraid not. He was found dead yesterday evening along the service road."

"Oh dear. How dreadful! What happened?"

"We're still in the early days of the investigation. We need to check his room now, and then I'll send someone back to collect his belongings. Please don't allow housekeeping in until we give the all clear."

"Of course," she said, opening a drawer to pull out her passkey. She took a quick look at her register. "He's in room seven. If you'll just follow me."

Jack pulled out his notebook. "Before we go, could you tell me when he checked in and for how many nights?"

She sat back down and looked at the register. "He arrived Saturday night, and he was to check out tomorrow morning. He paid up front with cash."

Jack flipped open his pad to jot notes. "And your name?"

"Oh, I'm so sorry. I'm Gladys. Gladys Wilson. My husband Sam and I bought this motel last year."

"One more thing, Gladys. Did he by chance register a vehicle with you?"

"Let's see…yes. He registered a silver Acura, plate number 8KMR49."

"Thank you. Let's go check his room."

As we left the office and walked down to room seven, Jack slowed to survey the cars in the lot. I walked next to Gladys while she explained she and Sam had bought this motel as a nice way to spend their retirement, and they were, little by little, trying to turn it into a boutique experience.

She turned the key in the lock and held out her arm to usher us in. "I'll use my passcode to open the room safe for you, and then I'm assuming you don't need me hovering, so just let me know when you're done."

"Thank you, and thank you for your cooperation," Jack said.

Jack and I stood inside the door, taking in the tasteful décor: a king-sized bed with crisp white sheets folded over the top edge of the dark brown duvet, and I recognized Maggie's hand in two large photo prints taken up at Flat Rock Falls State Park. Everything was spic and span, the carpeting looked new, and the quality of the furnishings bordered on upscale.

I nodded in approval. "You certainly can't judge a book by its cover, eh?"

"Nope. Nice room. I'd stay here." He moved toward the armoire. "Let's get started and see what we can figure out about Eddie Marks."

"Why would he have checked in under a different name?" I asked.

"There are lots of reasons people use an alias. Could be an affair, or a high-profile musician or actor, or even something like corporate investigation. It's not illegal. And when it's a motel like this, where there wouldn't be room charges, they often don't ask for ID. And it's possible he had a fake ID."

Jack opened the TV armoire, and I made my way to the closet and opened the bifold doors. I pushed back a feeling of sadness at the thought of pawing through a dead man's belongings and got started with the few items on the wooden hangers.

"Hunh, interesting," I said, more to myself than out loud, but Jack heard me nonetheless.

"What's that? Find something?"

"Oh, not really. Just looking at his clothing labels."

"I'm not really interested in his fashion sense." He said, tossing some items on the bed. "I'm striking out here. Just some shopping bags in the room safe."

"Here's his suitcase." I lugged it out of the closet and let Jack go through it while I looked in the shopping bags.

I pulled out a few books, a collection of note cards, and a wooden box. I recognized all of them. "He was at the festival!" I exclaimed. "These are JJ's watercolor cards, and this wooden box looks like it's from Wild Mountain Woodcarvers. It's more intricate, but I remember seeing some similar to this. And the Bennet Library stamp is on the inside of these books."

"Well, it's a start. We can make the rounds and see who remembers him."

Jack continued to root around in the suitcase and pulled out a passport he found tucked inside a sweater. He opened it and flipped through the pages. "Eddie Marks was quite the traveler."

"U.S. passport?"

"Yup. I haven't found anything to indicate what business he was in, but he's made frequent trips to London, Brussels, and Amsterdam."

"That explains some of the clothing labels. There's a tweed jacket with two shirts from a Savile Row tailor, and his boots are from an English maker." Jack gave me a quizzical look, so I simply said, "Don't forget, I used to know about such things in my old life. I still have a pair from the same maker," I said, pointing to the shoes. "They last forever."

"That must take some bucks."

I nodded.

"So Mr. Marks, what were you doing here, in Flat Rock?" Jack mused.

"Yeah, sort of off the beaten path. Did you find his wallet?"

"Not yet, which is the only real hiccup in this. With a hit-and-run accident, someone usually, well, *runs*. They don't stop to get out and take the victim's wallet."

"So what do you think? That they were trying to delay the ID, or they decided to rob him? Maybe there's another explanation—did you see his car? Maybe he left it in his car."

"I checked on the way to the room, and it's not in the motel lot." Jack pulled out his phone to relay the plate number to Matt at the precinct. "We'll drive

49

through a few parking lots around here. I also want to go to the accident site. You still have a little time?"

I looked at my watch. "Yup. I've got about an hour."

At the crime scene, I stayed in the truck while Jack and his deputy, Travis, examined the scene.

I opened the bag of chips and propped my foot on the dashboard. I'd watched this scene play out many times on TV, but seeing it in real life was different, and my eyes were glued to them as they first walked the road, then the cordoned off area where the body had been found. Travis pulled a shovel from the back of his patrol car, and they moved snow from one area to another, looking for anything they might have missed the night before. I had finished the bag of chips and was wiping my hands on my jeans when Jack got back in the truck.

"Don't know why I thought we might find something, but I had to try," he said, putting his hands in front of the heater vents to warm them. "So, there were no tire marks on the road. What does that tell you?"

I thought for a moment. "That means no sign of a hard brake; no burning rubber on the pavement."

"Signifying?"

A chill came over me. "It means the car hit him and didn't even try to stop."

"Right. Also, the body was partially covered with snow. Did it snow a lot yesterday evening?"

"Not enough to cover a body," I replied. "So was this murder?"

"Could be. It's vehicular manslaughter, obviously, but was it with malicious intent? Did someone intentionally run him over, then haphazardly try to cover the body with snow? Or was it a careless accident and someone tried to delay identification? We don't know yet. But we do know what this means for you, right?"

"What do you mean, me?" I asked, tilting my head.

"As per our earlier conversation, it means you watch your step."

"Oh, right." This might be murder, so I understood why he was warning me, but this incident wasn't related to me or the Workshop, so I wasn't really concerned. I gave him the two-finger salute, and said, "Don't worry. I got it. So what now? Parking lot drive-throughs to look for his car?"

"Yup."

After zig-zagging our way through multiple parking lots, we found it at the truck stop. Jack made quick order of opening the locked car—one of his cop-school skills. Within minutes, he found Eddie's wallet in the glove box. He had no ID on him because he had left it in his car. At least one mystery was solved.

To me, though, this opened up new questions. Why was he walking on the service road when his car was here at the truck stop? Why did he leave his wallet? Where was his cell phone?

Oh well, this was now Jack's problem to solve. At least that's what I thought.

Chapter 5

When we pulled into the Bennet House lot, Jack asked if I would mind discreetly showing the photo of Eddie around to see if anyone remembered him.

He explained, "I don't want to go in there all official-like and ask a bunch of questions. It puts people off. Particularly if there are customers around."

"Gee, you think?" I teased. Jack had a commanding presence, and you could sense him quietly percolating, so if you didn't know him, he could be pretty intimidating. "Okay, all joking aside, no problem. I'll ask the artists he bought things from if they remember seeing him." I climbed out and hefted my tote bag on my shoulder before grabbing the envelope with Eddie's photograph from Jack's outstretched hand.

After unloading my gear on the kitchen table, I tucked the photo envelope under my arm and went to the office.

"Hiya, Penny! How's it going this afternoon? Where's Clive?"

"Everything's good. We have one of the school groups arriving in about forty-five minutes, and as you coordinated, Spencer, Maggie, and Twila will be doing short talks with them as they tour each room. Clive is roaming the halls somewhere. Or maybe he's out having lunch."

"Okay. For now, I'm just as happy to avoid him. Can I show you something?" I pulled out the photo. "Do you recognize this man?"

Penny took the photo by its edges and looked at the image of Eddie that the medical examiner had strategically staged to look…how could I put this delicately?…less dead.

"Hmmm, no. I don't know him. Why?"

"He was the victim of a hit-and-run last night, and Jack and I found some purchases from the festival in his motel room. Jack has asked me to check and see if anyone remembers him."

"Oh, how awful. I wish I could help. Maybe someone else will recognize him."

"That's my hope. I'm going to start with the people he bought stuff from."

The phone rang at her desk, and she gave me a thumbs-up as she picked up the receiver, saying, "Bennet House," in her smooth professional voice.

As I jogged up the stairs, I could hear the buzz of happy patrons coming from all directions. This was good news for a weekday. I found JJ manning the book sale table, so I stopped to quiz her on her memory of customers.

I squatted by the side of her chair and discreetly pulled out the photo. "Do you remember seeing this guy yesterday? He would have bought some of your watercolor cards."

JJ frowned. "What's going on? Why are you asking?"

"He was the victim of a hit-and-run last night, and Jack's trying to get a handle on the timeline of where he was, when, and why. Perhaps he was with someone.

Anything you might remember would be a help."

Her look turned dark as she stared at me and then back at the image. I knew what was coming, so I sat back on my haunches and waited. She took a deep breath and tilted her head back, then slowly breathed in through her nose and out through her mouth three or four times before bringing her head back down and opening her eyes to look at the photo. She waved her hand over the image and closed her eyes again.

"I'm sensing many layers to this man. A complexity."

I needed to keep JJ on point, otherwise she would venture off into otherworldly tangents, so I gently prompted, "Um, so do you think you can remember if you saw him, and when?"

She opened her eyes and glanced at me over her glasses. "All right, all right…" She looked at the photo again, then handed it back to me. "Yes, he was here yesterday. I think it was probably mid-late afternoon."

"Did he happen to mention where he came from, or what he was doing here?"

"He didn't. He was cordial but not chatty. He asked me about the marbled papers and bought some watercolor cards. And I didn't see anyone with him. I wish I could be more help."

"No problem. At least it's something, and it will help Jack build the timeline. I'm going to check with Declan and Preston. He bought one of their boxes, so maybe they'll recall talking to him."

Back downstairs, I walked into the library and saw Clive talking to Maggie. I turned on my heel to exit the room—too late. She called my name, and I braced myself for the inevitable wrangling with Clive.

"Alex, I assumed you would adhere to the schedule for the school groups, and not *wing it*, as Maggie is now telling me," Clive said, barging over to me.

"Yes, there *is* a schedule, Clive, but I think what Maggie's trying to say is if the kids want to linger in one room or another, we're not going to herd them through like cattle. We want them to get as much out of this as possible."

"Well, I don't like it."

"Then maybe you should work in your office this afternoon so you don't have to deal with it. I was planning to monitor things, anyway."

He harrumphed and walked over toward Oscar, so I took the reprieve to show the picture of Eddie to Maggie.

"So this is the guy, hunh?" she asked. "I don't remember talking to him, but I think he might have been in here yesterday. I couldn't say for sure, though. We had a lot of people in and out of here. Maybe they'll remember him." She nodded toward Declan and Preston.

"Okay, I was going to check with them since he bought one of their boxes. Oh, and by the way, I saw some of your prints at the Whispering Falls Motel when we were tracking down where Eddie was staying. They look great!"

"Thanks! Gladys and Sam are real sweethearts, and I think they're doing a great job with the rooms there."

I looked over toward Declan and Preston and noticed a lull in customers. "Here's my window to talk to them. I'll catch you later." I approached them, and asked, "How are you guys doing? I hope you got some rest and had a good drive in today."

Preston adjusted his ball cap. "I decided to stay here, but Declan headed home for the night."

"Yeah," Declan said. "I had some things to tend to. It's an easy drive, so I didn't mind."

"Good to hear." Since we were past the pleasantries, I pulled out the photo. "I have a quick question for you. Could you please take a look at this and tell me if you recall seeing this man here yesterday?"

Clive scurried over and stood next to me. "What's this? What are you doing?"

"There was an accident on the service road last evening, and this gentleman from out of town was killed," I said. "He bought some things at the festival, so I'm helping Chief Maddox by asking around to see if anyone recalls speaking with him."

"Well, this is highly unusual, Alex. And unsavory."

Declan stepped forward and rescued me. "What a shame, that's just awful. Why don't we take a look? Maybe we can help."

I handed him the photo.

"Gee, I don't know. Preston? Do you recognize him?" Declan asked.

"I don't think so...but you know, I took a late lunch, so it might have been while I was outside in the tent."

"It appears he bought one of your intricate boxes, and he was likely here in the afternoon," I added, trying to be helpful.

Declan passed the photo and envelope back to me with a concerned look on his face. "He might have bought one our boxes, but I honestly don't recognize him. Sorry. We had a lot of people here yesterday."

Clive grabbed the photo from my hand, scanned Eddie's face, and tilted his head.

"Do you recognize him?" I asked.

He looked at Declan, as if silently chastising him for trying to be helpful, which had prolonged my intrusion, then thrust the photo back at me. "I didn't see him here. I'm genuinely sorry for what happened, but maybe now you can put that away so our patrons don't see you passing around a picture of a dead man." He then turned on his heel and walked out.

"Well, I think I've done what I can. At least we know he was here mid-late afternoon."

Preston cocked his head. "You said it was an accident, so why is all of this necessary?"

I looked over my shoulder to make sure there weren't any patrons nearby. "Truth is, it was a hit-and-run. My cousin is the chief of police here, and I occasionally help him with background work."

Declan had started to walk away but stopped and turned back to me. "Do you know what happened? And how intriguing, you assist the police."

"It was likely a wrong place at the wrong time kind of accident, and whoever hit him fled the scene. But Jack, he's the chief, likes to be thorough. Since we know he bought a few things at the festival, we hoped to trace his movements, or learn why he was here, and we thought it would be more discreet if I asked around."

Preston nodded. "That makes sense." He looked at Declan and added, "I feel kind of embarrassed I don't remember."

Declan put his hand on Preston's shoulder. "Hey, don't feel bad. You were probably out in the tent. I'm the one who should remember, and I don't."

"Which box did he buy?" Preston asked.

I scanned the tables, looking for a similar box. "It was about eight by six inches and intricately carved. I don't see another one here like it."

Declan nodded and knelt down to reach under the table. He shifted a cardboard box forward, pulled out three wooden boxes, and set them on the table, rewarding me with a smile. "Here we go. I was just getting ready to restock. These are our more elaborately carved boxes; they've been big sellers."

"Yes, it was similar to these."

Preston turned to help a customer, and at the same time Maggie sauntered over and turned on her charm. "Oooo, these are so beautiful! I may have to buy one," she said, batting her eyes at Declan. "You are so good with your hands…"

This was highly amusing, and I got ready to enjoy the show.

Declan swiped back a lock of hair that had fallen across his eyes and gave her a dimpled grin. "Thanks. I'll give you a discount since it's been such a pleasure to share the room with you. Do you still want to grab lunch later?"

"Sure," she said, coyly looking up at him. "Sounds great."

I did a mental eye roll, then made my excuses and left to go back to the kitchen to get some work done. But first, I stepped outside to call Jack and update him on the timeline. He said he'd get back to me after the ME report came in.

The afternoon flew by. The festival was a hit with the school groups, and it was fun to watch a budding interest emerge from some of the students. Deciding it was time for a break, I grabbed my coat and went out through the front doors. The sun was low in the sky, and the temperature was dropping quickly. Elliott was standing next to one of the ice sculptures intently observing something out of my sight line, so I buttoned up my coat and clomped down the steps.

"What's going on?" I asked, taking my gloves out of my pocket.

"Oh, hi, Alex. I'm just keeping an eye on Ryan. He and Clive are going at it again." He nodded toward the scene just at the curve of the path where the two were arguing.

I stomped my foot. "Oooh, that man! I'm really getting tired of his combative behavior. And Ryan has got to stop falling into the trap of letting him get under his skin."

"He's still young." He turned to look at me. "Do you want me to go snuff this out?"

I breathed out an exasperated sigh. "No, I'm just ticked off. I'll handle it. It's my job."

Patrons avoided looking at the scene as they passed, which made me bristle even more as I walked up to the pair. I was in no mood for tact and hissed at them, "What the hell is going on out here?"

Ryan was first to speak. "I'm trying to explain to Clive, if someone purchases one of the stone sculptures, we have to allow them to pull their vehicle in as close as possible to load in, which may mean the pond path if it's one of the pieces near the front entrance, and—"

I put my hand up to stop him from saying anything further. "Ryan, please wait for me over with Elliott." After Ryan stalked off, I leaned in close to Clive.

"Clive, you are embarrassing yourself and the festival by carrying on like this in public. Did you notice those people averting their eyes from this unprofessional display? It's got to stop."

"Ryan is acting like a bratty teenager, and I won't stand for it."

"I'll deal with Ryan. You are the face of the Bennet House, so if there's a problem, you don't deal with it in view of the public, and you know that. What if a board member saw it? What's really going on here?"

He crossed his arms and turned to look across the pond up to the library on the hill.

My shoulders dropped when I saw Clive for what he was—an insecure person overcompensating. He was desperate to fit in, and he wanted to be respected. I suddenly felt sorry for him.

I shifted gears. "Listen, you and I are in a similar position. You feel responsible for what happens here, and I feel responsible for making sure everything runs smoothly both for my people and the Bennet House. We all want the festival to be a success. So let's tag-team. You communicate with me and leave it to me to wrangle the artists. Since it's your first year, I'll just tell ya, artists are a creative bunch, and they're not always the best at following rules." I grinned at him, hoping to lighten things up.

Clive let out a tiny chuckle. "You're right about that. And I know I let things get under my skin, and I need to loosen up. But it's imperative the board feels confident in my ability to do this job."

"Okay. Let's clean the slate and start over. Let's work together and not fight each other anymore. That way we both come out of this looking good."

Clive seemed to relax. "Yes, all right. I think we can do that."

"So how do you want Ryan and Elliott to handle the sculpture pickups?"

"I was trying to tell Ryan it's best for the buyer to schedule a pickup with the Bennet House office. We'll give them plenty of options, but it will eliminate the safety issue of cars driving on the path during festival hours. If a purchase can be picked up in the back, then no problem. Anytime is fine."

"That makes perfect sense to me. I'll make sure they understand."

"Thank you," Clive said.

After Clive left, I went over to Ryan and Elliott. "Ryan, I need you to remember you represent the Workshop, and regardless of whose fault it is, this kind of bellicose behavior is reflecting poorly on us." He looked at me with a puzzled expression, so I added, "Bellicose...contentious."

Once I had pointed out the reflection on the Workshop, he morphed back into the more mature Ryan. "You're right. I hadn't thought of it that way, and I'm sorry. I'll smooth things over with him later, after things have calmed down, okay? Don't worry, I won't let it happen again."

"Good." I then restated what Clive wanted and explained why it made sense. When they both agreed it was a logical solution, I said, "And from now on, come to me before things escalate."

Ryan put up his hand for a high-five, which I ignored. "Ahh, Alex, don't leave me hanging," he said, pleadingly.

With a laugh, I gave him his high-five, and said,

"Now let's end this day on a high note. Get back in there and make happy with the customers."

I decided to take a walk around the pond to clear my head, stopping on the far side to appreciate the scene at the mansion. As evening approached, the dusk-to-dawn path lights were on, and the task lighting on the ice sculptures created a beautiful glow emanating from each piece. Small clusters of people had gathered to *ooh* and *ahh* over the sculptures. The animated voices and laughter as patrons entered and exited the building made me relax.

My phone rang as I was walking back to the mansion. "Hey, Jack, what's the news?" I asked.

"We confirmed the info on his license. Marks is from Cleveland, and the local cops are looking for family for the notification."

"What about the coroner report?"

"Well, that's complicated because the window is fairly wide due to the body temperature, but it appears he was badly injured and died later due to shock and exposure."

I shivered, suddenly cold at the thought of this. "That's just cruel! He could have been saved if the coward hadn't fled the scene."

"I know. And we're running out of avenues to find who did it."

"It's so unfair." The fragility of life struck me as I watched people leaving the Bennet House, smiling, with their bags of merchandise hanging from their hands, just like Eddie had. But Eddie was hit by a car and left to die.

"Nothing else can be done?" I asked.

"I've interviewed the clerk at the truck stop, and

they've requested the surveillance video from the security company for us. Maybe we'll see what time Marks was there, and if he was with anyone. If there's family, they may know what he was doing here. But if we don't get anywhere, we'll have to write it up and put it in the unsolved files."

"That stinks."

"Yup. I don't like it."

I hated that there would likely be no justice for Eddie Marks, but Jack had done what he could for him. Soon, Eddie would make the journey back to Cleveland. I stood for a moment at the pond's edge, thinking about how upset I would be if it were my loved one who had been left to die. When I started to feel the cold seeping through to my core, I shoved my hands in my pockets and made my way inside.

Back in the kitchen, I found Oscar making some tea. "Hi," I greeted, as I sat down in front of my laptop. "Help yourself to any of the snacks in the cabinet. And don't mind me, I'm just getting some work done while I'm here."

"Thank you. I'm good with just the tea. Do you mind?" he asked, gesturing to the seat opposite me.

"Of course not. Please sit down. How are things going for you so far?"

"Good, really good. Your patrons are eager to buy, which is not always the case."

"Yes, we are fortunate that people around here are very supportive of the arts. I hope you're not running low on stock, though, because I may want to buy one of your beautiful lamps, and I know Annie's interested, too."

Oscar became bashful and took a sip of tea. "That's

63

too kind. I should have plenty of lamps to get me through the week."

"Good." I looked down next to my laptop and saw the corner of the photo of Eddie sticking out from the envelope. "While you're here, can I ask you something?" I pulled out the photo and handed it to him. "You don't recall seeing this man here this past weekend, do you?" I gave him a short version of what had happened to Eddie.

He scrutinized the photo. "I think he came by my tables. We talked for a couple of minutes, but he didn't purchase anything. That would have been yesterday afternoon, I think."

"Thank you, it confirms the timeframe he was here. He didn't say anything personal, did he? Like if he had traveled with anyone or was meeting anyone here?"

"No, he was just asking about some of my lamps. He said he has clients he buys for, and asked if I had any other festivals lined up this winter or spring."

"Well, that's interesting, and something new. Thank you!"

Oscar raised his eyes to mine as he handed me the photo. "I also saw him purchase a box from Declan after he talked to me. They chatted for few minutes before he moved on."

"That's helpful. We know he bought something from them, but neither Preston nor Declan remembered him, so now we know for sure when he was there."

I found it interesting Oscar recalled what Declan did not. It further demonstrated why I was drawn to Oscar. He was observant.

****

Once the festival was officially closed for the day,

a group of us went to the Café for dinner. The Main Street Café, which my aunt Claudia had owned for as long as I could remember, was really more like a diner. We had spent many summer and holiday breaks here when I was a kid, and after my mom passed away, Aunt Claudia became a mother figure for me—a role she's a natural at, since she treats her staff and all her regulars at the diner like family.

As we swarmed through the door, Aunt Claudia's eyes widened, watching our group grow in size. "Wow, look at you guys!" she said. "Give me two minutes to pull some tables together for ya."

"I'll help," I offered, and in short order, we were all seated.

Menus flew down the tables, and a happy cacophony ensued, with multiple conversations mingling with the sounds of plates, glasses, and cutlery. Later, after the dinner plates had been cleared and we were waiting for dessert, I got up and walked over to one of the booths.

"Hey! How was dinner?" I looked around. "Where's Ryan?"

Hannah tucked a strand of her long hair behind her ear and said, "Dinner was great! Take a seat. Ryan said he had to get some work done."

I slid into the booth. "Too bad. He loves the desserts here. So, how are your sales going?"

Ethan said, "We're doing great. We've probably got enough inventory to get through, but we have some pieces ready to fire, and we'll knock those out in the mornings this week so we have a little extra stock for next weekend."

"How about you, Elliott? Going well?"

"Actually, yes. I have so many different sizes and designs I can attract a pretty good range of buyers. Ryan's had good luck too. His higher-end art sculptures have been a hit."

I shifted in the booth, folding my right leg under my left. "The week is flying by, and I'm kind of sad about that. It's been such a great burst of energy."

Hannah concurred, "I know. It's been so much fun to spend time with the people from out of town. We don't get to see them often. Plus the new folks…" She looked around, and added, "Oh! Did we forget to invite Preston, Declan, and Oscar?"

I swiveled around to survey the tables and noticed we were indeed short a few people.

Elliott answered, "No, I talked to the three of them before we left. They opted to head back to the lodge and make it an early night."

"Okay. That's good." She leaned forward and dropped her voice to just above a whisper. "I think Maggie and Declan might be doing the dating dance. Have you noticed?"

I chuckled. "You'd have to be blind to miss it."

"Yeah, Ryan's been teasing her about it," Elliott said.

Ethan rubbed his chin. "I just don't know why she's drawn to Declan. He's too smooth for my liking."

Hannah grinned. "That's because you're a guy. Declan's got the bad-boy charm, which can be very alluring." Ethan's eyes opened wide, and she hastily added, "He's not my type, though."

Eliza came over, so I vacated the booth and let her take my place. When I got back to my chair, I noticed I had missed a call from Clive. Since I was finally off the clock, I decided not to call him back, figuring anything he was calling about could wait until tomorrow. I later realized this was a fatal mistake.

Chapter 6

Tuesday

The next morning, I knew I should do a little cleaning around the apartment before settling into work, but I was procrastinating, trying to think of something else I could do instead. Then I remembered the missed call from Clive. I pulled my phone out of my bag to see if he had left a voicemail. Yup, there it was. I put the phone on speaker so I could make another cup of coffee while listening to the message.

"Alex, Clive here. Um, I need to talk to you about something…so please call me back when you get this, or we can talk at the Bennet House tomorrow morning. It's…it's about the photo you were showing around this afternoon. Okay…well…that's it. Thanks, bye."

Huh. Maybe he thought of something to help with the Marks case, but why not just leave whatever it was in the message? It was still early, but I went ahead and tapped his number. I waited through the rings until his voicemail picked up, then left a message.

"Mornin', Clive, it's Alex. Sorry I missed your call last night. Just trying ya back. Feel free to call me, and I'll look for you when I get to the Bennet House later."

I put my phone down and mindlessly tapped my nails on the kitchen counter while thinking. Even though the festival wouldn't open until noon, I could load up and go to the Bennet house to work. I needed to sort through the receipts and ticket sales anyway, and then I would be there when Clive arrived.

It was a gorgeous morning, with a bright blue sky and no breeze. I was humming a little tune as I walked down the hill from Park Street toward the path around the pond, enjoying the chirp of the birds and the occasional burst of red coming from a cardinal flying from branch to branch in the trees. How could anyone not love this weather?

Seeing the glint of sunshine reflecting off the ice on the pond took my breath away. I stopped to enjoy the beauty of the moment, taking in the scene of the library sitting regally on the snow-covered hill. Then my eyes drifted to the opposite end of the pond, nearer to the Bennet House.

Something cluttered the landscape, and I squinted to get a better view. I couldn't tell what it was, but the snow had been trampled near the pond. I hitched my bag up on my shoulder and continued walking. Now I could see one of the ice sculptures had been knocked over.

What the heck? Maybe some raccoons got a little raucous during the night. I started walking faster, already thinking about what we would need to do to clean things up before the public arrived.

As I approached, I saw one of Elliott's ice sculptures on the ground, and the snow was trampled around the whole area down to the pond. I set my tote bag on the path and tromped through the snow to get closer. I was standing with my hands on my hips, surveying the damage, when I looked at the pond.

What is that? Something was lodged under the ice.

I gingerly walked down the slope to take a closer look, then I stopped mid-step, paralyzed, with every nerve ending in my body prickling.

Clive was staring back at me from under the ice.

"Oh my God, oh my God..." I gasped. Clive's body was fully submerged, his pale face pressed against the ice, with his eyes wide open. Tiny air bubbles clung to his bushy eyebrows in the icy cold water, and his dark blue wool coat weighed his body down a few inches. Farther out was the splintered hole in the ice, where he had obviously broken through.

I opened my mouth to scream, but only a high squeak came out, fear seizing my vocal cords. My head was spinning and I turned to climb back up to the path, but my legs weren't moving in tandem with my brain. I tripped over my feet and started sliding closer to the pond, only stopping myself in the nick of time by frantically digging my heels into the soft earth under the snow.

I lay there, breathing heavily, then suddenly snapped to, realizing I had just trampled all over what had to be a crime scene. Clumsily, I reoriented myself to be on my hands and knees, pushed myself up, and retraced my steps back to the path. I pulled off my snow-caked gloves and called 911. After relaying the pertinent information, I called Jack.

"Jack, it's me. I need you here at the Bennet House. I've just found Clive, dead, in the pond."

"On my way. Did you call 911?" he asked in a controlled voice, which starkly contrasted with my frantic tone.

"Yes."

"Do you see anyone else around?"

"No, no one else is here from what I can tell," I said, looking wildly in every direction.

"Wait right there."

"Okay. Hurry."

The silence was deafening as I put my phone back in my pocket. The hideous sight at the edge of the pond was a macabre contrast to the glorious scenery around me, and I couldn't wrap my head around the two irreconcilable images, so I paced back and forth in a ten-foot swath until I heard the sirens. Emergency personnel approached, followed by Jack and Travis.

Jack strode up to me saying, "Tell me what happened."

"I don't know what happened," I said, a bit too loudly. "I walked today, and when I got here, I saw the ice sculpture turned over, and then I saw Clive under the ice."

"Did you walk down there?" he asked, pointing to the pond's edge.

"I'm sorry, but yes. I didn't know there was a body at that point. When I was trying to get back up here, I slipped, and I'm sorry, I made a mess of the area down there. I did walk out via my footprints…for all the good it will do you."

"It's okay. We just need to know what's what. I've got to get to work here, but we need to talk, so don't stray too far."

"Of course, I'll be right here."

"No, go inside. It's too damned cold to stand out here much longer."

"I'm not cold."

"It's shock. You will be. Look at your jeans. They're wet, and your legs are shaking. Seriously, go inside. There's nothing you can do here."

"Okay. I'll be in the kitchen," I replied with a whimper.

Jack turned and greeted the emergency personnel, who were discussing the location of the body and how to extricate it from the ice. This made me shudder, so I picked up my bag and walked up the pathway to the parking lot. No one else was here yet, so I pulled out my loaner key and entered the building.

I was sitting at the kitchen table, resting my head in my hands, when the click-clack of high heels on the wood floor alerted me someone else was here.

Penny hurriedly entered the kitchen and dropped her things on the table. "Alex, what's going on out there? I saw Jack when I pulled in, and he told me to wait in here."

"Oh, Penny, it's awful. I found Clive this morning. He's dead."

"*What?* What are you talking about?"

"He's dead. He was submerged under the ice in the pond."

She pulled out a chair and sat down heavily, with a bewildered look on her face. "I don't understand. What happened?"

"I don't know. The snow had been trampled, and one of the ice sculptures was toppled over. It took a minute for me to realize he was there, under the ice." I looked down at my damp jeans and brushed some of the dirt clinging to my knees, as if trying to swipe away the memory of what I'd seen.

"Oh my gosh," was all she could say. She looked shell-shocked.

"Let me get you some tea," I said quietly.

It felt good to have a purpose, so I got up and put the kettle on to boil and rummaged in the cabinet for some of the packaged foods we had gotten for the break room. I set her tea in front of her and put a heap of granola bars and muffins in the middle of the table. "Drink your tea and eat something. It's going to be a long day, and you're going to need your strength." I also knew sugar was good for shock.

Penny went through the motions without argument. I got another cup of coffee and followed my own advice and grabbed a muffin.

We sat in silence until Penny found her voice. "So, I've not heard the word 'accident' yet."

"I honestly don't think it was an accident," I said.

"I just can't believe it. What on earth happened?"

She sounded genuinely bewildered. Jack might think otherwise, but I knew if Penny was going to kill Clive, she would have done it in a very neat and tidy way, not in the manner I saw outside. My instinct told me she had no part in what happened to Clive, so I was comfortable talking with her about it.

Before long, the back door clanged open and shut, and moments later Jack entered the kitchen, the cold air clinging to him like a cloud.

"Good, you're both here," he declared, tossing his hat on the table and pulling out a chair to sit.

I got up to get a mug for Jack and set the coffee maker in motion again. "What in the world, Jack? What happened out there?" I asked.

"We're trying to sort things out right now. The scene has been documented, the emergency crew is working on getting him out of the pond, and I've got Matt and Travis combing the area for any evidence.

Someone went to the trouble to cover up some blood near the bank of the pond, so this was no accident." He pulled out his flip pad and pen. "I need to ask you both some questions, okay?"

"Of course," Penny said softly.

I put the steaming mug in front of Jack, then took my seat. I sat on my hands to keep them from shaking and asked, "What do you need to know?"

"I'll get to you in a minute, Alex. Penny, just to get the formalities over with, where were you last night?"
"Of course. I know you have to ask. I was here until about seven thirty, and then I went home. My mother and my aunt are in town, and they were waiting on me for dinner. I called my mom from the car to tell her I was on the way."

"And was Clive still here then?"

"No—he left before me, and I didn't see anyone else on the premises. I always check before locking up for the night."

"Okay, thank you." He looked at both of us and asked, "Do either of you know of any reason why someone would want to kill Clive?"

Penny took a deep breath and exhaled. "I'll be honest. Clive was a difficult person. He rubbed a lot of people the wrong way, but badly enough for someone to kill him? I can't even fathom that."

"I agree," I added. "He was argumentative, snide, and a general pain, which caused some aggravation. But I can't imagine someone killing him for being a jerk." I felt badly for speaking ill of the dead, and added, "Sorry, that wasn't very nice, but you need the truth, right? And it's the truth."

"Yes, I need an honest assessment. Who had issues

with Clive?" he asked.

"Well, I did," I admitted, chewing on my thumbnail. "Penny handled him better than me. She's the consummate professional and manages to do her job and not let him rattle her. But, yes, Clive and I got into a couple of times. And pretty much everyone has had one story or another, complaining about his behavior."

Penny said, "When he left last night, he almost seemed in good spirits. I mean, he wasn't overly friendly, but he wasn't brusque like he often is." She shook her head. "I think your list will be long if you count anyone who had a run-in with Clive."

Jack muttered to himself, "This is going to be a real mess." Then he looked at Penny. "Do you have surveillance cameras here?"

"Yes. Both exterior doors and one in the lobby."

"We'll need to look at the footage."

"I'll call the security company. It's all kept off-site."

"Okay, thank you. The next order of business is to contact all the artists so we can go through their interview process as quickly as possible. Alex, can everyone meet over at the Workshop? That way they won't be muddling around here, near the crime scene."

"Sure," I said. "What will happen to the Festival? Not to be callous, just thinking logistics. Will we be able to open up today at noon?"

Jack looked at his watch. "It depends on how quickly we process the scene. Penny, we'll set up a blockade so people can't enter the path, and I'll leave it to you on how you'll deal with patrons in the event you can't open up today."

Penny nodded and pushed back her chair. "I'll start

contacting the artists. Alex, how about I tell them to be at the Workshop at ten? And in a little while we can confer with Jack and decide if we should remain closed today."

"Good plan," I said. "I'll call Maggie to let her know what's happened and to get the lounge ready when she gets in. I can't focus enough to think straight about whether we should open up today, but the sooner we can answer that question, the better."

Penny went to the office to make the calls. Jack held up a finger just as I tapped Maggie's number.

"When you're done with Maggie, I want to talk to you further."

"I figured as much—oh hi, Maggie, no, I was talking to Jack." After giving her the quick recap, staving off questions I knew I had no answers to, I hung up and turned back toward Jack.

He leaned his elbows on the table and looked me square in the eye. "I need a rundown of everyone here. The short version of who's who."

I tried not to squirm under his gaze. "All right, but this feels weird, Jack, because some are Workshop people. And most of the out-of-towners I've known since moving here."

"I know. But it would be a big help. Just give me the basics: who dealt with him, who had problems with him, and what you've seen or heard since the festival started. Best case, since this is a public event, we'll be able to at least eliminate this pool of people from the seemingly endless suspect list."

I nodded in understanding. "Well, Clive had a habit of sniping at people. He also skulked around a lot, which didn't set well. So, let me think back. As I told you, I've had my own run-ins with him since last Thursday when the festival setup started. I know Oscar witnessed one of those. But Clive and I ended on a good note the last time I saw him."

Jack was scribbling in his notebook. "What about other people from the Workshop?"

"Maura is his ex-wife, but she seems to understand him and doesn't let him bother her. Ryan has had a few altercations with him because of logistics with the sculptures and the path."

"Were their problems resolved?"

"I think so. Ryan said he was going to make things right with him."

"What else?" he prompted.

"At the Lodge, when a group of us gathered at the end of the weekend, there was a general discussion about his behavior. Almost everyone chimed in about something. So, he's offended pretty much everybody at one time or another. But nothing stands out as escalating to the point of murder. I mean, nowhere close to that level."

"When did you last see him?"

"Yesterday, at a little before five p.m. That was when he was arguing with Ryan. But, as I said, we resolved our issues, and it felt like things might get better."

"And that's it, you didn't talk to him again?"

"No, but he left me a voicemail last night." I must be in shock. That was the whole reason I'd come early this morning, and I'd almost forgotten about it. "I listened to it this morning. He wanted to tell me something about the photo of Eddie Marks. It didn't sound urgent, and he said we could talk today if I didn't get back to him last night. I just thought maybe he remembered seeing Eddie and wanted to be more helpful. But could his message be significant? Could it have something to do with what happened to him?" I asked, becoming anxious.

"Did he say anything specific in the message?"

"No. I tried to call him back, but he didn't answer, so I thought I would just catch him here when he arrived." My voice dropped to a hushed groan. "Oh, that means when I called him this morning he was dead under the ice out there! I feel kind of sick." I had a mental image of his phone in his wet coat pocket, the muffled ringing under the ice breaking the silence of the scene. I squeezed my eyes shut to block it out.

Jack clasped my arm. "Hey, hold it together. I'm going to need you focused, so put that imagination of yours on hold."

"I'll try," I said, but in truth, I didn't know how I could possibly hold it together enough to get past what I'd seen.

****

Back at the Workshop, Maggie placed the large coffee urn on the table and asked, "With the artists, volunteers, and Bennet House staff coming, will this be enough?"

"It's fine," I said. "Under the circumstances, I don't think anyone is going to expect us to put out a spread."

She leaned her hip against the table and crossed her arms. "I know. I'm just trying to focus on something else. What the heck, Alex. This is crazy!"

I motioned for her to follow me around the corner into the kitchen, where I started opening cabinets.

Being a nervous eater, I was looking for something to munch on.

"It was awful. I can't get the image out of my head. And I can't fathom what happened, and why."

"So you actually found him? What did the scene look like to you?"

I pulled a container down with crackers and started mindlessly crunching on them. Between mouthfuls, I relayed what I was comfortable saying out loud, which wasn't much.

Maggie gasped. "Oh my gawd. Who could have hated him so much?"

"I have no idea. Nobody we know would have been pushed that far. Hell, nobody we know would commit murder. Period."

The voices of the festival crew coming into the lounge reminded me of my duty. I really wanted to be by myself and curl up in a ball on my bed, but I fielded a steady stream of questions and had repeated a general statement about Clive's death more than a few times by the time Jack poked his head in and motioned to me to come into the hall.

"You mentioned being at the café last night. What time did you all leave the Bennet House, and what time did you leave the café?" he asked.

"We left after the festival closed, so sometime after seven, and then we stayed at the café until a little after closing, so after ten p.m. Why? Do you have a time of death already?"

"Not exactly, but his watch got broken at some point, which helps narrow it down. It stopped at a little before nine thirty p.m."

"So anyone who was at the café is in the clear,

right?" *Omigosh.* Was it possible Clive's murder would clearly, and definitively, not have anything to do with my people? That would be an incredible relief.

"Presumably so. I need a list of everyone who was there, and if anyone came and went at any point during that timeframe."

"Okay. Let's go to my office."

Once we were there, I closed the door behind us and made a list of who had been at the café: me, Annie, Spencer, Ari, Maggie, Ryan, Ethan, Hannah, Shelby, Lena, Eliza, Becca, Clara, Twila, Hank, JJ, and Bitsy. I handed it to Jack.

"There was another small group of volunteers and some of the amateur artists who came on their own," I said. "But I doubt any of them had any contact with Clive. They were only involved on the periphery of the festival. If you need their names, Bitsy may be able to help. Her brain remembers everything."

"Did anyone leave? And who wasn't there from the festival?"

"Oh, Ryan left early, I think to get some work done here. And Declan, Preston, and Oscar didn't join us. They were going directly back to the Lodge. We know Penny went home, and I don't know about Maura."

"Thanks. This is a big help."

We walked back to the lounge, and Jack made a brief statement to the group. "Good morning, thank you for coming. As I'm sure you've heard, Clive Collins was found dead this morning near the Bennet House. I extend my condolences to each and every one of you. I will need to speak with you one at a time, but we'll do this as quickly as possible. Once I've spoken with you, you'll be free to go about your business. Alex?" He indicated to me to say something.

I quickly gathered my thoughts, and said, "I know Penny has communicated with all of you. We'll decide shortly if we can open the festival today, so please keep an eye on your phones. She or I will text you updates."

Jack interjected. "Once you're done here, if you return to the Bennet House, use the parking lot entrance, and if they still have it cordoned off, show your ID to the officer. Penny has given him a list of your names."

He looked back at me, so I continued. "And, of course, the Workshop will be open all day for our out-of-town guests. The lounge and kitchen will be at your disposal, and there is studio space if you would like to get some work done."

He looked at the paper I had given him, and called out, "Maura, could you please come with me?"

One by one, Jack pulled people across the hall to have a chat. A little over an hour later, Travis arrived, and asked me where Jack was. His congenial face was unusually deadpan, so after a few minutes, I poked my head out the door and saw Jack and Travis in the hallway having a quiet, but earnest, conversation.

"What's up?" I asked, walking toward them.

Jack jerked when he heard my voice and turned to me with a serious face. "How many are left in the lounge?"

"Just Preston, Annie, and Spencer. Preston is the last to be interviewed," I said.

Jack turned to Travis. "Go get Preston's info and tell him he can go, but I'll need to talk to him later." To me, he said, "I need to speak with Ryan."

"You already talked to him. What's this about?"

"Not now, Alex. Is he still here?"

"Um, let's see. He's probably in his studio," I said, trying squelch the rising panic in my gut.

"Take me there."

I walked him down the hall. "Jack, what's going on?"

"Just doing my job. You can either wait for me in the lounge or you can come with me, but you have to keep your cool if you stay with me, okay?"

I swallowed, suddenly finding my throat was dry, and squeaked a soft "Okay."

Jack knocked firmly on the studio door and entered without waiting for a reply.

Ryan looked up from a stone sculpture he was working on. "Hi! All done with the interviews? Any news?" he asked.

Jack stepped forward, and in his most official voice said, "Ryan, I need you to come with me to the station to answer some questions. Will you come voluntarily?"

Chapter 7

I sputtered in protest, "What the hell is going on, Jack?"

Ryan's face paled and his mouth hung open in disbelief. He looked like a frightened teenager, and I was incapable of helping him.

His head swiveled back and forth looking between Jack and me. "I'm happy to answer any questions here. Why do I need to go to the station?"

I rushed to his side and said, "Wait. Ryan, don't say another word. Jack, you haven't answered me. What's going on? Are you arresting him?"

Jack stood mute, his eyes imploring me not to ask any more questions. "No. But based on evidence found at the scene, he needs to come in for formal questioning. I'll ask again, Ryan, will you come voluntarily?"

Ryan's face scrunched in confusion. "Um, I guess. What evidence are you talking about?"

"Jack, you better mirandize him," I snapped. "Ryan, do not say a word until I can get an attorney there with you. And I'll be at the station as soon as I can."

On the way to the car, I texted Maggie to call Penny and tell her we shouldn't open today. Once in the car, I connected my phone to Bluetooth and called Bitsy's husband, Jim. He wasn't a criminal attorney, but he was a lawyer and I knew he could help. As soon as Jim answered, I felt some comfort in his confident and calm voice.

After I explained the situation, he said, "I'll meet you at the station in about fifteen minutes."

"Thank you," I said. I couldn't believe what was happening, and wondered if my reaction was over the top. "Jim, surely Jack knows Ryan didn't have anything to do with this. I mean, we don't actually know why he wants to question him. Do I really need to be all *Law and Order* about this? I even barked at Jack to read him his rights, for crying out loud."

"You are absolutely doing the right thing. And Jack's doing exactly what he's supposed to do, especially under the circumstances of you two being family, and both of you having a friendship with Ryan. Everything must be above board. Don't worry, I'll be there shortly."

****

The inside of the precinct hadn't changed since I had been here earlier in the fall. The long, reclaimed church pew, which served as a visitor's bench, sat against the wall across from the chest-high reception desk, with the scarred wood swinging half door at the end of the counter. The same sticky plastic tablecloth covered the coffee table, and the coffee looked just as undrinkable as it had before. The only changes were the thumbtacked postings on the cork bulletin board with advertisements and announcements.

Matt, behind the reception desk, looked slightly awkward as he hopped up to greet me. "Alex, Jack wants to see you in his office. Ryan is in the interview room."

Instead of going to Jack's office, I went straight to the interview room and stuck my head in the door. Ryan looked like a deer in headlights.

"Bitsy's husband, Jim, is on the way. You didn't say anything on the way here, did you?" I asked.

"No. And neither did Jack. I'm really confused, Alex. Do they think I killed Clive?"

"Hold on, I'm going to see what I can find out."

I squared my shoulders and marched into the precinct room and entered Jack's office. "Okay, Jack, will you tell me what the hell is going on?"

Jack leaned back in his chair and motioned for me to sit, which I did, reluctantly.

"I'm sorry to have done it that way, but because of our family relationship, and your friendship with Ryan, I have to do this strictly by the book."

I knew I looked angry, but I couldn't help it, and I snapped, "That didn't answer my question."

Jack continued in a calm voice, which just ticked me off more. "So, the ME report says Clive was stabbed just below the sternum. He then stumbled, or was pushed, out onto the ice. He probably thought he could flee across the pond. The ice cracked, and he went under and couldn't get out. He drowned, but with the stabbing, he wouldn't have lasted very long in such cold water."

"Oh my God." My pulse quickened. "What does this have to do with Ryan? Ryan would never do this."

He held up a bag for me to see. "This was found at the scene."

Inside was a long, pointed metal object, with dried blood covering half of it. I recognized it immediately as a chiseling tool, like Ryan and Elliott used for their stone sculptures.

I could feel my face blanch, and I gasped. "Oh my gosh. This has to be a mistake."

"There's no mistake. The blood type matches Clive's. We're just waiting on a DNA match. Ryan's prints are on this chisel. He's in the database from the fall, when everyone had their prints taken for elimination purposes—"

I interrupted, "It's a sculpting tool, and Ryan's a sculptor. So of course his prints would be on it."

Jack ignored my snippy attitude, and continued. "From the statements taken earlier, Ryan was seen having arguments with Clive, his tool was used to stab Clive, and he left the café early. That's motive, means, and opportunity, which means he's become a person of interest."

"Where was this found?"

"Buried in the snow, near where the ice sculpture was tipped over."

"Oh, come on, Jack. Why on earth would he leave it there if he had just killed Clive with it? This makes no sense."

"Did you see Ryan leave the café?"

"No. When I went over to sit with Elliott, Ethan, and Hannah, he'd already left."

"Okay." Jack scribbled a note in his flip pad.

A moment later, Jim entered Jack's office. I got up and stood to the side while they talked.

"So what's this about, Jack?" he asked.

Jack told Jim what he had just told me.

"This is purely circumstantial, and I'm sure you know that," Jim said, with efficiency.

"That's why he hasn't been charged. But I've got

to question him, and we're going to have to search his apartment, car, and art studio."

"Well, get on the horn and get a search warrant. I will advise him you must get one before carrying out a search."

"I would have expected nothing less," Jack said evenly. "I've already got a call out. I should have it shortly."

"Give me two minutes with Ryan, and then you can come ask your questions."

My legs felt like they weighed a ton as we walked down the hall a few minutes later. Jack went in to the interview room, and I went to the little room on the other side of the glass to watch.

Jack turned on the recorder, recited who was in the room, then read Ryan his rights. Once finished, he said, "Thanks for coming in, Ryan. I need to ask you some questions, and you may confer with Jim at any point."

"Okay. What do you need to know?"

In a friendly voice, Jack asked, "Ryan, can you tell me what you did last night? Say, between seven and eleven p.m.?"

Ryan seemed to visibly relax. "Oh, is that all? Well, we all went to the café when the festival closed, so around seven thirty or so."

"Did you drive on your own or with someone else?"

"I knew I needed to finish up some work, so I drove on my own."

"What time did you leave the café?"

Ryan thought for a moment, then said, "Had to be around eight or a little after. I ordered a club sandwich and took it with me."

"Where did you go then?"

"Well, to the Workshop, of course. I worked in my studio until about ten p.m. and then went home."

"Was anyone else there? Did you see anyone?"

"Um, nooo," he said slowly. "I didn't see anyone at the Workshop, and I live alone."

Jack then placed the evidence bag on the table. "Can you identify this?"

Ryan leaned forward. "That looks like a chisel."

"This was found at the scene of Clive's murder. It has your prints on it. Can you give me any explanation for how it got there?"

Ryan looked at the tool, his anxiety clearly visible. "If my prints are on it, it must be my chisel, but I have no idea how it ended up at the crime scene."

Jack moved in a new direction. "It's come to my attention that you have recently had some public disagreements with Clive. Would you say that's an accurate statement?"

Jim leaned over toward Ryan, but Ryan blustered and said, "It's no secret we didn't get along, but Clive and I straightened that all out before he left for the day…the evening he was killed."

Jim stepped in now. "Ryan, I really must advise you not to say anything else."

Ryan shook his head in frustration, then bolted upright. "Wait a minute! Hold that up again." Jack complied. "That's part of the tool set I took to the Bennet House for the live demonstrations. I left my most expensive chisels in my studio, and I put a canvas bag with more generic tools in the entry closet for when I do demonstrations. Someone must have taken it from there. It was totally accessible to anyone."

Jim stopped Ryan from saying anything further and addressed Jack. "So this makes what was already circumstantial evidence, even more convincingly so. That tool was accessible to hundreds of people. And from what I've heard, plenty of people had run-ins with Clive. Going to the Workshop that night to work in his studio, without witnesses to give him an alibi, is hardly cause for suspicion."

Jack nodded, then said, "Perhaps. But there's no getting around the fact we still have the trifecta of motive, means, and opportunity. Clive didn't simply annoy Ryan, they actually had verbal sparring. He doesn't have an alibi, and his tool was used in the crime. So here's what we're going to do." Jack looked at Ryan. "I have to follow procedure and tick some boxes. Do I have your permission to search your apartment, studio, car, phone, and the tool bag at the Bennet House?"

Jim answered, as Jack expected, "No, you do not. You will need a warrant."

Ryan was growing impatient and said to Jim, "Let's just get it over with. I don't have anything to hide, and I don't want this to take any longer than it has to. I didn't have anything to do with Clive's death."

Jack hesitated, then said, "Ryan, please take Jim's advice. I would not normally say this, but because of our relationship and my family connection to Alex, I actually suggest waiting for the warrant. There cannot be even a whiff of impropriety. Do you understand?"

"I guess so."

"Thank you. I'm going to have to ask you to stay here while we do our search. You are not under arrest, but we can hold you for up to forty-eight hours."

Ryan nodded in resignation. "All right. I'll wait here."

Jack pushed his chair back, got up, and turned off the recorder. And once he and Jim left the room, I went in to talk to Ryan.

"Oh my gosh, Alex! I didn't do it. I swear. This is really scary. Someone took my tool and left it to frame me!"

"I know. I wish I could say something to make this easier. One thing I'm sure of, Jack wants nothing more than to be able to clear you. And you're in good hands with Jim. Just follow his advice, sit tight, and hopefully this will be over before the end of the day."

"Are you going to be here?"

"It's going to take a while for them to get the warrant and carry out the searches, and I need to be at the Workshop when they search your studio. Plus, I want to get to work and try and help you get out of this mess, so I'm going to take off. Do you want anything? Need anything?"

"No, I'm okay," he said, but he didn't look okay.

I reluctantly got up and quietly closed the door behind me. I caught Jim in the hallway on his way out. "Thank you for coming so quickly. I really appreciate it."

"No problem. Glad I can help. But look, if this goes any further, he'll need a criminal defense lawyer. But let's hope it doesn't come to that. I'll be in touch."

It made my stomach sick to even consider Ryan needing a criminal lawyer. And speaking of feeling sick, I really didn't want to talk to Jack right now, but I had to.

He looked up from his desk and said, "Now you

know why I had to do things by the book, right?"

I sat heavily in the chair next to his desk. "I do. But honestly, Jack, you don't think Ryan did this, do you?"

"You know I've got to follow the evidence, and right now, it means putting him under scrutiny. I'm hoping we find enough to clear him, or at the least, we don't find anything to warrant holding him. The weapon is circumstantial. Yes, his prints are on it, but it's his tool, so they would be."

"Exactly." I started to get up, then stopped in my tracks. "Wait, what about the message Clive left me last night wanting to talk to me about the photo. Are you even considering that this could be linked to Eddie Marks?"

"As far as I'm concerned, two violent deaths are too much of a coincidence. So yes, it's a possibility. Right now, though, we have to deal with the evidence in front of us, and that evidence points to Ryan. But it doesn't mean I'm not thinking two steps ahead about other scenarios."

"Damn it. This feels like deflection, and it's wasting valuable time."

"We're going to work as quickly as we can. And in my public statement, I'll be asking anyone who might have been in the area last night to please come forward. We may get lucky and find a witness who saw someone near the Bennet House last night."

"I don't know if his chisel was taken out of convenience or to frame him. If it was to frame him, what if other evidence was planted?" I asked.

"Let's hope that's not the case. We're either going to find something else or we'll go a long way to clearing him."

"What about the interviews with the artists? Did you get anything useful from them?"

"Not really. Most admitted Clive was cantankerous at times, but they all said he was great with the public. And no one saw anything unusual. Declan, Preston, and Oscar went back to the Lodge instead of going to the café with the rest of you. They had a quick dinner, then made it an early night and went to their rooms. Maura said she met friends for dinner, then went home."

I didn't want anyone I knew to be a suspect, but I felt encouraged Ryan might not be the sole person without an alibi. "So there's a window of time when some of them can't be accounted for, right?"

"Right, but other than Maura, they only met Clive at the festival and only had limited interaction with him. So as of now, none of them have motive, whereas Ryan does."

I clenched my fists. "Oh, this is infuriating!"

"I know it is. And I also know you're not going to like what I have to say now."

"What?" I looked at him with squinty eyes.

"You're benched. You're too close to this situation. So until Ryan is cleared, or charged, you need to stay out of the investigation."

The seconds ticked by as I stared at him. "Okay. I guess you're right."

"Well, that was easier than I thought," he said.

I smiled benignly at him. *That's what I want you to think, you big oaf. There's no way in hell I'm going to sit back and do nothing!*

****

I dreaded telling Maggie what was happening with Ryan. They were close, and I knew this would be dropping a bombshell on her.

She looked up with anticipation when I entered. "Is there any news?" Her forehead crinkled in concern. "Excuse my bluntness, but you don't look so good."

I looked down at my mud-stained jeans, which only served to remind me of the crime scene, and said, "Oh my gosh, I still need to change."

"I don't mean your clothes, although yeah, they look pretty rough, too. I mean your face is pale, and your eyes are sunk in your head. The shock of Clive is bad enough, but you seem worse now than earlier. Are you okay?"

I pulled up a stool and perched on it. "Not really, and I've got to tell you some hard news. Take a seat."

Maggie tentatively pulled up another stool to sit. "What is it? You're scaring me."

"Ryan has been taken in for questioning—"

"What?" Maggie interrupted.

"Evidence was found at the scene—one of Ryan's stone chisels. It has his prints on it, and what appears to be Clive's blood."

Maggie blanched. "This can't be. No. I won't believe he had anything to do with this," she said, her eyes welling up.

"Please don't panic. You and I both know Ryan wouldn't hurt a fly, but Jack has to follow the evidence. And hopefully, following the evidence will clear Ryan and send them in another direction."

Maggie sniffled and wiped the tears with her hand, smearing her mascara in the process. "How's he doing? Where is he? Can I see him?"

"One thing at a time. He's still at the precinct and will be there at least until the search of his apartment, car, and studio, are complete. I want to be here when they search his studio, so do you want me to check with Jack and see if you can sit with Ryan while he waits?"

"Would you? I don't want him left there afraid and alone, and I'll just be here stewing."

I pulled my phone from my pocket. "Let me text Jack," I said, tapping out the message. Within a few minutes, Jack texted it would be okay, so I gave Maggie a hug and told her to try not to show any anxiety while with Ryan. "He needs to know we're going to get him out of this," I said, trying to exhibit more confidence than I felt.

She nodded in agreement, and seemed to pull herself together knowing she had something to do. "I'll pick up some sandwiches. I bet he hasn't eaten."

"Good idea. I'm going to talk to Spencer and see if he'll cover the front desk while I'm upstairs getting to work."

Since the festival was canceled today, Spencer was working in his studio, so I repeated the process I just went through with Maggie. Other than tears and smeared mascara, it went about the same with Spencer as it had with her. He quickly agreed to man the front desk so he could alert me when the deputy arrived to search Ryan's studio.

I ran up to my apartment, dropped my tote on the couch, gave Baxter a pat on the head, then headed for the bedroom to change into fresh clothing. When I took off my jeans, I noticed dark streaks of dirt on my knees. I felt like I couldn't get away from myself, so I stripped down and took a blazing hot shower. After putting the mud-stained jeans in the laundry room, I headed for the coffee machine. The sound of the grinding beans and the aroma as it dripped into the cup helped my mental state.

The first order of business was to call Michael for some legal advice. He was a top-tier attorney and my ex-husband. The short version of the story was we were considered to be a power couple back in Philly, but we realized our marriage had been built out of professional convenience, and thankfully, before it was too late, we decided we were better suited as friends.

"Hey, stranger," he answered, with a friendly voice.

"Hey, how are things there?"

"Busy. I'm in the middle of a big case."

"I won't take much of your time, then. I just need some advice." I recapped the whole story for him.

Michael was all business when he spoke. "You did the right thing to bring Jim in to represent Ryan, and the interview sounds like it was textbook. Jack's also doing the right thing to stick to procedure."

"What if it goes further, and he's arrested?"

"At that point, he'll need a criminal attorney. You get in touch with me, and I'll find someone who can represent him. Don't just google and pick somebody out of a hat."

"Okay. I can't thank you enough. That's a load off."

"Let's hope you won't need my help. And in the meantime, just do what you do, and keep focused."

"I will. And I know you're super busy, so I'll try not to bother you."

"You are never a bother to me. Text me either way. If he's cleared, great. If not, I'll call ya after I do some checking around and give you some names."

"Okay."

"You stay out of trouble, and we'll talk again soon." Michael knew I tended to leap before I looked.

After we hung up, I was ready to get to work. This was my wheelhouse. In my old job as a political strategist, I always felt the most relaxed when I could strategize and implement a plan to problem solve. I guess it had something to do with feeling in control of a situation totally out of my control.

I put my cup of coffee on the table next to the couch and pulled out my laptop. The first order of business was to create a document segmented into columns, listing those who were at the café the entire time on Monday night and therefore eliminated from the suspect list; those who still needed to be cleared; and, of course, the third column for the to-be-determined outsiders.

Then I created a page with questions:

Who had a motive to kill Clive?

Who had access to Ryan's tools?

Is this person someone from the festival or someone who had attended the festival?

What were Clive's movements the last few days?

Who had something to gain from his death?

Did we have any photo or video history of the weekend?—ask Penny and Maggie.

Could outside influences have provoked this?—ask Maura and Penny.

I texted Maggie to look through photos later for any including Clive. I had a feeling there would be few to none, but I had to cover all bases. Then I perused the lists I had made, looking for a starting place. My conclusion was that I had a pathetic amount to work with.

Feeling at a loss, which is unusual for me, I unfolded myself from the couch and paced back and forth in the living room while chewing on my thumbnail. *Think Alex, think*, I admonished myself. Out of nowhere, I had an overwhelming urge to talk to Walter and picked up my phone.

"Alex, your timing is perfect," he said. "I've been knee-deep in paperwork all morning and was up at three a.m. for a conference call in London, so I could really use a break. How are things on your end?" Walter had a gentle but confident voice, and as he spoke, some of the tension left my body.

I couldn't help myself and started right in, pouring out the story of Clive's murder. He then calmly asked me follow-up questions, which I answered to the best of my ability.

Walter was a businessman who also had a history of being a behind-the-scenes political confidant and advisor for a select few at the highest level of government. His demeanor was unflappable.

He said, "I can hear you pacing, so first, sit down and take a deep breath."

"You nailed it. Okay, I'm sitting down. The situation with Ryan has me all discombobulated. He's counting on me. Jack has sidelined me, but I'm not going to just sit around and do nothing."

"Cut yourself some slack. I'd say finding Clive's body this morning is more unsettling than getting Ryan out of trouble. You can help Ryan, and Jack's really good at his job, and he'll get to the bottom of this. The issue is figuring out how to get past the shock of seeing a dead man under the ice."

I sat up a little straighter. "You make a good point. I need to muddle through the psychological issues and then focus on the tangibles, which will help Ryan, and keep me somewhat distracted from the hideous nature of this crime."

"That's all you can do," he stated, then added, "Would you like me to come?"

I realized I actually did want him to come, but instead said, "Oh, I'll be all right. You don't need to drop everything and come here."

He was silent for a beat, then said, "Then why don't you get in touch with the gang and have them come over and brainstorm with you? I would feel better knowing you aren't wearing a hole in the floor pacing all by yourself."

"That's a good idea. They don't know about Ryan yet, and I don't want them finding out via the gossip hotline."

"And keep me in the loop. Call me later, and let me know how things are going."

"I will, and thanks. I can't tell you how much it's helped to talk to you."

We said our goodbyes, and I sat for a moment holding the phone, marveling how talking to a person I hadn't known but five months felt like putting on a warm, cozy sweater. I shook myself back to the task at hand and put out an SOS text to Annie, JJ, and Bitsy. They all chimed back they would be here in an hour, so I grabbed my keys and went downstairs to the front desk to talk to Spencer, who was hanging up from a phone call.

"I was just getting ready to text you. That was Matt. He'll be here in a few minutes to look over

Ryan's studio. Do you want me to wait here for him?"

"No, it's okay, I'll do it. And hey, Annie, JJ, and Bitsy, are coming to help me brainstorm later. Do you want to join us?"

"I sure do. I can't really focus while Ryan is waiting to be cleared, or, I can't even say it…charged."

"I know. I feel the same way."

A few minutes later, Matt entered the lobby with an apologetic look on his face. "I'm sorry, Alex. I know this is rough, but I've got to search Ryan's studio."

"It's okay. Jack told me someone would be coming. I'll need to join you because this is on Workshop property. Don't worry, though. I won't interfere with what you need to do."

"I appreciate it. This is hard enough."

We walked down the hallway to Ryan's studio, which looked forlorn in the absence of his zealous energy. I dragged a chair over to the door and perched while Matt went methodically around the room. There was a large piece of stone waiting for hammer and chisel to continue chipping away at it to reveal a piece of art. Small chunks of stone were on the floor, and Ryan's safety goggles were sitting on the height-adjustable work stool.

I inhaled deeply and took in the odd scent of the room, a combination of stone and wood, and my eyes followed the abstract design of footsteps in the blanket of white stone dust covering the floor.

Matt had moved from the shelves and was slowly walking along the wall of windows which looked out onto the courtyard.

"Can you tell me what you think you might find?" I asked.

He avoided my gaze. "This is awkward, Alex. I know you've helped Jack out before, but Ryan's a person of interest and he's a close friend of yours, so I really can't say anything."

"I understand. Well, I don't understand *any* of it, but I get what you're saying."

"I can imagine how hard this is," he said, sympathetically. "Look, I doubt I'll find anything, but we have to tick every box."

I thought about the searches taking place. Was I fooling myself? Did I need to face the hard reality they might find something? I squeezed my eyes shut to stop my imagination from creating the scene where Jack would find a shirt with Clive's blood on it in Ryan's apartment.

Chapter 8

Tuesday, late afternoon

While waiting for the gang to arrive, I distracted myself by doing a quick twirl of a clean-up. Once Baxter's floating fur had been corralled and dumped in the trash and my own mess had been straightened, I surveyed the results and did a mental pat on my back for a job well done. I fully embraced what I called deceptive tidiness.

Once I stopped moving, though, an unyielding energy drain hit me, and I gave in and lay on the couch, closing my eyes. I needed to come to terms with what I had seen this morning. Sometime later, I opened my eyes and the changing light through the windows told me it was late afternoon. I should have realized this by the rumbling of my stomach and got up to take a quick assessment of what food I had on hand.

I opened the fridge and took stock. Ketchup, salad dressing, and leftovers far enough past their prime they were unrecognizable. That wasn't going to cut it, so I opened the cupboard and grabbed two bags of microwave popcorn. While each bag was popping, I pulled out a can of mixed nuts and a bag of miniature chocolates leftover from my post-holiday sale candy stash. This perfect blend of salty and sweet almost looked intentional, and I had just placed the filled bowls on the coffee table when there was a knock on the door.

"The phone tree is in full force. Spencer called Annie, and so on. So we're up to speed," Bitsy declared, taking off her wool cape, which had been held in place with a bright cardinal pin. She kept on her jaunty beret, which had a goldfinch perched on the band. Baxter instantly became intrigued.

JJ removed her jacket and starting digging in her purse. She pulled out some incense sticks and looked at me. "May I?" she asked. After I gave the okay, she lit one and started walking around the room waving her arm in a wide arc. "This is benzoin. It provides clarity of the mind and clears negative energy. It also eases sadness and anxiety."

Annie, Spencer, and I looked at each other and shrugged. At this point, we'd take any help we could get. I wasn't sure what to expect and feared the worst, but the benzoin had a nice vanilla and slight balsam scent.

"I have tea, coffee, or water. Who wants what?" I asked.

After we settled around the coffee table with our drinks, I sat on the floor in front of my laptop, and the elephant in the room was finally acknowledged.

"Do you feel like talking about it?" Bitsy asked me, with empathy in her eyes.

"It was awful, you guys. I don't think you need to hear the details of what I saw, and I think I'm better off focusing on solving this."

"Well then, let's get busy," Annie suggested, knowing I would want to move on from talking about the nitty gritty details of the death.

I reached to the top of my head and pulled my

glasses down before opening the laptop. "Let's start by compiling what we know."

"We obviously know Ryan didn't kill Clive!" Spencer proclaimed.

"Yes, we know, but we can't prove a negative. So let's talk about what we do know." I opened the desktop folder and pulled up the page with columns. "Let's separate who was and was not at the café."

"Is that significant?" Spencer asked.

"Possibly. We were there during a big chunk of time that evening, and Jack is issuing a public statement with a request for anyone in the vicinity of the Bennet House during those hours to please come forward."

"That should put all of us who were at the café in the clear, right?" Annie asked.

"That's the theory I'm working from. So, let's confirm my list of everyone who was there."

One by one, names were thrown out, and I scanned the list I had already made. As I suspected, Bitsy's memory recalled a few others from the festival who were at the diner that evening.

"Who's left?" JJ asked.

"Maura," Annie contributed.

"Oscar," Bitsy added.

"What about Declan and Preston?" Spencer asked.

"Yup, you're right," I said and typed their names in the "unaccounted for" column. "Let's take them one at a time. Maura: what do we know?"

"She was married to Clive, right? Do we know anything about their history?" Annie asked.

I leaned back against the couch. "Maura was talking about it the other day when I stopped in the craft room. She didn't seem to hold any antipathy toward him. Although, she was a little exasperated he ended up taking the job and moving here last year."

Bitsy said, "Maura is really grounded. Her life is good here, and I don't see her harboring any resentment or ill will toward anyone."

"I think you're right," JJ added.

Spencer brought us back to the reality of murder. "Look, we really don't know what goes on behind closed doors. Should we so easily dismiss her?"

"You've got a good point," I said. "Maybe I can ask her some questions and get her talking." I found it unsettling to think Maura should be considered a suspect, but the priority was to shift the investigation in another direction, and off of Ryan, so I shook it off and moved on to Oscar.

"He is such a sweetheart," Annie said.

Bitsy added her character assessment. "He's an introvert and a gentle soul. And once he gets to know you, his social awkwardness vanishes. It would be totally out of character for him to strike out in a violent manner."

"I agree," I said. "As far as I know, he didn't have any run-ins with Clive. He did witness a tiff I had with him, and I found it endearing he didn't probe and ask me about it. I don't think he's interested in drama of any kind." I finished typing up notes on him and then said, "Now we have Declan and Preston. Let's take Declan, first."

Annie chortled. "Oh boy, he's a bit of a player, isn't he? He's been courting Maggie big time."

Spencer wasn't as amused. "I think he's a bit of a jerk." He saw us look at him in surprise, and defended his assessment. "One minute he'll be somewhat dismissive, and the next he's turning on the charm, thinking he can win over anyone he wants by showing those dimples. So yeah, I think he's a jackass. And what is the name of the song he keeps whistling? Man, it's so annoying."

I laughed. "Don't hold back, Spencer. Tell us how you really feel."

"I'm just telling it like it is."

"I think Spencer can see through him, whereas we are blinded by those moody eyes and nice hair," Bitsy contributed, laughing.

"You may be right." Thinking about the lunch conversation with Lena, I said, "His kind of looks are a dime a dozen to me, so he's not my type. And anyway, it's one thing to be a player and another to be a killer."

"What about Preston?" JJ asked. "I haven't had much opportunity to talk to him."

Spencer spoke up. "I've actually found Preston to be quite friendly. He just has boundaries about how much he gets involved, particularly in other people's business. But we've had great conversations about hockey and, of course, art. I like him."

Annie asked, "Did any of these guys have any run-ins with Clive?"

Nobody had heard about anything, so I added, "I'll try to casually talk to them and see if I can get a read on what they thought of Clive." I finished the notes on the two of them and put my glasses on my head, moved my laptop to the side, and grabbed a handful of popcorn. "So we've covered everyone we can think of. Now let's just talk and see what crops up." I looked sideways at the laptop screen. "These are the questions I came up with earlier…" I read out the list.

"Who had a motive?" Annie pondered.

Spencer got up to look in my fridge and turned to me with a smirk of disappointment on his face. He mouthed *no beer*, and I pointed to my coffee mug with a cheery smile. He just shook his head, then grabbed a mug out of the cabinet.

While brewing his cup, he said, "Clive pretty much annoyed everyone he interacted with, so the field is wide."

"How Penny put up with him I have no idea," JJ said.

Bitsy grabbed a handful of nuts and paused with a cashew halfway to her mouth. "Wait? Penny's not on either of those lists. Where was she? She wasn't with us at the café."

I pulled my laptop back over and started typing. "Dang, I forgot. I was there when she told Jack she went home from the Bennet House after locking up. Her mom and aunt are in town and were waiting for her to have dinner. I can't imagine Penny lying, can you?"

"No," Bitsy said. "And this doesn't feel like a woman's crime."

Spencer looked at her with a raised eyebrow.

"Seriously. Think about it. There was clearly some sort of fight, a stabbing with a chisel, chasing Clive so he rushed out onto the ice, and then leaving him to die. I think historically, women tend to be more subtle, like using poison."

"What about Lizzie Borden?" Spencer asked, with a grin.

"The exception, not the rule," Bitsy said decisively.

"I tend to agree with Bitsy on this one," I said. "As I told Jack, Penny would be neat and tidy if she committed murder. But we won't check her off the list until Jack confirms her alibi. So, back to motive. Let's list the most common ones."

Each one in turn threw out a motive, and I wrote them down: greed, jealousy, a love conflict, money, or caught doing something illegal.

I sat back again. "What about wrong place, wrong time? What if he saw something he shouldn't have? Maybe it's not about what Clive did, but what someone else did?" I relayed Clive's voicemail and my thoughts on it connecting to the Marks case.

"Oooo, how interesting," Annie said with intrigue. "But what? What would he have seen at the festival? It's a pretty innocuous bunch, both the artists and the patrons. And no one noticed much about Eddie Marks when he was at the festival, so it's not like there was a big *aha* moment."

I blew out some lip flutters in frustration. "I don't know. I'm just spit-balling at this point."

"It's a good process, even if it doesn't give us much to go on," JJ acknowledged. "What about family? Other than Maura, does he have any family here?"

"No. Her family is here, but his isn't," I said.

"What about relationships outside the Bennet House? What do we know about his personal life?" Annie asked.

We all looked at each other.

"How sad," she said. "We really knew nothing about him, did we?"

I added a note to my list. "I need to ask Penny about his personal life. And maybe someone at the library knows something about him since the two organizations are connected. I should remind Jack to talk to the Bennet House board and see if any of them knew him well."

"Good point," Spencer said.

I moved to the next question. "Who had something to gain?"

"A will? Did he have money?" JJ asked.

"I'll add finances to the list of things to ask Jack about," I responded, my fingers tip-tapping on the keyboard.

Spencer asked, "What about Ryan's tools? Where did he keep them?"

"He said the chisel was from the set he brought to the Bennet House, and he stored them in the front hall closet," I answered. "That means anyone in the building could have taken it."

Bitsy groaned. "That will be impossible to track!"

"I know. Penny said there are some security cameras, so maybe one covers the entry hall closet. I'm sure Jack has thought of all of this stuff already, but it hasn't even been twelve hours since I found Clive, so everything goes on the list. Okay, the last thing is Clive's movements over the last few days. Maybe we can ask some questions and track who he interacted with, and when. And that's about all we've got to work with for now."

"Boy, two deaths in less than a week. I don't think we've ever experienced that," Annie said, shaking her head.

"That's right. What's the word on the poor guy who was the victim of the hit-and-run, Alex?" Spencer asked.

"There's still not a lot of information about him."

"But you said Clive left you a voicemail about his

photo," Spencer said.

I nodded. "When I left Clive on Monday, we had resolved our differences. I think he probably knew something when he first saw the photo but was being intentionally unhelpful, so it was likely just to concur he saw him at the festival on Sunday or maybe he spoke with him briefly. Knowing Clive, if it had been important, I'm certain he would have said so."

"Is there anything else we can think of to help Ryan out of this mess?" Spencer asked.

We all looked at each other and came up empty. I closed my laptop and said, "At least now I have some sort of list to tackle."

There was a sudden ding-ding-ding coming from our cell phones. We all dug around to pull them out and found a text from Penny relaying the police had released the crime scene. The festival would open at the normal time tomorrow, at noon.

"All righty then," said Bitsy. "I guess we're back in business, but boy, it's going to feel weird."

"I know. At least we'll all go through it together. For now, I need a break. Who's ready for dinner?"

Spencer quipped, "From looking at your fridge, I know you don't mean you're going to cook something."

"Of course not. I was thinking of Fat Daddy's barbecue."

"I'm in," everyone chorused.

****

Fat Daddy's was on a side street at the end of Main Street, and we managed to pass another hour talking about Clive and Ryan, with the table full of every kind of barbecue imaginable, stress-eating clearly in full swing.

109

Later, back in my car, even though I was stuffed to the gills, I made a detour to the Bushel Basket market. It was time to restock my fridge and pantry. Plus, it was another way to distract my brain.

I was lugging in my grocery bags when I found Maggie and Ryan sitting on the stairs in the lobby.

"I'm happy to report I've been released," Ryan said. He sounded exhausted but relieved.

I put the bags down and gave him a big hug. "Let's go upstairs."

We hauled everything up to the apartment and unloaded the groceries while Ryan relayed that the search of his car and apartment turned up nothing. They took his clothing from the night before and found no evidence of blood. His car was clean. They even scraped under his nails to make sure there was no physical evidence.

"So I'm basically in the clear," he said. "Jack told me, off the record, because of the nature of the crime, if there was something to find they would have found it. And they went overboard to make sure there was no conflict of interest due to our relationship."

"What a relief," I gushed. "Wait a sec, I've got to text the gang." I quickly tapped a group message to the foursome and received ding after ding of cheers.

"Maggie was incredible. She kept me sane," Ryan said, throwing his arm around her for a tight squeeze.

"I wouldn't have wanted to be anywhere else. But what a day," she said. "I'm going to go home, take a hot bath, and crawl into bed."

"I think I'll be asleep before my head hits the pillow," Ryan said, with a yawn.

I walked them to the door, then grabbed Baxter's

leash, and we went for a long walk. By now, the night was quiet. The sky was perfectly clear, and the stars were so bright it felt like I could reach up and touch them. The air was cold, but still, so I let Baxter drag me around longer than usual.

Back inside, I could tell, even though I was exhausted, I was subconsciously reluctant to go to sleep. Normally I can't wait to crawl into my cozy bed, but not tonight. Once under the covers, I patted the quilt and Baxter jumped up, circled a few times, then plopped down next to me. I focused on his breathing and then his little doggy snores, hoping it would lull me to sleep.

A couple of hours later, I was still wide awake. My mind was twirling around the lack of evidence and the difficulty of narrowing down suspects and motives. Suddenly a new thought struck me, and I turned on the bedside lamp and grabbed my phone to call Jack.

He answered with a whisper. "Hold on." A minute later he continued. "Sorry, I didn't want to wake Annie. What's up? It's a little late, is everything okay?"

"I was trying to get to sleep when I thought of something to run by you."

"Go on, what is it?"

"Have you been able to corroborate Preston, Declan, and Oscar all stayed in their rooms during the time when Clive was killed?"

"Not yet. We've had to deal with Ryan and buttoning up the Marks case."

"Don't hotels have a record of when swipe keys are used?" I asked.

"Yup. So you're thinking we can check to see if they left their room even though they told me they

111

turned in early."

"Yes!"

"That was on my list after clearing Ryan."

"Oh," I said, somewhat deflated. "I'm sorry to have gotten you up, then."

"Hey, don't feel bad. This is my job. I think it's great you came up with it on your own. We'll talk more in the morning. For now, try and get some sleep."

I read until I could no longer keep my eyes open. As I feared, a nightmare looped over and over, and I woke up an hour later in a cold sweat from the repeated sight of Clive under the ice, his phone ringing in his coat pocket with my name on the caller ID.

****

Wednesday

The relentless ringing of my own phone pulled me awake, and I muttered, "Geez. What the heck is so important? It's only…" I looked at my clock. Oops, it was after seven thirty a.m. I must have turned my alarm off in my sleep. I quickly grabbed my phone and answered before the ringing stopped. "Hello," I said, trying to disguise the sleep in my voice.

"You never answer my calls with *hello*, so I must have woken you up," Jack said, with humor in his voice.

I sat up, put my phone on speaker, and scrubbed my face with my hands to clear the cobwebs and get the blood flowing. "Ugh. Sorry, yeah, I didn't get much sleep last night."

"I'm not surprised. Nightmares?"

"Yeah." I sighed.

"Well, up and at 'em. I want to meet and talk about where we are with things. Can I swing by?"

I threw the covers off and got out of bed. "Give me twenty minutes, and I'll be ready."

Being a man who likes to conserve his words, Jack responded by disconnecting the call.

I made coffee, quickly showered, and threw on my clothes. I had just put Baxter's kibble down when there was a knock on the door. "It's open," I called out.

"Hey," Jack said by way of greeting, while removing his coat and hat.

"Coffee?" I asked, making my second cup.

"You betcha."

I filled the counter with English muffins, cream cheese, fruit, pastries, and a box of cereal. Since it was Valentine's Day, I added two of the chocolate-covered strawberries I had picked up at the market the night before. And then I stood back with a satisfied grin.

"Look at you!" he exclaimed, in a mildly patronizing tone of voice. "Shamed into going to the market, huh?"

I chuckled. "Actually, yes. It had gotten pretty bleak here in the food department. Happy Valentine's Day, by the way," I said, pointing to the strawberries.

"Same to you. I'm not sure I can eat something sweet this early in the morning, but thank you, nonetheless."

"Ah, come on, it qualifies as fruit!"

"Right," he said, unconvinced.

We filled our plates and perched on the stools at the counter.

"Ryan and Maggie were waiting for me when I got home last night, so is it true? Has he really been cleared?"

"Yes. We had his clothing from the night before

and there was no dirt, no blood, no mud on his shoes from the area around the pond. No mud in his car. Nothing. And from a follow-up interview with Elliott, we know what clothing he wore. We even inspected his drains. His washing machine hadn't been used in days. There was no evidence in his studio, either. Because of the personal connections, we went overboard to ensure there would be no appearance of looking the other way. So yeah, I feel like he's in the clear."

"I can't tell you how relieved I am. Does this mean I'm off the bench?" I asked.

He looked at me and smiled. "Yes."

I rubbed my hands together and said, "Well let's get started."

Chapter 9

It felt good to be on the same team again, so while Jack ate, I dove right in. "The gang came over last night for a little powwow. We just worked through various motives for murder, and then, well, it wasn't really gossip, but we just talked about the various personality types at the festival. I've actually been making some lists, both of people to talk to and questions to ask."

"I figured you wouldn't sit idle. What did you come up with?"

"Probably everything you have already. The people who weren't at the café need to be looked at more closely. That's Preston, Declan, Oscar, Maura, and Penny. We looked at motives, and who would gain from his death. Did he have money? A will? How did he spend his off-work time? Was he in a relationship? Was this a wrong place, wrong time situation? Clive did like to meddle. Could he have seen or heard something he shouldn't have?"

"All good avenues, and yes, so far those are the same lines we're looking at."

"I figured as much. How will you go about finding some answers?"

"Other than what we talked about last night on the phone—checking the alibis at the Lodge—we're going to start combing the video cameras to try and track Clive's movements. We did a search of his house and got his tablet and laptop. And we're going to look at the other relationships, such as Maura and even Penny. Plus, we have to talk to anyone who knew Clive outside of the Bennet House to find any other personal or professional connections. And that's just Clive's case."

"You guys have a lot of work to do. How can I help? I can stop by the Lodge this morning to ask Dustin about the swipe keys." Dustin was the owner and manager of the Lodge.

Jack nodded. "That would be helpful. I'll call and tell him you have clearance to get the information. Then you report straight to me about it, right? Don't start asking people pushy questions."

"Pushy? Me? Never," I said. Jack's eyes narrowed, so I added, "Seriously, I promise. Do you want me to check with Penny about the security cameras at the Bennet House?"

"She's getting the feed from the security company, and then I'll be able to take a look."

"Okay. I'll be checking in with her later this morning anyway because there should be an emergency board meeting to appoint her as acting manager. Maybe I can finagle going to the meeting to see if any of the board members knew Clive outside the job."

"Good, maybe someone will have something to tell us. We still have to dot the i's and cross the t's on the Marks case, so we're stretched pretty thin. How'd you like to do some basic research on him, too? The kind of stuff you did in your old job. Just a neat and tidy background report I can put in the file."

I popped a tangerine slice and mumbled through partially closed lips, "Sure, I'll do that. I'm going to do a little snooping around online anyway, just to see if anything stands out with the festival crew. But wait, you keep bringing up the Marks case. I thought that it was essentially closed."

"Almost. The Ohio boys found and notified Eddie's wife. She's coming tomorrow. Arrangements have to be made to release the body and transfer him back to Ohio."

"So at that point, his investigation will be done," I said as a statement, not a question.

"I still have some follow-up I want to do. I don't know," Jack said pensively. "For some reason, I'm just not ready to give up on this one yet. I still don't like the coincidence of two deaths back-to-back, and something doesn't feel right. Too many unanswered questions."

"Such as…"

"Why was he walking down the road when his car was a few miles away at the truck stop? Did he get in someone else's car? Did he know someone who lived down that way? If so, why has no one reported him missing? There are too many questions."

"Hmm. Can I look at his stuff again before his wife takes everything?"

"Sure."

"Okay, I'll swing by later."

After Jack left, I cleaned up the kitchen, tossed some newly purchased snacks in my tote bag, locked up, and went downstairs to walk the halls. As expected, I fielded a number of questions from people regarding Ryan, and it was a relief to be able to say the investigation was moving in other directions.

A little later, I made the short drive to the Lodge. The lobby had the gentle hum of guest activity. The business clientele was up and dressed for the day, getting breakfast with their lanyards around their necks in anticipation of their first meeting of the day. There was a smattering of tourists mixed in, some in robes, getting coffee to take back to their rooms, others eager to start their day, with backpacks by their chairs.

Dustin was tending to a guest, but he had his assistant take over, then motioned for me to follow him to the end of the counter. In a soft voice he said, "Jack called me, but I haven't been able to pull everything yet. Give me two minutes."

"Sure, no problem," I said and turned to scan the lobby and people watch while I waited.

"Here ya go. This is a printout of the swipe card records for the names Jack gave me. If you need anything else, just let me know." Dustin had helped with the inquiries in the fall and knew better than to ask questions I couldn't answer.

"Thanks so much. I'll let Jack know."

I sat in my car with the printout leaning against my steering wheel. I looked at Oscar's comings and goings first. As I expected, once he entered his room after dinner, he did not emerge until the next morning.

Declan entered after dinner, and a few minutes later he left for about five minutes, then nothing until after ten p.m., when he left his room and came back about forty-five minutes later. Maybe he went to the bar for a nightcap.

Preston left his room and came back an hour later. The timing overlapped with the murder. Would an hour have been enough time for him to get to the Bennet House, kill Clive, and come back? Maybe, but it could have been as simple as he went to the lounge. I knew Jack should be the one to follow up on these, but maybe

I could quiz them later, asking if they'd had an opportunity to hang out in the bar. Innocent questions.

I took a photo of each page and sent them to Jack, but I continued to sit and think. On impulse, I drove around the building and pulled into a parking spot where I could see the back of the Lodge. According to the room numbers on the sheets, Preston's room was on the second floor, and Declan and Oscar were on the first.

The rooms at the Lodge had small balconies with slider doors so people could let in the fresh mountain air. I sort of remembered the room schematic from the fall when Jack and I were searching one of the rooms, and I guesstimated where these three rooms were. Could someone climb out and exit the building without going through the hotel?

A cartoon figure of Jack sat on one of my shoulders, telling me not to do something stupid. On my other shoulder, a figurative form of my inner voice was telling me to just take a quick look around. In order to stop the debate going on between these two, I got out of the car. I'd just take a little stroll and scope things out. A happy medium.

A sidewalk ran alongside the building, about twenty feet from the first-floor rooms, and I felt a little like a voyeur. Through the sheers, I could see the silhouette of someone blow-drying their hair, and others eating at the table with the TV on. But I was not there to look in windows. I quickly determined it was unlikely someone could exit from the second floor. It wasn't impossible, but they might break an ankle in the process. But it *was* possible to climb out the first-floor rooms, so I scanned the ground to see if there were any telltale signs that someone had done so.

I had moved off the sidewalk to take a closer look when I heard "Good morning."

The voice startled me, and as I clumsily tried to get back to the sidewalk, I tripped and landed in the snow.

"Oh dear," a voice said, and I looked up to see Oscar peering at me through his sliding door a few feet down from where I lay.

Oh crap. This was not good. Jack was going to throttle me. "Hi, Oscar," I said, nonchalantly.

He opened his door farther and said, "Do you need some help?"

I got to my knees and pushed myself up. "No, no, I'm fine," I singsonged, wiping the snow from my jeans.

He opened the screen door and said, "I have an extra towel. Why don't you come get that snow off. Otherwise you'll be both cold *and* wet."

I walked a few feet over and awkwardly climbed over the railing into his room, thusly proving my hypothesis that it was possible to get in this way. While Oscar shuffled into the bathroom, I tried to come up with a rational story for what I was doing. I came up blank.

"Here you go," he said, handing the towel to me. "And if your jeans are wet, you can use the blow dryer."

I suddenly started laughing at the absurdity of the situation I was in. "Oscar, you amaze me. You haven't even asked what the hell I was doing out there!"

He avoided eye contact and tidied up the already tidy room. "Well, it's not really any of my business. I don't like to interfere in someone else's personal life."

Oh my gosh, he probably thought I was sneaking out of someone's room! I instinctively knew Oscar was not a suspect in Clive's death, so I sat on the edge of the desk chair and said, "I appreciate your discretion, but I'm not here on a personal matter. I was trying to scope out if it would be possible for someone to leave the hotel from their room, without using the exit doors." I gave Oscar an apology shrug and added, "I'm just grasping at straws, trying to figure out what happened to Clive."

Oscar gingerly sat on the edge of the bed. "I see. That certainly seems a worthwhile endeavor."

"Yes, but I'm afraid I bungled it, and I'm just lucky it was you who saw me out there. Can I ask you to please not mention to anyone what I was doing here?"

"Of course. Your secret is safe with me. However, you didn't really bungle it. You have determined it is indeed possible to enter a room in this manner."

I smiled at him. "You're right! And now I'll demonstrate someone could leave the room the same way."

I handed him the towel and after taking a quick look to make sure no one was around, I climbed the railing and quickly got back to the sidewalk.

Oscar waved to me from the still-open sliding door, and I said, "Thanks, Oscar. I'll see ya later at the Bennet House!"

I got back to the car, took a deep breath, and tried not to think about the fact I was going to have quite the reckoning with Jack.

Chapter 10

I picked my way through the parking lot of the Bennet House, avoiding the slick spots the morning sun hadn't yet reached, and bustled in through the back door. After dropping my tote in the kitchen, I went to find Penny and found her in Clive's office.

Her poised, professional demeanor and prim pale-pink skirt and sweater set still made her look like an efficient secretary, but I also saw a glimpse of the potential leader in Penny as she sat behind the big mahogany desk.

"You look like a natural in this office," I said, taking a seat across from her.

Penny looked up and twisted her mouth. "I don't know about that. Right now it just feels weird, but the business has to keep going, and for now I need to do it from here."

"Is there going to be an emergency board meeting?" I asked.

"Yes, They're coming this afternoon to install me as interim. We'll meet in here since the festival will be open."

"I'll help you set up, and if you think it's okay for me to be there, I told Jack I would see if any of them knew about Clive's life outside of the Bennet House."

"Sure, what a good idea. I'll introduce you after they finish the House business." Penny's cell phone rang, and her face registered concern as she answered.

"Mom? Is everything okay?" She listened to the voice on the other end, and then soothed, "Don't worry, Mom, that's standard procedure...really, it's okay, you and Aunt Marcie did exactly what you should have...yes, yes, I will...love you too...bye-bye."

She hung up and tossed her phone on the desk. "Jack stopped by my house to confirm my alibi."

"Sorry. I hope he didn't upset your mom and aunt."

"No, it's best to get it out of the way. They'll be fine. I assumed people's stories would be checked. I'm just grateful there are people to corroborate my story, unlike poor Ryan."

"Well, at least it's over with, and one less thing to worry about."

She smiled, her eyes flickering with humor. "Trying for the glass half full, huh?"

"What else can we do? If we don't try, we might lose our minds," I said, with a laugh. Penny's phone rang again, so I got up and started toward the door. "I'll leave you to it. I've got to pop out later this morning, but I'll be back around opening time."

I came across Preston in the library. He was organizing the display tables, shifting wooden boxes and other decorative pieces to add more stock. From a large cardboard box with packing paper overhanging the edges, he pulled out two intricate wooden boxes. He placed them on elevated stands, which highlighted the items with special craftsmanship. These pieces made me think of the box Eddie had purchased.

"These are a little different from what I saw earlier. How lovely!" I enthused.

Preston beamed at me, running his hand over the

smooth wood with brass inlay. "You have a good eye! These are puzzle boxes. Very special indeed."

"Puzzle boxes? What are those?"

"They're for people who like the aesthetic beauty of the piece but also like a brain-teaser challenge of a puzzle. Each box is different, with a trick of sliding and shifting pieces to open a secret compartment. The super deluxe ones have more than one compartment and can involve hundreds of moves." He demonstrated by shifting and sliding pieces until a secret drawer slid open. His hands moved at lightning speed, like a Rubik's Cube master.

I blinked, and my mouth gaped. "Incredible. Your hands were moving so fast I couldn't keep track of what you did! There's no way I could retrace your steps to get in there."

Preston chuckled. "And I'm not as good as Declan. He's the real genius at making these."

"Very cool." I looked around and added, "I take it Declan will be in later?"

"Yeah, he's got something to do this morning, and then he and Maggie are going to lunch before the festival opens."

My protective nature kicked in, and I couldn't help myself from saying, "It's hard to believe he's not already in a relationship. He's not, is he?"

Preston pulled a stool over and perched on it. "No, don't worry. Declan likes to have fun, but he's not a creep. Because of his schedule and being on the road a lot, he's not ready to settle down, and from what I can tell, he makes that clear from the get-go. Let's just say I haven't heard anything about him leaving a string of angry women in his wake."

"I'll take your word for it, because if someone messes with Maggie, they'll have to deal with me."

Preston chuckled. "I can well imagine you're a force to be reckoned with."

"So I've been told," I joked, then changed the subject. "Are you both on the road a lot?"

"I'm not as much as Declan is. He's developed some business in Ohio and New York, so along with our festival circuit, he's gone more than I am."

"It's not an easy life, is it? I mean, actually, it's a great life to earn a living as an artist, but I bet the festival circuit isn't easy."

"Nah, it's not bad at all. We're in a few galleries and shops, which is where we earn a good chunk of our income. And the festivals are fun because we get to be around more people and other artists, so personally, I don't mind the time on the road."

"That sounds like a pretty good combo. I'm glad you guys decided to join us this year. Your collection is a good addition to our festival, but hopefully you aren't regretting the decision to come. Clive's murder has had a drastic effect on things." I hoped this intro would prompt some productive talk.

Preston's face turned serious. "No kidding. I feel awful I had some negative thoughts about him. I might not have liked him all that much, but I wouldn't have wished him any harm. Is there any word on the investigation?"

I gave Preston what would become my standard response, which was to state an official line without really saying anything. Then, I asked, "Do you recall seeing anyone interact with Clive who would be of interest? Maybe something didn't seem out of the

Sydney Abrams

ordinary at the time, but now might register as unusual or noteworthy?"

Preston shifted his eyes to the ceiling while he thought about it. "Honestly, nothing stands out. I usually just saw him rushing from one room to another. I never witnessed him having any intense conversations or anything close to an altercation. I wish I could help more."

"No worries. You guys are usually busy with customers, so it was a long shot."

"People were talking at the Lodge this morning, and I heard Ryan was taken in for questioning. I was relieved to see him working with Elliott outside this morning, and assume it means he had nothing to do with it."

"Thankfully, the police have closed the line of inquiry involving Ryan."

"I'm sure you're all relieved to be out from under the stress of having a friend under scrutiny."

"That's for sure," I said, heartily. The moment presented itself to ask him about the night of the murder. "So speaking of the Lodge, are you enjoying your stay there?"

"I like it. It's really comfortable, both the rooms and the woodsy atmosphere in general."

"Yes, it has a nice vibe. And if you haven't already, the lounge is a great place to hang out."

"It is. I've become a frequent customer," he said, with a grin.

"Good, I'm glad you like it there. We locals particularly like it in the winter. It keeps us from hibernating too much. I hope it hasn't been too busy when you've been there?"

"Nah, I've always found a seat at the bar, which suits me fine since I can watch whatever game they have on."

That was as far as I wanted to push it, and after a few minutes of discussion, we wrapped up the conversation by chatting about the weather, and I answered a few questions about places to shop and eat before I made my excuses and left him to his work.

I found Preston to be an open and friendly guy, but could that just be a front? I would let Jack talk to him about the time he wasn't in his room the night Clive was murdered. Maybe using discretion now would lessen Jack's annoyance with me when he found out about my earlier escapades at the Lodge.

I stepped out the front door and was grateful to see Elliott and Ryan cleaning up the crime scene area. I had left my coat in the kitchen but still had on my thin down vest, so I zipped it up, and put my hands in the pockets.

"How's it going out here?" I asked, approaching them.

Elliott cheeks were bright red from the cold. "Good. Travis gave the okay to clean things up, and we're just about done."

They had righted the pedestal and raked the snow on the ground to cover the muddy footprints from the investigation. My eyes couldn't help but drift down to the pond, even though my stomach rolled at the prospect of seeing a remnant of the blood trail in the snow or the jagged hole farther out in the pond where Clive had broken through when trying to run. Thankfully, by now, fresh snow had covered the ground, and the pond's surface already had a thin frozen layer on top, concealing the icy grave within. I looked back to where Elliott's ice sculpture lay on the ground.

"What about the sculpture? Can you salvage it?"

"We're going to find out right now," Ryan answered. He and Elliott leaned down with gloved hands to get purchase under it.

Elliott counted down. "Three, two, one, lift."

They slowly lifted the piece and wrestled it onto the pedestal. It was the sculpture of the penguin with the hockey stick. Elliott gently wiped snow and dirt from its surface, and little by little, the figure revealed itself.

"It looks pretty good!" Ryan exclaimed with glee.

"Yup." Elliott smiled. They did a gloved high-five, and then Elliott looked closely at the area where the hockey stick met the penguin's hand. "I might need to do a little repair work here"—he pointed to a slight crack—"but, all in all, it's good."

Ryan smoothed the snow around the base of the pedestal and then came over to stand next to me, leaning on the handle of the flat-edged shovel.

"Did you get some sleep last night?" I asked.

His boyish smile slipped, and he pressed his lips together before saying, "I woke up a lot. I won't lie, I was scared. I'm still scared, but I'm trying to focus on being relieved they let me go. I know Jack is going to get to the bottom of this, and I'm really grateful you're helping."

I loosely draped my arm around his waist. "I know. I'm scared too. I'm still trying to get over finding Clive. We just need to keep our heads and focus our energies on figuring out what happened here. Now, let's talk about how we should proceed with the festival. What are you thinking?"

He thought for a moment, staring at the Bennet House. "I think I should lie low right now. I already talked to Elliott, and he can cover both his and my pieces with the customers. I was thinking maybe I should stick to the Workshop—just until the air around me clears."

I was glad he brought it up first, since this was my inclination as well. "Okay, you do what you think is best."

"It's tough. I don't want people thinking my absence means I'm somehow involved, but at the same time, I just don't feel right being a distraction for the artists and the customers until the focus of the investigation fully shifts off me. They've said I'm no longer a suspect, but I won't relax until the killer is caught."

I looked at Ryan, feeling a swell of bittersweet admiration. "You know, Ryan, you're handling this better than I probably would, and I'm proud of you."

"Thanks," he said, humbly.

"I could use your help keeping tabs on things at the Workshop while I'm off site, anyway. So, let's go with your plan. And why don't we get the gang together at the Lodge tonight? That way everyone can get over the hump of talking about it with you. Plus, we can all celebrate Valentine's together. Sound good?"

"That would be great. I would rather not spend the day apart from everyone and then be alone at home tonight."

I was growing cold and stomped the ground with my boots to get the blood moving in my legs. "Dang, it's a little chilly to be out here without my coat. I'm heading inside, but I'll check in with you later. In the meantime, you hang in there. Everything's going to work out all right." I waved to Elliott, who was busily working on the sculpture repair, then made a beeline back inside.

Before I knew it, it was time for lunch, so there was an extra pep in my step as I made my way to the car. The food trucks were only here for the weekends, so a few minutes later, I parked in the café lot and crunched my way to the door. After dislodging the ice-melt pellets from my boots, I entered and inhaled the aroma of comfort food. At this hour, it was busy with the local workforce, as well as the old-timers who got together for their weekly dish over current events and gossip. I nabbed a spot at the end of the counter and pulled a menu from the clasp on the napkin dispenser. I knew what I was getting but still wanted to see the familiar pictures on the glossy interior of the menu.

After Aunt Claudia finished up with a customer, she side-stepped over to stand in front of me with her glasses perched on her nose. "Well, it looks like you're in the thick of things again, aren't you?" she admonished.

I put the menu down and looked back at her with my glasses perched on my nose, and mimicked her tone. "I should have known you would have heard. News sure travels fast around here." I then dropped any pretense of normalcy. "Oh, it was awful, Aunt Claudia. Just awful. I'm having trouble getting the images out of my head. It's like they're on a loop." I'm normally a pretty tough cookie, but Aunt Claudia embodies the warmth and protection of family and her maternal nature always allowed my inner child to emerge.

She came around the counter and gave me a sideways hug. "I know," she cooed. "You poor thing. Anyone who can experience such a horrific thing without some kind of lingering effects is just not normal. How's everyone else holding up?"

I proceeded to blurt the whole story in a rushed whisper, and when I finished, I had to grab a napkin to blow my nose and used another to dab my eyes.

"Okay, now, now," she purred. She then gave my shoulder a hard squeeze before returning to the other side of the counter. "You've proven your whole life you have more strength than most. You just tap that brain of yours and start looking for answers. Between you and Jack, you'll get to the bottom of this." Now she leaned in close and pointed a finger at me, close to my nose. "But you leave the dangerous stuff to Jack, right? I've had enough years taken off my life worrying about your father and my dear Arthur when they were cops, and now Jack. I don't need to be worrying about *you*."

I looked at her in earnest. "I promise."

"All right." She stood up straight and asked, "Now, what do you want for lunch?"

"BLT and fries, with mayo on the side for the fries, of course, and a big slice of the Died and Gone to Heaven chocolate cake, please."

She cocked an eyebrow at me but only said, "You got it," before swiveling the order to the kitchen window.

While I was waiting, Lena came in and sat next to me at the counter.

"Hey! Are you going to join me for lunch?" I asked.

"I wish I could. I called in an order for some soup

to go. I need to take care of a few things at the library before the festival opens. How are you holding up?" she asked.

"I'm doing better now since Ryan's been cleared."

"Oh, what great news. I knew he would be, but it's such a relief." She turned solemn, and said, "I just can't get over this, Alex. Who would do such a thing to Clive?"

"I'm having difficulty with it, myself. You haven't been here long, but neither had Clive. Did you have any interaction with him at the library?"

"I did. He came in frequently to check out books, and we often talked about the latest best-sellers, or he would ask me for suggestions for certain genres. He was a very different person when he was there. I never saw the exasperating side until the festival work started."

"I am so relieved to know he had a fairly good life. I really hated feeling like people, including me, disliked him so much, and I wish I had been able to get to know him better." I shook my head, disappointed in myself.

Janice approached with a paper bag. "Here ya go, Lena. I put some crackers in on top."

"Thank you," Lena said, sliding off the stool, preparing to leave. She put a hand on my shoulder and said, "I believe Clive knows you are working hard to find out what happened to him. Take comfort in that."

I swiveled on the stool to watch her leave and was surprised that it did give me comfort.

****

I arrived at the station and waved at Matt as I swung through the half door at the end of the reception desk. I could hear a buzz of activity coming from the precinct room before I got there and entered to find Jack, Matt, and Travis congregated around the white board, discussing Clive's case. Ryan's name and photo on the board made me uneasy, but I was relieved to see he was no longer under the suspect list. Jack felt my presence, looked over at me, then held up his hand to indicate he'd be with me in a minute.

Taking quick strides, he approached, saying, "I want to talk to you about a few things, and you're here to look at the Marks stuff, right?"

"Is this a bad time?" I really didn't want to talk to him about my mishap this morning if he was in a foul mood.

"No, come on, let's go to my office."

I put the printouts from the swipe keys on Jack's desk. "I sent these to you, but these are easier to read."

"Right." He picked them up. "So even though Preston and Declan said they called it an early night, they both left their rooms. I want to talk to them again."

"I chatted with Preston earlier, and he said he's been going to the lounge a lot in the evenings, and he usually sits at the bar, so maybe you'll be able to confirm he was there." I didn't want to look him in the eye, so I looked in my tote for some yet to be determined important object.

Jack cocked his head while I fidgeted, then narrowed his eyes and asked, "What's going on? What'd you do?"

He knew me too well. I let my tote bag drop to the floor and said, "Okay, so after I read over the printouts, I started wondering if someone could leave the building via their window or balcony, so I drove around to the back of the building to take a look. I remembered from the fall the even-numbered rooms are on that side."

"Right," he said, drawing out the word slowly.

My words then came out in a rush. "Anyway, I ended up getting out of the car to scope things out. And I determined it was possible to climb out of a first-floor room and get to the parking lot unseen."

"Then why are you so nervous?" he asked suspiciously.

"Well, it's possible not to be seen, but I *was* seen. Oscar saw me, he startled me, I fell, then he had me come into his room so I could towel off the snow."

Jack stared at me for a very long few seconds, then said, "I told you not to go off half-cocked! What if the wrong person saw you? Did you even come up with a cover story?"

"I found it to be a teaching experience, and I learned the invaluable lesson to come up with a cover story *first*."

Chapter 11

Jack pursed his lips and shook his head. "You are unbelievable. If I thought it would do any good, I'd tell you to stay away from any investigations from this minute on. But I know you'd just do it behind my back. So somehow, I have to get it through your thick head to think before you leap. Whether it's someone from within or outside of the festival, if you trip over the wrong person, you could be in serious danger."

I couldn't look him in the eye. "I know."

"I don't think you do. You see, when we, meaning police officers, don't know what we're dealing with, we watch every step because we can't anticipate where the danger could come from. We are always on alert. And we are trained to know what to do if danger comes our way. This is the difference between being a trained officer and being a consultant. We know that, and you don't."

I put my hands up. "I get it. And I promise, it won't happen again. Earlier, when I saw Preston, I didn't ask him any questions about where he was the night Clive was killed. I *knew* I should leave those questions to you."

"Good," he said, emphatically. He took a moment to calm down, then said, "I would actually have paid good money to have watched that unfold at the Lodge." I could see laughter in his eyes, and he couldn't help but grin. "You are such a doofus."

"I know. I felt pretty ridiculous."

He looked at me for a beat, then asked, "So, do you want to look at Marks' stuff?"

When we were kids, Jack and I would get into it about something or the other, and then we would be back to normal thirty seconds later. I was relieved to see things hadn't changed. "Yes, if you don't mind."

We left his office and went to the table with plastic evidence bags. "So this is everything?" I asked.

"Yes, we've examined and documented everything, so you can take out anything you want. But put things back in the appropriate bags. I'll need to cross-check before boxing up anything we can release to his wife tomorrow."

"Okay, will do." I looked at the assortment of bags and asked, "Still no sign of his phone?"

"Nope. His wife gave us the number and the carrier, but no trace of it. It's either off, or if stolen, the sim card has been pulled out and replaced."

Jack went back to the white board, and I started sifting through the bags. There was a new batch of items taken from his car. I looked at those first, smoothing the plastic to determine if I wanted to pull anything out for a closer look. Stuff often clogged up the storage areas in a car, and Eddie's was no different. There was a flyer for the festival with the address circled, probably to put in his GPS. The remaining bags held two pens, sunglasses, a business card from the motel, receipts, some loose change, and a box of matches.

There was nothing terribly exciting there, so I moved on to his clothing, remembering the labels from

London. I bent forward to place my hands on the table and rotated my shoulders to release some tension. *Who are you, Mr. Marks? You were well-heeled enough to have clothing from London tailors, so what brought you to our little corner of the world?*

I wasn't going to get any answers just staring at the table, so I pushed back from my leaning position and grabbed the bags with his purchases from the festival. Looking through the books again, there was nothing specific in the genres or titles he purchased, so I moved on to the wooden box. I took it out of the bag and ran my hand over the intricate carving. It looked like one of the fancier boxes with the puzzle compartments Preston showed me. I turned the box this way and that, looking underneath and on all sides. I could find no indication this was one of the puzzle boxes, but my gut told me it was.

"Jack?" I called out, holding up the box, "can I take this with me for the evening? I think this is one of Preston and Declan's puzzle boxes."

Jack walked over to me. "I don't see why not, but you have to bring it back in the morning when his wife comes. What are you thinking?"

"Oh, nothing. I'm just curious about it. Preston showed me one of these this morning. It has hidden compartments, but they're really tricky to get in to. I want to see if this is one of those."

He gave me a sidelong look. "I can think of better ways for you to spend your time, but sure, go ahead and knock yourself out. Don't forget, tomorrow morning. She'll be here at nine thirty, after she makes the formal identification at the morgue."

"Yessir," I retorted, putting the box back in the

evidence bag and into my tote. "I'll be here with bells on."

****

I made it back to the Bennet House in plenty of time to help Penny set up for the meeting. Within minutes, the board members arrived, and I took a seat at the back of the room and waited while the president made the motion to install Penny as interim director. The motion was seconded, and all votes were in the affirmative. At this point, Penny gave a report on how the festival would continue seamlessly, and her outline for covering her responsibilities and Clive's in the interim.

When the meeting was finished, Penny motioned to me and relayed I was there in conjunction with the investigation, seeking information about Clive's life, both professional and personal, and to talk to me if they had anything to contribute.

Once the meeting adjourned, all of the board members stayed for a few minutes to greet me and express their dismay at what happened to Clive. There was the usual round of excuses to distance themselves from the situation, such as, "He's only been here this past year, and I haven't had a chance to get to know him," or "We don't really run in the same circles," or "I can't say I've ever seen him outside of the Bennet House."

In the eyes of a few, there was a modicum of guilt they hadn't attempted to get to know Clive, but truthfully, there would be no reason for them to do so unless they had a common interest. At any rate, I came away empty-handed and relayed to Jack that, well, I had nothing to relay.

Walking toward the parlor, there was a whoosh of cold air as the front door opened and a group of red-cheeked women bustled in. I didn't want to get in their way, so I backed up to the library. Maggie was bagging up one of her prints for a customer, and once finished, she turned to me with a smile still on her face.

"How are ya holding up?" she asked me, turning more serious.

"I'm doing okay. How are things here?"

She tucked a bright green strand of hair behind her ear. "I feel guilty saying it, but I'm fine. I'm feeling so much better knowing Ryan isn't still down at the police station. Actually, where is he? We talked this morning, but I haven't seen him since."

"He's back at the Workshop. We decided it might be best for him to lie low until the investigation points in another direction."

Maggie nodded, deep in thought. "I can see how that might be good. Boy, we've got to figure this out. Poor Clive. I may not have liked him, but he deserves justice. And so does Ryan. I'm hopping mad someone used his tool to kill Clive."

"Jack's doing his best. I'm hoping Maura will have something to add about Clive's personal life. Speaking of personal life, I heard you had another date with Declan today for lunch. You haven't spilled your guts like usual, so how's it going?"

Maggie batted her eyes and said, under her breath, "I really like him. He took me for lunch today to celebrate Valentine's Day. He even paid! I know that sounds stupid, but you know the duds I've dated lately, and he's a real step up in the gentleman department." She ticked off points on her fingers, one by one. "He's well-traveled, well-read, really cute, and we can talk about art all day long. Plus, he seems genuinely interested in the people here. He's shown concern for Ryan and asks how the investigation's going. He cares about how us locals are holding up."

I couldn't help but smile at her enthusiasm. "I'm glad you're having fun and that you think he's a good guy. Are you planning to see him after the festival is over?"

"Well, he only lives a few hours away, so who knows? Maybe. I could deal with a long-distance relationship, just like you and Walter!"

I sputtered, and hissed, "Walter and I are *not* in a relationship. We're just friends. You know—"

Maggie stopped me mid-rant by laughing. "I'm just kidding! But seriously, I wouldn't mind seeing Declan after the festival. He might be a keeper."

Personally, I wasn't sure his type was a keeper, but I wanted to be supportive and said, "I told Ryan a group of us would probably be at the Lodge tonight, so why don't you bring Declan along. I wouldn't mind getting to know him better since you think so highly of him."

"Cool, I'll ask him. And since we'll already be at the hotel, maybe our V-day celebration will continue into the wee hours." She winked theatrically.

There were no words, so I just rolled my eyes.

After leaving Maggie, I moseyed across the front hall to see Annie and Spencer. Both agreed meeting at the T-bird would be fun, but our chat was interrupted by the sounds of music drifting down from the second floor.

I cocked my head. "What the heck?"

Annie gave me a puzzled look in return and then

asked Spencer to cover her customers while we went up to see what was going on.

I stood on tiptoe to see around the shoulders in front of me and saw Bitsy holding court reading a book and JJ standing behind her with her accordion. The kids in the reading circle were enthralled by the story and the music.

I smiled as my eye took in Bitsy's headgear. She had on one of her elaborate hats with a bird on the end of a wire, gently bobbing as she moved her head, and JJ was wearing a squirrel costume. I could easily visualize JJ's spare bedroom stuffed with costumes for any occasion.

Lena pulled me aside. "Isn't this *fun*?" she whispered.

"Yes! When did you hatch this plan?"

"On Monday night when we were all at the café, and from the positive response, I think we'll add it to the programs at the library this summer. JJ created little musical themes to go along with the different animals in the story. So clever. And Bitsy is putting me to shame with her storytelling."

"Well, they've been doing this for years. JJ was a professional musician before retiring, and she used to play the cello with the readings until she took up the accordion."

"Ah, well that explains it. Accordion is an interesting choice. I'm not sure I would have thought of it, but it works, doesn't it?"

I pulled myself away from the scene and wandered down the other hallway to stop in the arts and crafts rooms, hoping to find Maura so I could ask her a few questions about Clive. Shelby and Eliza and a few folks from the Workshop's adult classes were there to cover customers, so I asked Maura if she had a few minutes to talk.

We moved down the hallway where we could talk in private. "I'm so very sorry about Clive," I said to her, extending my condolences. Ex-husband or not, they had a history, and at one point, a happy one.

"Thanks, Alex. I'm just so saddened by this and even more perplexed. Why would anyone kill him?"

"It's beyond reason. Can you give me a glimpse into anything about his private life here? Did he have any relationships outside of the Bennet House?"

Maura crossed her arms and shook her head. "We only talked occasionally. As I told you, Clive had hardened over the years, but he trusted me, and every once in a while, I would see a little of the old Clive when we talked. He loved the Bennet House and the job. I told him he needed to lighten up, and he admitted it was hard to go with the flow. His insecurities made him overcompensate, and he knew it."

"What about outside the Bennet House?"

"I don't know if he had developed any friendships yet. Mostly, he worked and went home to his cat, at least as far as I know. Oh, by the way, I picked up his cat, Bella, and I'll take good care of her."

"Oh my gosh, I'm so glad you did. I had no idea he had a cat!"

"Yes, he doted on her. I hope I didn't misstep. I was his 'in case of emergency' person, and he had given me a key after he moved here, so I picked her up shortly after I heard the news."

"I'm certain you did the right thing. Otherwise, she might have ended up at the shelter. While I've got you, can I ask you a few questions?"

Maura checked her watch. "Sure, I've got a couple of minutes."

"Clive didn't try and reach you the night he died, did he?"

Maura furrowed her brow. "Why do you ask?"

I told myself to tread lightly. "I'm embarrassed to say he called when a group of us were at the café, and I didn't call him back. He left me a non-specific voicemail, and I didn't get it until the next morning. I'm just thinking if it was something important, he might have called you."

"Oh, I see. No, I'm certain he didn't call. I was out with friends, but I had my phone out and on the table in case any of the festival craft folks needed to reach me."

"Well, it was worth a shot. So, where did you go?"

Maura grinned at me. "Why Alex, if I didn't know better, I'd say you were questioning me."

I sputtered in protest, and Maura laughed and said, "It's okay. I want to do whatever I can to help. So to answer your question, we went to Thai Blossom, next to the supermarket on Barkley. I already gave Jack the info on who was with me and when we were there."

"Sorry, I really didn't mean to poke my nose in."

She gently grabbed my forearm. "Hey, you poke all you want. I'm grateful you care enough to try and find out what happened to Clive. So, what else? Ask me anything."

"What about money or possessions? Did he have anything worth killing for? Who could benefit from his death?"

"He was always pretty good with his savings, but no, he didn't come from money, if that's what you mean. And I have no idea about his will. Surely, he would have changed it after we divorced."

"Jack is checking into it. I'm just trying to make some sense of this." I noticed a new batch of customers had migrated toward the craft rooms. "I know you need to get back to the patrons, but thanks for taking the time to talk to me, and please let me know if you think of anything."

"Of course."

I stood for a moment after she left, with melancholy descending like a low-lying fog, until I heard my name being called from across the landing. Annie, Bitsy, and JJ had emerged from the lounge and were beckoning me to join them for a cup of coffee.

The break helped me get my head back on straight, and upon returning downstairs, I got to work on my makeshift desk at the kitchen table. Thankfully, it was quiet enough I could do a little online snooping for Jack. I started with social media searches for Eddie Marks, and then for Clive, Oscar, Preston, Declan, Twila and Hank, Becca, and Eliza.

Eddie was absent from social media. There were some articles or references to his work buying art for private clients, but otherwise, nothing. Coincidentally, Clive didn't have a social media presence either. I could easily imagine he wouldn't have any interest in it. Heck, I didn't have any interest in it. Oscar had an Instagram and Facebook account for O&C Lamps, but no personal accounts popped up. Although, if he enabled all the privacy settings, he wouldn't show up in a search.

I heard light whistling, and then Declan sauntered past the kitchen toward the back door. He was on my list to talk to, so I quickly closed down the laptop and rushed out to try and catch him. This time, the inner voice on my shoulder yelled in my ear, loud and clear, *No probing!*

"Hey, Declan," I called out, "hold up. Can I have a minute of your time?

"Sure," he responded, grinning.

I half jogged to where he waited on the sidewalk. "Sorry to stop you, this won't take long. I'm just asking around to see if anyone might have seen something to shed light on what happened to Clive. Even something seemingly insignificant might help."

Declan put his hands in his pockets and swayed slightly. "Aren't you quite the junior detective," he said, somewhat patronizingly. "First showing a photo around of an unidentified man involved in a traffic accident, and now Clive's murder. You'll need a badge soon." He chuckled.

"Um, I feel a responsibility to help in any way I can, and to make sure the festival is a safe environment for all of you. So I'm asking around to see if anyone saw something, particularly if Clive interacted with a patron or someone from outside the festival in a notable way. There have been a lot of people coming through the Bennet House, and you artists are here the whole time, so you might have seen something I missed."

He lightly tapped me on the arm. "I'm just teasing you," he said, smiling enough to reveal his dimples. Then he became serious. "Well, of course, Clive got on my back about putting boxes in the lobby closet…and no, I didn't kill him because he scolded me. I just ignored him."

"I wasn't accusing *you* of anything," I said. I was

145

finding him exasperating and felt this was a waste of time. "I was just hoping you might be able to help. Thanks anyway." I turned to go back inside.

"Hey, don't go! I'm sorry, I'll be serious now."

I stopped and turned back to face him.

Declan spoke with sincerity. "I honestly didn't see anything significant. Mostly, I noticed him lurking. But I will say he seemed to get on well with the patrons. I didn't see him having an argument or anything unusual with anyone." His mouth twisted in concern. "Except I heard he and Ryan got into it pretty good. I also heard Ryan was taken in for questioning, and his tool was the weapon used to kill Clive."

I cocked an eyebrow.

"Oh please, don't get the wrong idea. I'm not engaging in idle gossip. Maggie confided in me because she's been so worried."

Of course, Maggie would naturally turn to Declan for comfort under these circumstances. "I'm sure she's been grateful to have you to lean on, and I would imagine, then, she's told you Ryan's been cleared."

"She did. Let's hope Ryan's part in this is over and done with now. We all know he wouldn't cause anyone harm."

"No, he wouldn't. I won't keep you any longer. Thanks for talking, and if you should think of anything, please let me know."

"Will do," he said, before continuing down the sidewalk and around the building.

I stood until he was out of sight. For the life of me, I couldn't see what Maggie saw in him. I found him arrogant, and dimples or not, I couldn't get past that. But Maggie was smart, so he must be showing her a different side. Maybe I would start to see it, too, when I got to know him better.

Back at my makeshift desk, I decided to go ahead and tackle Declan and Preston. They had multiple social media accounts for Wild Mountain Woodcarvers, and they each had personal Instagram accounts, where they posted some pics of their individual work. Neither posted with regularity, which I liked. These days, everyone seemed to think their every thought, mood, and meal needed to be relayed to the world. It didn't surprise me about Preston, but I was encouraged Declan didn't feel the need to post his every move on social media.

Hank and Twila were an open book, just like their bigger than life personalities. I actually loved their prolific posts because most had a touch of humor or a special zest for life. Lastly, Eliza and Becca had Facebook only, with the usual friends and family types of posts.

I opened the deeper search tools, which I had held onto after leaving my job in Philly. I hated spying on people's lives, but desperate times call for desperate measures, so I approached it with a clinical attitude. In the end, I found absolutely nothing of significance. No criminal records, court documents, or bankruptcies, thank goodness. Having done what I could, I compiled everything together for Jack and dispatched it to him in an email.

I was frustrated I had diddly squat to send him. Oh well, at least I had checked some things off the list, but it also meant the field would be impossibly wide if the killer was a member of the public who had attended the festival. I really didn't want to think about that, and slapped the laptop closed in frustration.

****

When I got home later, Baxter jumped down from the sofa and galloped between me and his food bowl, conflicted between welcoming me home and letting me know he was ready for dinner. I filled his bowl with kibble and then pulled my bag up on the counter to unload. It felt heavier than usual, and I remembered the wooden box. I set it on the counter and brewed a cup of coffee to savor while I puzzled over the puzzle box.

I perched at the kitchen counter, staring down at the box in front of me, trying to see if there was a fine line or a visual clue for a secret compartment. The box had both brass and wood inlay. I opened the lid, which exposed an interior of deep green fabric. I probably wouldn't have noticed had I not seen the puzzle boxes Preston showed me, but the interior was smaller than it should be. *Aha! It's definitely one of those!*

I mentally congratulated myself, closed the lid, and gently shook the box. There was no audible sign something was hidden inside. I then gently placed my fingers on the top and tried to move different pieces of the inlay. I was getting ready to give up when one piece of brass moved forward. Now I was excited. I tried moving nearby pieces. Nothing.

Baxter was watching me intently, so I looked at him and said, "What? You think you can do better?" He wagged his tail in response.

I kept working at it for another hour. I would get one piece to move but would then hit a dead end. I had reached a point of extreme frustration, so I put the box back down on the counter with deliberate care to keep myself from hurling it against the wall.

"Let's take a walk," I told Baxter, grabbing his leash. He was waiting for me by the door before I could even put my coat back on.

****

Later, at the Lodge, our usual gang, with the addition of the out-of-towners, had commandeered the lounge area, and after we got past the initial round of discussion about Clive's murder and Ryan's status, the ensuing friendly chatter was just what the doctor ordered.

Hank regaled us with stories, which had me laughing until my stomach hurt. Even Oscar came out of his shell and engaged in an animated conversation with JJ about chakras and color auras. And Jack joined us to spend a short Valentine's time with Annie.

Maggie and Declan sat close together on one of the lounge settees, having shared their plates of bar food. He casually draped his arm around her as she leaned in toward him. I had to admit, they made a cute couple. At one point, though, he tilted his head to whisper in her ear, but at the same time, he leveled his gaze at me for a little longer than made me comfortable.

Had Preston told him my concerns about his intentions toward Maggie? I hoped not. But then again, I didn't really know Preston, so why would I think he would hold my concerns in confidence. Did I just create unnecessary drama? Geez, the last thing I needed was to have to add *smooth things over* to my to-do list.

Chapter 12

Thursday

The next morning, after another restless night, I shuffled into the kitchen and, without flipping on the lights, turned the coffee machine on. I hit the programmed button, and while it brewed, I walked over to the living room windows. There was a hushed stillness to the scene outside. A light snow had fallen overnight, gently blanketing the grounds in front of the Workshop. The road glistened under the street light from the ice melt spread during the night. All of nature's little creatures were still tucked into their nests, and no cars were on the road yet.

I felt very solitary looking out into the darkness from within a dark room, and I stepped closer until my breath fogged up a small circle on the window. I reached out with my finger and drew a line through it, enjoying the coldness of the window pane against the warmth of my skin. The coffee machine's final gurgle broke the spell, and I returned to the kitchen to grab my cup, climbed back in bed, and read the news on my tablet. The bedside lamp bathed the room in a warm glow, and sitting cross-legged under the quilts, with the smell of coffee filling the room, I was grateful I had set my alarm to give me some extra time this morning.

After my shower, I dug around in the back of my

closet. Today, I would dress with care. I was going to meet Eddie Marks's wife, and the somber event warranted a more professional appearance. I pulled out pieces from my old wardrobe: gray herringbone slacks, a white blouse, a black V-neck sweater, and my go-to low-heeled black oxfords. They could handle the salt and snow. I dried my hair and let it hang below my shoulders instead of pulling it back in a ponytail as usual, and finished with my more comprehensive cosmetic routine. Afterward, I assessed myself in the mirror and nodded with satisfaction. I could never pull off a totally refined look, but I could convey professionalism. That had always been enough, and it would be again today.

I still had an hour before I had to leave, so I pulled out the puzzle box. Maybe with a fresh morning brain, I'd have better luck. I sat hunched over the kitchen counter, moving the pieces this way and that, trying to keep a rolling memory of what I had tried so I wouldn't keep retracing my steps. It reminded me of those golf-tee peg-board triangles where you keep eliminating tees until only one remains. I rarely succeeded, more often having the aggravating result of two tees left, the five-dollar toy's way of taunting me with my lack of puzzle acumen. Granted, this box was way more sophisticated, but the reminiscence only served to lessen my confidence.

I had moved a few of the pieces and picked up the box to give it a little shake. Something shifted. It was barely perceptible, and I thought maybe I had imagined it. Could Eddie have put something in here? Surely not. We found it in the shopping bag with his other purchases. And what would he have squirreled away in a puzzle box? Something he happened to pick up while traveling? It didn't make sense, but it spurred me on to keep trying.

After the hour, I gave up. Maybe Jack would let me hold on to it a little longer, and then mail it back to his wife. If I couldn't get into it, perhaps Declan or Preston could open it for us.

****

I arrived at the precinct early and found Jack in his office. "Mornin'! Anything new on your end?" I asked, with more enthusiasm than I felt.

"Not much, although if you can stick around, we should have the security tapes from the Bennet House this morning."

"Sure thing. Why does it take so long to get security footage?"

"Because most businesses don't keep it on site anymore. It's stored at the security company, and we have to go through the red tape to get it."

"Hunh, I didn't know that. You got my email, right? With the data I've collected so far?"

"I did. Thanks for putting it together for me."

"No problem, but as you can see, I've been hitting dead ends at every turn. I've got my fingers crossed we'll see something on the security footage."

"You and me both. By the way, I talked to Preston, and he said he went back out to the bar to watch the hockey game. Dustin was able to pull the room charge from the bar tab, and it lines up with his statement, but it doesn't totally eliminate him."

"Well that's annoying. What else?"

"Since we have the two investigations going, I had Travis pick up the security video from the truck stop where Eddie's car was parked, and we've been looking through the few street cameras we have in Flat Rock to see if Clive went anywhere. It's a long shot, though. Unlike bigger cities, we don't have many street cameras."

"Well, we'll hope for something. Anything is better than where we are right now. As I reported, none of the board members were able to tell me anything about Clive's personal life. Maura didn't have much to offer either, other than some insights on his personality. Lena actually had more interaction with him than Maura did. Have you checked for a will? Anything in his finances? What about his laptop?"

Jack flipped open his notebook. "Nothing unusual in his finances. Regular auto deposits from the Bennet House, and standard bill paying or ATM withdrawals. Fortunately, his attorney's contact info was in his address book. Clive did have a will, and I'm going to the attorney's office later to go over it with him. And I'm in the process of checking Maura's alibi."

"I talked to her, and she seemed genuine. But what have you always said? You look close to home first."

"Right."

"What about his laptop? Any communications between them or anyone?"

"His laptop was clean; there was some general email correspondence, but mostly Bennet House stuff. There were no texts or emails to or from any of the festival artists."

I had leaned forward with my arm on his desk, tapping my fingers in a quick staccato.

"Stop that racket. You're making me tense," he chided.

"Sorry, trying to think," I said and leaned back in the chair. "It's just frustrating. The suspect field is too wide. How do we do this when we can't find a motive for his murder, and most or all of the people connected to the festival, Workshop, and Bennet House have been cleared? If it's some random person, I don't know how we'll ever get to the bottom of this."

"I do. We're going to keep digging until we find something. That's how it works. Trust me."

"I know, and I do trust you. I'm just impatient." I remembered the box and reached down into my bag to pull it out. "As I told you, Preston showed me puzzle boxes like this one. You shift the inlay around, and a secret compartment opens."

"That's interesting, but since it was still in the bag with the other stuff he bought, do you really think he put something in it?"

"My gut is telling me he did. And if he did, it might give us a clue as to what happened to him."

"How strong is your gut?"

I waffled my hand back and forth. "Fair to middling. This morning I had some of the pieces moved and gave it a shake—out of frustration, I might add—and I just barely felt a weight shift."

Jack rested his jaw on his hand and looked at me with interest. "Okay. I'll tell her we need to hold back some of the evidence, and we'll get everything back to her as soon as possible."

"Great. I'll do my best, and if I can't do it, I know Preston or Declan can open it."

"Not a good idea. If there's something in there, we need to see it first. So don't even mention you have it."

"Got it."

There was a sudden commotion coming from the hallway, and Matt was talking rapidly, his voice rising nearly an octave.

"Ma'am, if you'll please wait out in reception, I'll let Chief Maddox know you're here...I'm sorry, you'll have to wait out there."

A female voice, thick with disdain, cut him off. "Get out of my way. I don't have time to sit around and wait."

Jack shot up from his desk and, while rushing to the doorway, motioned to Travis to flip the whiteboard over so everything was hidden from view. I slowly rose from my chair, steeling myself for what was coming.

Jack said, "Good morning, you must be Mrs. Marks. Matt, thank you. Would you please have Travis put Mr. Marks' effects together and bring them to the interview room?" He then put his hand on her elbow and said, "Please, come with me," managing to gently steer her away and move her down the hall.

I followed a little behind, intending to go to the viewing room on the other side of the two-way glass. Mrs. Marks was tall, and her expensively highlighted hair fell just above her shoulders. She wore cream-colored wool slacks with a matching long coat made of the same material. I found myself walking in the wake of her perfume. It was a distinct scent, but I couldn't quite put my finger on the brand. Anything else about her would have to wait until I watched her meeting with Jack.

I pulled a chair up to the glass and switched on the intercom. From the woman's demeanor, this was going to be an interesting interview. I wished I had some popcorn.

"Please accept my condolences. I am very sorry for your loss," Jack said, with the appropriate decorum. "Would you prefer Mrs. Marks, or may I call you Gina?"

Gina crossed her long legs, revealing a slender ankle above a foot encased in a cream-colored leather pump. She wore a white silk blouse, tasteful gold jewelry, and her face was perfection—a smooth, creamy complexion, lightly powdered to eliminate any sheen, the merest touch of blush, perfectly shaped eyebrows, and understated eyeshadow highlighted her green eyes. Her manicured nails were painted the palest pink I have ever seen.

She folded her hands in her lap and looked Jack squarely in the eye. "You may call me Gina. And thank you for your sympathies. Do you have an update on what happened to my husband?"

Jack leaned his arms on the table. "As you know, he was a victim of a hit-and-run. I'm not willing to close the investigation yet, but I'm sorry to tell you we have very little to go on. I would chalk this up to a tragic accident, except I have not come to a conclusion yet about why he was walking on that road, particularly with how cold it was. His car was at the truck stop with his wallet in the glovebox, so I still want answers about how he got there, and why."

"I see," she said, exhibiting very little emotion.

"Can you tell me if Edward knew anyone here? Why he was here?" Jack asked.

"I can't imagine he knew anyone here. As to why, I'm not sure. My husband is...*was*...a buyer for art collectors. He has clients both in the US and in Europe. As a matter of fact, he was scheduled to leave for

Brussels this week. He was on the road doing some buying, and then he was to fly out of Philadelphia."

"Could he have been here to purchase art for someone?"

"I can't imagine why he would look here," she responded with just enough disdain to get my dander up.

"Actually, we have some very fine professional artists living here, both in Flat Rock Falls and the surrounding area, many of whom have a national reputation. An art festival is going on this week at the Bennet House mansion, and we have an artist collective here, called the Creative Workshop, where many of these artists have their studios. Do any of those names sound familiar to you?"

She raised her eyebrow. "My mistake, I had no idea, but no, he didn't mention anything to me. I would imagine he was just traveling through, read about the festival, and decided to stop. He sometimes preferred the backroad routes for that very reason. Anyway, maybe he just wanted to take a walk and was in the wrong place at the wrong time."

"When did you last speak to him? Oh, and to follow up since you gave us his cell number, we have not yet found his cell phone."

She looked at her watch and sighed, clearly impatient with the questions. "We don't talk every day when he's on the road, so I wasn't expecting to hear from him until he reached Philadelphia. Surely you don't think there was foul play, do you? I mean other than it being a hit-and-run, which is foul enough," she said, with distaste.

"I cannot say definitively. I just have some nagging

questions. For example, do you know why he might have checked into the motel using a different name?"

"What are you talking about?"

"He used the name John Middleton."

Gina's brow puckered, but she made no comment.

"I don't mean to ask an indelicate question, but could he have been meeting someone here and he didn't want it traced back to him?"

Now she looked at him snidely. "What, you mean a girlfriend?"

Jack nodded. "I'm sorry, but I have to ask."

"No. Absolutely not. That's not Eddie's style. I would more think that the motel entered the information incorrectly."

Jack took a moment to assess her before speaking. "Perhaps. Even still, until I have a better understanding of what took place here, I'm not ready to close out the case."

Gina uncrossed her legs and shifted in her chair, indicating she was done with the meeting. "Well, I'm sure you will keep me up to date with any developments in your investigation."

I could sense Jack's surprise from the tightening of his shoulders. He leapt up as she stood, and said, "Um, would you like to see his personal effects?"

"I don't need to see them, and I'm in a hurry, so please just package them up for me to take. And I need to know who to make arrangements with about transferring his body to Ohio, and a transport company to bring his car."

"Of course, however, there are a few items we will need to keep here until the investigation is over. We'll either get them to you before you leave, or courier them to you. Please give me one moment to put everything together for you. Can I get you anything while you wait?"

A scowl marred Gina's perfect complexion, and she said, "I thought you were essentially done, so why must you hold on to any of his things? You've asked me your questions. What more is there to do?"

I found her tone irksome, but Jack exhibited patience when he said, "It's standard procedure to protect the chain of custody until we are certain the case is closed. Please be assured we will get these things to you as quickly as we can."

"I would hope so. Before I leave town would be best."

"Of course. Now, is there anything I can get you?"

"No, thank you, I'm fine," she said, with a touch of frost.

I met Jack out in the hall as he exited the room. "Wow. She is quite the snow queen, isn't she?" I said in a stage whisper.

He was unfazed by her demeanor. "Grief is not one size fits all. Everyone reacts differently in this kind of situation."

"You're right. May I go in and introduce myself?"

Now Jack looked at me like I had two heads. "If you want to. I need to put this stuff together for her and call the morgue to prepare for the transfer. So, I need a couple minutes, anyway."

I knocked lightly on the door and entered the room. Gina looked at me in surprise, expecting Jack. "Who are you?"

"Mrs. Marks, my name is Alex Montgomery. I'm a consultant for Chief Maddox."

She raised her hand. "Mrs. Marks is Eddie's mother. Please call me Gina."

I sat in the chair Jack had vacated, relieved I had taken the extra care with my appearance. Having my old wardrobe on helped me present a cool professionalism to match her aloof exterior, and I mirrored her body language to make her feel at ease and cultivate rapport. This was a technique I used in my old job.

"Okay, Gina, I just wanted to step in and tell you I'm so very sorry about Edward. Please accept my condolences."

"Did you know him?"

"No, I'm afraid not, but I was with the chief for part of the initial investigation, so I feel a connection to the case."

She didn't say anything, so I continued. "Did you drive in this morning? If so, you must be exhausted."

"I stayed the night on the road, so I'm fine." she said, brushing an invisible piece of lint from her slacks.

"Will you be heading back directly, or are you spending the night here?"

"When I spoke with Chief Maddox by phone, he gave me the information for the hotel where Eddie was staying, so I called and asked them to put me in the same room. I'll be leaving tomorrow if I can make the transport arrangements today."

"I see." The sentimentality of wanting to stay in the same room contradicted her outward emotions, so maybe Jack was right. "I'm sure this has been quite a shock. Do you have family to help you?

"No, they're all on the West Coast, but I can manage fine."

"Well, please let me know if there is anything we can do to make your stay here easier."

"Thank you."

Jack reentered the room and took the chair next to mine. He put two sets of papers and a pen on the table, along with the wallet and keys. He took one set of the papers and swiveled them around in front of Gina.

"This is an inventory list of what was found in Edward's car and hotel room. If everything looks correct, please sign at the bottom."

Gina took her time and carefully looked over the list. I noticed her green eyes widen for a split second. It was an almost imperceptible change in expression, but I caught it. She let out a sigh and placed the paper on the table.

"I didn't know everything he took with him, but these things look like what he would take on the road." She picked up the pen and signed, returning the page to Jack.

"Thank you. The next page is a waiver, stipulating you are taking the wallet, keys, and car, but leaving the rest of his personal effects with the department until they are released to you." Jack then pointed to the other page with the list of Eddie's effects. "Would any of the purchases from the art festival be for you? Perhaps a gift for you?"

After quickly scribbling her signature on the waiver, she pulled the inventory page back over to look at the festival items. This time, her eyes remained neutral but lingered a little longer than necessary. "No, I can't fathom why he would buy any of these as a gift for me. Well, I take that back. Maybe the wooden box or the cards, but it's doubtful he would buy a gift for me now, when he still had the trip to Brussels ahead of him. It's more likely the box is for a client, who will now be waiting for it. So, the sooner these things can be returned to me the better."

"I understand. We'll work as quickly as possible," Jack said, then passed the wallet and car keys across the table. The last item remaining in front of him was the hotel key.

I said, "Gina is going to be staying at the Whispering Falls Motel and would like to stay in the same room as Edward did."

Jack slid the hotel key toward her. "I'll let them know I gave you the key. Don't let the exterior put you off. It's actually a very pleasant room."

"And Gladys is nice," I added. "She spoke kindly about Edward."

Jack then went through the steps with Gina to have the body released for transport, and he gave her a business card for a vehicle transportation service.

When he finished, Gina's hard exterior melted just a notch, and she said, "Thank you very much for putting this all together for me. You both have been most kind." She stood up and extended a long slender hand first to Jack and then to me before walking toward the door. "You have my information if you have any updates for me. And if I don't speak with you again, thank you for everything you did for Edward. You've done your best."

"Please take care," I said to her departing back as Jack ushered her out.

He returned a few minutes later, and I said, "I'm glad we're holding onto the box. Did you see the subtle shift in her eyes when she saw the list?"

He said, "I did. It's why I held back his clothing, too. I don't want her to think we're focusing on anything specific. So, keep plugging away at it. And definitely keep it under wraps." He had a laptop under his arm and he set it on the table. "Hang tight a sec. We can stay in here to watch the security footage."

A few minutes later, he had the laptop hooked up to the monitor mounted on the wall at the end of the table. He opened a folder on the desktop and cued up the first video.

"This is Bennet House footage from Monday. I'll fast forward to seven p.m."

"Digital sure is easier than the old tape format, isn't it?" I mused, as he quickly scrolled through the day to closing time. "Now where are the cameras? I haven't noticed them."

"There are two exterior cameras at the front and back doors. There's also one interior of the lobby. It's not a museum, so there's really no call for every room to have them."

"At least we have something," I said.

"Okay, here we go. This is the back door."

Over the next few minutes, we watched as a procession of artists left through the back door to go to the parking lot, mostly in small clusters. It was weird to see everyone, including myself, blissfully unaware of being watched and recorded by the camera. Penny exited at about seven thirty, just as she said in her statement. She locked the door, did a test pull to double check it was locked, then walked out of view in the direction of the parking lot.

"I didn't see Clive leave. Should we back it up?"

Jack moved the video back to around six p.m.

"Let's see if this does it," he said.

While we watched the minutes tick by with no significant activity, Jack and I hashed over where the investigation would go next if nothing came of the video. It wasn't a promising conversation, and I was grateful when we were pulled back to viewing the tape. At six twenty-seven p.m., Clive exited the building, and he was alone.

Jack made a note on his pad and said, "Okay, let's look at the front entrance for the same time frame. Then we'll have to look at both cameras again later in the evening to see if Clive comes back, and who else is in the frame. If they bypassed the building altogether, we're going to be out of luck."

"I'm crossing my fingers."

We observed the cluster of artists in the front lobby, when we were discussing who was going to the café, and then we watched everyone split off, presumably to get their stuff before leaving. I pointed to a door in the wall on the side of the lobby. "That's the closet where Ryan had his tools, right?"

"Yup. I'll have one of the guys go back through hours and hours of footage to see who accesses that closet."

Jack returned to the back door camera and sped up the tape so we could get through the lull time more quickly. Even still, we had time to kill. I was getting stiff from sitting, so I got up and walked back and forth across the room. Jack kept an eye on the screen but decided it was a great time for a chitchat.

"So how's Walter doing?" he asked innocently.

I stopped and scrutinized his face to see if there was any hidden agenda in his question. "He's fine. I talked to him on Tuesday, after Ryan was taken in for questioning."

"I thought you might want to talk to him. He's good in a crisis. Any plans for him to come visit again?"

"Are you fishing?"

With his eyes still glued to the screen, Jack's mouth curved into an impish smile. "Who, me? Fishing? I never pry into your personal life."

I stopped and put my hands on my hips. "Yeah, right."

"Have you told Michael about him?" Jack and my ex were still friends, so I wasn't surprised by the question.

"There's nothing to tell, is there?" I paused, then said, "Well, that's not true. I have told him Walter is investing in the Workshop."

"That's what I meant, about the Workshop. What did you think I meant?" he asked, again with an impish grin.

I wanted to wipe that grin off his face. "You're taunting me. Geez, it's like we're back in high school."

Jack let out a deep laugh. "Sorry, can't help it. I like to wind you up."

I flipped him a bird.

Jack darted a look at me before returning his eyes to the screen. "Seriously, I do like Walter, and I'm glad he's still considering…" Jack stopped mid-sentence, sat up straight, and said, "Hold up. Here we go."

I rushed back to my seat and leaned forward. "What do you see?"

Jack rewound a few seconds and pointed to the screen. "There's Clive. He's come back."

We watched Clive approach the back door. He looked over his shoulder before he unlocked it.

"What's the time?" I asked, peering to look at the screen.

"Eight fifty-six p.m."

"So now what?"

"Let's see if anyone joins him."

About fifteen minutes later, we saw a figure approach the door. "Look! Someone's going in!" I exclaimed, feeling a rush of butterflies in my stomach.

"Can you tell who it is?" Jack asked, freezing the image on the screen.

I looked at the figure in all dark clothing, with a navy or black hoodie covering the head. There were no distinguishable characteristics to give away the identity.

"I can't tell with the hoodie on," I lamented. "Male? Female? I can't really tell. The gloves mean we can't see the hands, which would help us determine if it's a man or a woman."

Jack restarted the video.

"What's interesting to me is this person seems to know there's a camera here. Notice how he or she turns so there's no shot of the face?" he asked.

The hair stood up on the back of my neck. "Oh, hell's bells. First of all, this is someone who knows something about the Bennet House. It's someone who has been there."

Jack sat back, and said under his breath. "Yes. it also means Clive's murder was likely premeditated."

We looked at each other and then he asked, "Are you ready for what happens next?"

166

Chapter 13

"What do you mean?" I asked.

Jack explained, "We need to go to the front camera to see what happens prior to Clive ending up down at the pond."

"Oh." Of course. I was so thrown by seeing the hooded person I hadn't thought ahead.

"You won't see the murder, but you might see the beginning of the chase. Can you handle it?" he asked, with concern in his voice.

I chewed my thumbnail, and said, "I don't want to, but I feel I owe it to Clive."

Jack wordlessly switched to the lobby camera. He once again sped up the tape, but this time, instead of light banter, we sat in silence while the minutes ticked by.

At nine twenty-one, we saw Clive dart into view, repeatedly looking over his shoulder. He scuttled from one side of the lobby to the other, then finally, he threw the bolt and opened the front door. He looked back one last time and then hurled himself outside and out of view.

Seconds later, the figure entered the screen, walking at a leisurely pace, taking a quick look in the parlor and drawing room to make sure Clive hadn't opened the door as a ruse. Then the figure approached the open door, and in a split second of time, the light reflected off the chisel in the killer's hand.

My right leg started shaking uncontrollably, and a tear slid down the side of my face.

Turning to Jack, I said, "Oh my gosh, Jack. We've just watched up to the moment where Clive is killed. It's like watching a horror movie, except it's real. This is just too horrible."

I sensed the anger swell in Jack, and he said, "Yes, and I'm going to nail the bastard who did this." He turned off the video stream. "I'll put Matt and Gabe on video duty. The timeline is narrowed down now, so we need to scour the street cameras to see where Clive was before coming back to the Bennet House, including the day or two leading up to this. Plus, all those hours from the start of the festival to see who went into the closet." He shook his head at the prospect of how long this was going to take.

As Jack spoke, I was busy reviewing what we'd seen. "I feel like it's a man, Jack. There's something about the way he moved. It was a man's walk."

"I tend to think you're right, but I'm not going to rule out a female yet. Based on statistics, this kind of a violent crime points toward it being a male, but the video doesn't make it clear. But I will say this has cleared Ryan. I know Ryan's physique, and how he moves. He's taller and thinner than the person on the tape. Plus, did you notice which hand held the chisel? That was *not* Ryan."

I bolted upright. "Of course! Ryan's left-handed, like me. The guy in the video was holding it in his right hand!" I was too busy being creeped out, and it hadn't registered to me that the figure was *not* Ryan. "Thank goodness. You'll call and tell him, right?

"Of course. This officially clears him."

This news bolstered me a wee bit, and recalling Jack had been talking about the daunting task of looking through the videos, I made a suggestion. "Why don't you give a batch of the recordings to me to look at? I can take time off from the festival to do this."

Jack tapped his fingers on the table as he mulled this over. "It would certainly help speed this along, but you have to really pay attention to every minute. We won't have time to go back over them to cover missed ground."

"That kind of work is right up my alley. If I start glazing over, I'll take a break. I promise, I won't let you down."

"Okay. I'll have you handle the festival footage and Matt and Gabe can take the street cameras. Document everyone who goes in and out of the front closet. It could be a lot, or only a handful, but maybe we can start eliminating people."

"Got it. I'll document everything."

"Perfect. Come on, let's get out of here. I'll send you a secure link for these, and then I'll call Ryan."

I was grateful to leave the interview room. Even though I was incredibly relieved Ryan was now officially off the suspect list, I was reeling from watching the moments leading up to Clive's death. I went to the water cooler a few feet down from Jack's office and filled the little paper cup three times. I usually can't stand the taste of those paper cones, but right now, I didn't care. The cold water helped squelch the queasiness in my stomach.

****

Back in the car, my energy drained, and I rested

169

my arms on the steering wheel and put my head down on my arms, contemplating my next move. I swiveled my head to the right to see the clock on the dashboard; it was almost noon. The first order of business was to see if Penny was comfortable covering things so I could work on the surveillance tape at my apartment. I pulled out my phone and tapped the office number.

After a few rings, she answered with a smooth, professional voice, "Hello, this is Penny."

"Hi, Penny, it's Alex. Jack and I started going through the surveillance videos, and since there are hours and hours to weed through, I've offered to help him out. Do you think you can handle things without me this afternoon?"

"Of course. The festival is basically running itself at this point, and I was planning to be here until closing anyway."

"You're a gem. I really appreciate it."

Penny seemed to easily slip into her new leadership role as she said firmly, "We'll be fine here. You just take care of what you need to do, and I hope those videos prove to be of help."

It was comforting when you were part of a good team, and I felt better after talking to her. I took a deep breath, then drove to the Workshop.

As I walked in the door, I got a call from Ryan. "You heard the news, right?" he asked, joyfully.

"Yes! I'm assuming you'll be back at the festival today?"

"You bet. I can't wait." He paused, then asked, "What should I tell people?"

I thought about it, then answered, "Tell them the investigation is going in a new direction. That your part of it is now closed."

"Perfect. I'll see you over there."

"Actually, you won't. I'm working on some stuff for Jack, so Penny will be handling everything today. But I'm sure I'll see you later if we all meet up for dinner."

"Roger that," he said, back to his perky self.

Annie and Spencer rounded the corner, and I went through the same explanation about what I was doing.

Spencer asked, "Why don't we come by after the festival closes. We can bring some take-out. Annie, does that work for you?"

"Great idea! What do you think, Alex?"

"That sounds perfect. By then I'll be ready for a break, and the company."

Upstairs, I settled on the living room floor, with the laptop on the coffee table and my legal-sized notepad in hand to make notes on who went to the closet, when, and what they were doing. *Okay, roll tape!* I said to myself and began the mind-numbing process.

I started with Thursday morning. The camera showed the lobby with the storage closet in clear view. I pressed pause a number of times to make notes. Thankfully, as my eyes grew accustomed to staring at the screen, I was able to speed things up, and within three hours, I had covered Thursday.

I needed to stay sharp, so I went to the kitchen, drank a glass of water, and made myself a mid-afternoon coffee. Back in the living room, I scanned my notes for a memory recap of who had visited the hall closet. Spencer went in for a broom and dustpan, and Annie returned them. Hank put two boxes in the closet, Declan put one in. Ryan put his canvas tool bag on the closet floor. Midafternoon, Clive opened the door, looked inside, then he closed the door and strode off.

Later, Penny made several trips to the closet as she set things up for the festival, pulling out an ornate easel, a coat rack, a lectern, and then a stool, and a stack of coat tags. *Geez.* That closet was like the black hole of storage. I was waiting for clown cars to emerge from it.

Watching the videos once the public arrived the following day would be more arduous, with lots of people coming and going. To continue my job, I needed to have fresh eyes, so I closed the laptop, swapped my shoes for my knee-high rubber snow boots, put on my coat and scarf, and grabbed Baxter's leash. "Come on, big boy. Let's go for a walk."

We went down the stairs and out through the double doors off the lobby. We passed the courtyard and went farther into the grounds. In kinder temperatures, the courtyard was our hang-out spot. There was a stand of old growth trees lining the back of the property, and we had taken over one of the school fields to plant new trees, smaller ornamentals, and flowering bushes. This summer, we would create the paths, install the benches, and complete the new sculpture garden.

The fluffy snow came up above Baxter's knees, and his wagging tail left a swath of partial snow angels as we plowed around the grounds. Eventually, I let him off his leash so he could have a good romp. I loved to watch dogs in the snow; nose goes to ground, with their front paws extended out, as if playing with a toy. And just like I did when I was a kid, Baxter liked to eat the snow. We traipsed back and forth across the fields a few times until my hands started to go numb from the cold.

"Okay," I called. "Let's go!" He pranced over to me and we made our way back, the snow kicking out from my boots and his paws as we walked at a faster pace.

Refreshed from our walk, I returned to my laptop, opened up the link for Friday, and kept my eyes glued as the first patrons arrived for the festival. I cringed seeing myself on screen while I interacted with the guests and had to stop myself from analyzing how stupid I looked and just focus on the danged closet.

As the hours ticked by, I stopped a few times to make some notes, but nothing new had cropped up. I had finished getting through Friday when I noticed the light from the window had shifted from dim to dark. I looked at my watch and was shocked to see it was already after six. Baxter looked at me expectantly, clearly ready for his dinner, so I swung my glasses up on my head, got up from the couch, and ambled into the kitchen. I pushed the button for my last cup of the day, maybe, and put kibble in Baxter's bowl as it brewed.

I was leaning on the kitchen counter, wondering if my sifting through these videos was an exercise in futility, when my phone dinged with a text. It was Annie, saying they were going to pick up Chinese takeout to bring over, and what did I want? I went with my usual order of Sesame Chicken, then got back to work.

It was now Saturday on the tapes and I watched, made notes, watched, made notes—wash, rinse, repeat. By midday on Saturday, I had listed six individuals who had entered the closet: Penny, Ryan, Spencer, Hank, Declan, and Mindy. So far, all seemed perfectly harmless; Hank and Declan had each squirreled away a box, Spencer grabbed a roll of paper towels, Penny got the broom to sweep up tracked-in snow, and Mindy picked up more coat tickets.

I was trying to decide whether to stop or continue on when there was a rapid knock at the door. "Come in!" I called out.

Annie, JJ, Bitsy, Maggie, and Ryan all entered. "Spencer is on his way," JJ said, taking off her many layers of winter gear. "He left a little bit before us to go get the food."

"Just throw your coats on the guest room bed," I suggested.

Annie looked around. "Where should we eat?"

I said, "Here, I'll clear off the table."

I never sat at the long barnwood table to eat. Instead, it was covered with catalogs, art magazines, and a couple of projects I had been toying with over the holidays, including a collection of bottles I'd been decorating with paint pens and some colorful papers for experimenting with folding techniques before applying them to a canvas.

JJ came up to me in a swirl of gauzy fabric, a look of concern on her face. "Your chakras are all out of whack."

"I'm not exactly sure what you mean, but out of whack isn't far off from how I'm feeling right now."

"Hold on, I have just the thing." She went over to her bag and pulled out a vial with some kind of liquid in it. "Come stand over here, where it's quieter." She motioned me toward the alcove leading to my bedroom.

She poured a dime-sized amount of oil in her hands and rubbed them together to release a pleasantly soft and musky scent with a hint of citrus. "Close your eyes," she commanded.

I complied. I could sense movement, and opened one eye to see her flicking her fingers at me.

"Keep them closed," she admonished, and then intoned meditative song-like phrases, while flicking. "Breathe deeply. Lower your shoulders. Feel the calm descend upon you like a gentle rain. Your neck is released from tension. Hear the babbling brook, and the clear water rolling over the rocks, while the sun warms your soul. Breathe in deeply and exhale slowly." After repeating the breathing exercise three times, she took each of my hands and gently massaged some of the remaining oil on the inside of my wrist.

"Okay, that's better!" she said in her normal voice. "Your aura colors are more balanced, now."

I opened my eyes just as she finished stroking the air around my head and shoulders. I blinked a few times and said, with hesitation, "I think I actually feel a bit better."

"Of course you do."

I sniffed my wrists, taking in the heady scent, only to be brought back to present by a thunking sound at the door. Annie rushed to open it, revealing Spencer, loaded down with take-out bags.

A few minutes later, the table was laden with paper pails of aromatic food. Bitsy suggested we not discuss the murder during dinner, so instead, we talked about how sales were going at the festival and laughed at each other's stories about customer experiences. Once sufficiently stuffed, we cleared the plates, loaded the dishwasher, and convened in the living room.

Ryan sat on the floor with his long legs stretched

out in front of him. "Since I've been officially cleared, I need to catch up on the investigation. Where are you with things?"

"I wish I had more to report," I replied. "Jack and I watched the surveillance footage from the Bennet House and saw what led up to Clive's murder. It's unsettling, so I'm not going to talk about it." I looked around the group and didn't see an argument brewing. No one wanted to hear about the terrifying last moments before the murder.

I continued, "I've spent the day going through the videos from the beginning of the festival."

"Oh my gosh," Annie exclaimed, "are we on tape the whole time we're in the Bennet House?"

I patted the air with my hands. "No. They only have cameras at the front entrance and the back door for security purposes."

She breathed a sigh of relief. "Whew."

Spencer let out a laugh. "What are you nervous about? Getting caught picking your nose? Or maybe a wedgie?"

"Oh my gosh, you are worse than my brother!" she chided.

"All right, simmer down. Nobody's been caught on tape doing anything. And that's sort of the point. I'm going through the mind-numbingly boring video hoping to see who goes into the front hall closet where Ryan's tools were, and, if there were any noteworthy interactions with Clive."

"Have you seen anything interesting?" Ryan asked. "Did anyone go near my tools?"

"I wish it was so clearcut. So far, it's just been people going in and out for the usual business of the festival. But I'm only partway through. Maybe further into the weekend I'll see something relevant."

Spencer asked, "Other than those videos, what else is there to go on?"

"We need to learn more about Clive. He was an enigma." I paused, then added, "Not really an enigma. He just didn't seem to have much of a life outside the Bennet House."

"Oh no," Betsy said, with sadness in her voice.

JJ said, "Surely there was something, or somebody, he was involved with. No hobbies? No memberships to any clubs or groups?"

"I haven't found any yet, but I'll keep asking around. Some people are loners, though. His job kept him busy, and he had his cat and his books. Maybe he didn't need anything else."

Maggie spoke up. "By the way, I looked through the photos I've taken so far, and I mostly focused on specific subjects, like an artist with a customer, or a close-up of one of the pieces."

"That's what I thought, but we had to cover the bases," I said, opening the laptop to check it off the list.

Bitsy said, "All of us at the festival have been talking amongst ourselves at various times, which is normal under the circumstances, and no one saw anything suspicious. It's just so frustrating there's nothing to go on."

Annie chimed in. "Not to change the subject, but what's happened with the other death, Alex? You know, the hit-and-run? Jack's been stretched so thin I don't want to bombard him with questions when he gets home."

"I know, we rarely have one unexplained death and

now Jack has two on his hands," I said. I gave a brief recap of Eddie Marks for the rest of the gang, then said, "Earlier this morning, I met his wife, Gina."

"What was she like?" Maggie asked.

"She's something else," I said. "I've dubbed her the snow queen. She was dressed in white, and her personality was pretty cold."

"Wow, I would be a wreck if I lost my husband like that," Maggie said.

"Let's just say she was very low on the scale of exhibiting emotion."

Bitsy put a hand up in objection. "Now, everyone handles death and loss differently. Just because someone has a cool exterior doesn't mean they aren't feeling it inside."

I felt awful for even having the whiff of being gossipy. "I know, you're right. I'm judging based on reading her mannerisms on the surface, which is not fair under these circumstances."

Bitsy conceded, "It's okay. You're actually really good at reading people, so I shouldn't have jumped down your throat."

"Well, at any rate, I don't think she had anything helpful to contribute regarding why he was here.

"What a shame," JJ said. "It's just so sad."

"I know, and I'm afraid his case may never be solved." I got up from the couch, brought my bag over, and pulled out the wooden box. "But I am curious about this."

Maggie leaned over with interest. "This is one of the puzzle boxes Declan and Preston make. Was this with the things Eddie bought at the festival?"

"It is." I shifted pieces of the inlay to demonstrate.

Bity's eyes grew wide. "Look at that! How clever. Have you gotten into it yet?"

"No!" I exclaimed in frustration. "I cannot get this thing open."

"Why don't you just get a hammer," Spencer suggested with a chuckle.

"Nooo," Maggie burst out. "You can't destroy such a beautiful piece of work!"

Spencer winked at Maggie and shrugged. "I'm just saying, if you can't get into it, you may have to take drastic action, and one bang of the hammer would do it."

"Believe me," I interjected, "I've had to control myself from throwing it against a wall, but we can't do either of those things, since we have to get it back to Eddie's wife. And I should mention, Jack doesn't want anyone to know I have the box. So lips sealed about this and, as I'm sure you know, everything else we've talked about." Everyone nodded, but I looked at Maggie, and added, "I don't care how close you and Declan are getting, you can't say anything to him, okay?"

"Of course," she said through pursed lips. "I may be smitten, but I don't know him nearly well enough to let him into our circle."

"Glad you got your head on straight," Spencer said to Maggie. Then he held out his hand to me. "Here, let me take a turn at it." When I hesitated, he said with a laugh, "I promise, I won't break it."

I passed the box over to him and he started sliding pieces, hitting the same dead ends I had with it. Next, it went to JJ, then Annie, then Bitsy, then Ryan. Maggie passed altogether after seeing everyone else fail.

179

Eventually, the box ended up back in front of me, and I moved it to the side of the table in order to open my laptop.

"Now you all understand my frustration!" I said. "Okay, dang it, let's put this aside and go back to Clive to see if there are any other questions we can check off for the investigation."

We spent the next hour talking over Clive's role at the Bennet House, and who we each had talked to. Annie, an amateur conspiracy theorist, concocted her own story.

"Maybe he had a secret bank account with a million dollars in it. And then a long-lost family member, whom he had never met, came knocking on his door. Or better yet, they just said they were a relative, but they really weren't, and Clive figured it out and they killed him to get his money."

Luckily, there was a knock at the door, and I left the gang to expand on her wild theory. I opened the door and found Jack leaning his head against the door frame with his eyes closed. It's quite possible I heard a soft snore.

Chapter 14

Jack opened his eyes when I tapped his shoulder.

"Long day?" I asked.

"You have no idea," he replied, taking off his coat as he walked through the door.

Calls of "Hey Jack!" came from the group, and he gave a perfunctory wave before asking, "You don't by any chance have any food, do you? I haven't eaten."

"As a matter of fact, you hit the bonanza. We have lots of leftover Chinese take-out."

His eyes brightened, and he rubbed his hands together. "All right!"

While reheating a loaded plate in the microwave, I pulled Jack over to the hall by my office. "Anything new today?" I asked, quietly.

"We went through hours and hours of video tapes from street cameras, store fronts, anything we could get our hands on. And I had a meeting with Clive's attorney."

"What'd he say?"

"Clive did have a will, and he hadn't changed it since he was married to Maura. He left everything to her. The estate doesn't amount to enough to warrant murder for financial gain, so nothing out of the ordinary there."

"Annie's going to be so disappointed," I said, with a chuckle. "She's come up with quite the conspiracy theory."

Jack's eyes crinkled with humor. "I can only imagine."

"What about the tapes?" I asked.

"That's a little more interesting. We backed up to Sunday to see where Clive went, which meant trolling street cameras first. He went out twice on Sunday, at least based on what the cameras picked up.

"Where'd he go?" I asked.

"We tracked him to the supermarket on Barkley Avenue."

"That's not very exciting," I said.

"Then he went out in the evening. We followed him down Main Street and watched him merge onto Buchanan Boulevard. We took a flier and guessed he might be going to get gas—the kind of Sunday chores a man who likes routine might do. So we looked at camera footage from Buchanan and the Junction, and we got lucky. We tracked his car to the Quick Pit Truck Stop. Just as we thought, he was getting gas before the start of the week."

I felt disappointment set in. "Oh well, not exactly earth-shattering, is it?"

"You might think not, but this is where it gets interesting. The camera angle showed him at the pump. He stood by his car, pulling his coat collar up to keep warm, when something caught his eye. He was looking to the right of the gas pumps, and something or someone held his attention long after the pump clicked off. A car behind him must have wanted his spot at the pump and called out to get his attention because he gave a sign of apology, put the gas nozzle back, hustled into his car, and drove off. We then followed his progress back toward his house."

"I wonder what caught his attention?" I asked.

"Well, we pulled up the Quick Pit footage showing the front door of the convenience store. Guess who we saw there at the same time?"

"Eddie Marks," I guessed, as a joke.

"Right you are," Jack said.

"Shut the front door!" I exclaimed, then lowered my voice. "Are you kidding me? What a coincidence. The moment Clive is getting gas happens to be the moment Eddie Marks was at the truck stop? What was he doing?" I slapped Jack's shoulder. "Why didn't you lead with that?"

Jack chuckled. "Sorry, I liked the buildup. But yes, Eddie was there during the window of time Clive was getting gas. The camera captured Eddie entering, then exiting the convenience store, stopping at the trash can by the door to open a pack of cigarettes, pull out some matches, and light up. He then walked off to the left, out of camera range, in the direction Clive had been looking."

"Well, I'll be damned. That is quite a coincidence," I said.

"Yeah. As a rule, I don't like coincidences, and this one sure does bother me, but I don't know yet how the two are tied together. At least we now know what time Eddie was at the truck stop, which narrows down his timeline."

"But we don't know how it affects Clive's case, if it even does," I lamented. "Maybe that's what Clive called me about. Something clicked, and he remembered he had seen Eddie at the truck stop. Although, surely, Eddie wasn't what caught Clive's attention since he didn't even know him. It would have been pretty random for Clive to remember seeing him unless Eddie had tripped and fallen or done some other grand gesture to pique Clive's interest. I do think it tells us, though, your instinct was right not to close out Eddie's case."

"Always trust your gut," Jack said.

The microwave had already dinged, so I led him back to the kitchen and pulled out his plate of food. "Ta-dah! Dinner is served."

Spencer vacated his seat on the couch to Jack, who gratefully sat down and dove in to the food. A few minutes later, he realized all eyes were on him, and he self-consciously looked down at his shirt.

"What? Have I spilled something?" he asked.

Annie, sitting next to him, patted his knee. "No, I think they're waiting for you to finish eating before pouncing with a bunch of questions about the investigation."

Jack nodded. "Give me a minute, I'm almost done," he mumbled, between forkfuls.

The group made small talk, trying to appear nonchalant as they waited. Eventually, Jack put his plate on the coffee table and said, "Okay. As you know, I can't tell you much, but ask away, what do you want to know?"

Ryan raised his hand, which made Jack smile. "First, I want to thank you for working so hard and for getting me officially cleared today."

"I was just following the investigation where it took me, Ryan. But I'm glad, too. I know you're all relieved." Jack leaned back on the couch and rubbed his eyes.

Bitsy said, "You look beat, and I think we should take pity on you and not bombard you with too many questions. But is it true? Those of us who were at the café are in the clear?"

Jack looked at me sharply, and I put my hands up and said, "I just told them your public statement asked for anyone to come forward who was near the Bennet House during the time we were at the café."

Jack knew these guys could be trusted. He also knew we would occasionally hash over details in a way he would never do himself, and he trusted me—well, mostly trusted me—to know what line not to cross.

He nodded. "Okay, this is not ironclad, but yes, based on the approximate time of death, those of you who were at the café are not considered people of interest. At this point, anyway."

Spencer said, "That was fairly noncommittal, but I'll take it."

JJ asked, "Can you tell us if you've found a link to anyone connected to us or the festival?"

"We have not found a link to the festival or Flat Rock Falls, but we also haven't found a link to anything else. So you should continue being careful. I know that's not much help, but it's all I got at this point."

Bitsy said, "That's somewhat comforting. But the unknown is always worrisome."

Annie spoke up. "We just have to be vigilant and keep an eye out for each other."

"That's good advice," Jack said, getting up to look for more food. "So, why don't you tell me what ground you covered today."

"We've all tried our hand at that blasted box," Spencer interjected.

"No luck, huh?" Jack asked, while eating an eggroll in two bites.

"No, and they didn't like my idea to hurl it against the wall."

"I know you don't want to, but we may have to ask Preston or Declan to help," I suggested.

Jack said, "Give it till tomorrow afternoon. If it's a no-go, then I'll think about how to proceed. I don't want to draw any attention to this," he said, pointing to the box, "so no one talks about it, right?"

"I already told them. And I'll keep trying to get into it." I then told him my progress with the Bennet House video. "I've gotten through midday Saturday, so I should have most of Sunday done by tomorrow afternoon if I get up and at 'em early in the morning."

"Then we should let you get to bed," Maggie said, looking at her watch.

Everyone started to shift and shuffle to gather their belongings, which excited Baxter to no end. His tail wagged furiously, making the back half of his big mountain dog body wiggle back and forth. Next thing we knew, there was a loud clunk as his tail knocked the wooden box from the edge of the coffee table to the floor. It fell with such force it bounced onto the wood floor, which startled Baxter, and he scooted next to Jack in the kitchen.

Some pieces had shifted during the fall and I was making sure nothing was broken when something caught my eye. "Whoa! Look at this!" I exclaimed, pulling open a drawer. Inside was a folded piece of paper.

"Wait!" Jack exclaimed. He went to the kitchen and got a napkin and a fork.

"What are you going to do with those?" Spencer asked, with a laugh.

"We need to keep our mitts off of this. So the fork will lift the paper up, and we'll hold it with the napkin."

"Clever," he said.

We used Jack's method to get the paper out, and I tucked the box under my arm as we awkwardly unfolded it. There was a handwritten sequence: two letters, followed by two numbers, followed by five numbers, followed by...I counted to myself...twelve numbers.

"What the heck is this?" I mused, passing it to Jack.

"What is it?" Bitsy asked. "Some kind of code?"

"It's a series of numbers after two letters," I answered.

"Maybe a cipher code?" JJ asked.

"What's that?" Maggie asked.

"It's where numbers are swapped with letters. You have to figure out which letter corresponds with which number," she answered.

"Maybe it's the key to a locker somewhere," Ryan suggested.

"Too long," I said, "but it could be a bank account. I've seen a lot of bank codes over the years, and it's not a US bank, but it could be foreign. What do you think, Jack?"

"I'll have to take this to Matt. He's the guru for cracking these kinds of things. It's short enough he can figure it out if it's a word code, and if a bank code, he'll find out where it's from." He carefully refolded the paper and went to the kitchen for a plastic bag to put it in. "I'll be taking this with me, but you keep the box.

Paper would not have made the slight shifting sound you heard, Alex, so you keep working to find another secret compartment."

"Will do." I went to Baxter's treat jar in the kitchen. "Baxter, you good boy. You did what we couldn't do, and saved us hurling the box against the wall!" I bent down and patted his head while he happily crunched his treat.

After everyone got leftovers to take with them, they donned their coats and scarves and made their way out. I spent the next half hour tidying up and was wiping down the kitchen counter when there was a knock on the door.

Thinking someone must have forgotten something, I opened the door wide, saying, "What'd you forget?" But it wasn't one of the gang. It was Walter, standing there with an overnight bag in his hand.

After closing my gaping mouth, I said, "Walter! What are you doing here?"

Walter sauntered in and set his bag by the couch to shed his coat and scarf. Bending down to give Baxter's scruffy ears a rubdown, he said, "Jack called me. He said things were heating up a little bit here." I started to bluster in aggravation, and he put up his hand. "No, he didn't ask me to come. I decided I needed a little time away, so I took it upon myself to come. Plus, I knew if I asked you if I could be of help, you'd say no, so here I am."

I stood for a moment, arms crossed, staring him down. Even at this hour, he looked the consummate professional, from his expertly cut salt and pepper hair to his expensive, but understated, wardrobe. He wore gray corduroy slacks with a crisp button-down shirt under a thick sweater. His dark brown eyes were deeply warm, exuding both sincerity and intelligence.

I made up my mind about how I felt and took a step forward to give him a hug. "I'm glad you're here."

I sensed an almost inaudible sigh of relief before he said, "Good. I'll just put my bag in the guest room, and then you can fill me in on what's happened since we talked."

I watched as Baxter followed him, then went to the kitchen and put a pot on the stove to make us some apple brandy hot toddies. By the time Walter emerged from the guest room I had taken our steaming mugs to the coffee table. We sat on either end of the couch, and Baxter curled up in the middle and was snoring within minutes.

It was getting late, but we sat for another hour, hashing over both investigations. Walter knew all the right questions to ask and how to ask them in an order that made sense, linking one aspect of each investigation to the next. Along with catching him up, it helped create some order in my brain.

Eventually, Walter noticed my eyes were sinking back in my head, and he got up and said, "Okay, time for you to get some sleep."

He reached out for my hand to help me extricate myself from the cocoon I had created in the corner of the couch. "Yeah, we'll pick this up in the morning," I replied, taking the empty mugs to the kitchen sink. "Do you need anything?"

"I don't need a thing. Just get some rest, and I'll see you in the morning."

"Well, feel free to root around if you do, and help yourself to anything in the kitchen. I actually have some food right now."

"I'm so impressed," he teased.

I laughed, then called Baxter to come with me toward the bedroom. He stopped midway and looked from Walter to me, as if deciding who he wanted to go with. He reluctantly walked toward me. "Good choice, my friend," I chided, as we entered the alcove to the bedroom. Before closing the door, I looked at Walter's retreating back. I had a feeling I would sleep much better tonight.

****

Friday

The next morning, I woke up before my alarm went off. I hopped up and took a peek out my door. Walter wasn't up yet, so I tiptoed to the kitchen in my flannel sleep shirt to turn on the coffee machine. I cringed, hoping it wouldn't wake him as it went through the mechanical grinding and brewing, and I walked in place to hurry it along. I grabbed the mug and dashed back to the bedroom. Climbing under the quilt, I leaned against the headboard, savored the coffee, and made a list on my phone of what I needed to tackle today.

I knew I wanted to go to the festival to check in, and then get back here by midday to continue working on the video feed for Jack. Being Friday, the festival would be busy, and I wanted to be there around opening time, so I reluctantly climbed out of bed and hit the shower.

By the time I emerged, fully dressed, Walter was sitting at the kitchen counter, reading the paper on his laptop.

"Mornin'!" I called out.

He raised his coffee mug in greeting and said, "Good morning to you! You look ready to face the day."

"I am. I got some good sleep last night. Have you eaten?"

"Not yet."

The sound of a loud thunk followed by a tambourine-like jangling came from the bedroom. Moments later, we watched Baxter saunter through the kitchen and out the doggy door.

"Now there's a dog living his best life," Walter observed, with a chuckle.

"Yes, he most definitely is." I put food in Baxter's bowl and then pulled out some English muffins and fresh fruit, opting to leave the mini chocolate donuts in the cabinet in an effort to appear more adult than I actually was.

As we were eating breakfast, Walter asked, "What are your plans for the day?"

"I'm going over to the festival first and will be on site for the morning shift, then I want to come back here and work on the video feed for Jack. How about you?"

"If you don't mind, I'll stay here and get some work done."

"Sure, that's fine with me." I looked at my watch. "I don't have to leave until a little before nine, so I'll probably take Baxter for a walk and then do some Workshop business before I go."

Walter looked out the living room window at the crisp blue sky and said, "I'll go with you for the walk. A little fresh air will get the mental juices flowing."

I smiled at our similar view of cold weather. "I couldn't agree more!"

After putting on our winter layers, the three of us bounded down and out the front door. I stood at the top of the steps and breathed deeply to take in the cold fresh air, then followed Walter and Baxter to the sidewalk.

"It's not far to the Bennet House, right?" Walter asked.

I had an inkling of what he was thinking. "It's about ten minutes. You want to see the crime scene, huh?"

"I was thinking that, yes."

We took a right out of the Workshop and followed the route to Park Street. I could sense Walter becoming more contemplative once we reached the path around the pond, and when we came to a stop near where the murder took place, we stood in silence. Even Baxter stopped in his tracks and sat quietly next to us.

"You'd never know anything had happened," he said, his eyes scanning the bank of the pond.

I pointed to the area around the penguin ice sculpture. "Elliott and Ryan sure did a good job of smoothing things over, and Mother Nature did the rest."

He turned his eyes to the Bennet House. "It is a regal mansion, isn't it?"

"Yeah, and the library on the hill above is pretty cool, too. We're really lucky to have this park." Walter furrowed his brow, and I asked, "What is it?"

"I'm just imagining how Clive must have felt as he ran from the mansion down here to the pond, knowing he was running for his life. I wonder at what point he knew death would win."

Chapter 15

I shivered. "I'm really trying not to think about that."

Walter looked out over the pond. "I'm Sorry. I shouldn't have said anything. I'm just thrown off guard because it's like there's still a heaviness to the air."

Normally, I might look at him like he was channeling JJ and her auras and vibes, but I definitely felt the heaviness he was talking about, and I wondered how long it would take before I didn't.

"Believe me, I understand. I think since I was the one who found Clive, I became part of that violent moment in some way."

Walter shifted his gaze to me, and I pretended I didn't see the look of concern in his eyes.

"Shall we head back?" I asked, breezily.

"Let's go. We both have work to do."

Back up in the apartment, I let Walter take the office so he could work in privacy, and I sat at the kitchen counter. The Workshop would be back to business as usual come Monday, and looking at the calendar, I realized it would be busy. Just another reason, albeit less important, I hoped the investigation would quickly come to a conclusion. Although, the way it was going, I wondered if we would ever know who had killed Clive or Eddie Marks. Jack might have two unsolved cases on his hands.

****

When I arrived at the Bennet House, I could tell from the number of cars in the parking lot that the festival was already busy. I tried to convince myself so many people were here on a Friday morning purely because of the success of event, and not the gory draw of a murder. I entered through the back door, but hearing laughter and voices coming from the lobby, I dropped my bag in Penny's office and headed to the front of the building.

There was a buzz around the drawing room, where Annie and Spencer were doing a demonstration with Q&A for the patrons. These two were engaging and hilarious, as if they were talking with their friends, all while imparting knowledge, and I loved that. To me, there was nothing worse than a pretentious and sanctimonious *artiste*. Maggie was taking some pictures for our social media, so I went over to her.

"I'm glad you're getting some shots," I whispered.

She looked at me with bright eyes. "Sure! This is good stuff." Her hair, streaked with blue, was up on her head in a bun with a colorful glass-beaded hair stick holding it in place.

"How's everything else going?" I asked.

She stepped to the side, so we could talk out of earshot. "Um, okay, I think," she said with hesitancy.

"What do you mean? Has something happened?" I asked, alarmed I had maybe neglected something here while doing the work for Jack.

"Oh, I don't know yet. Declan has seemed a little shifty toward me this morning."

Uh-oh. Trouble in paradise. That I could handle, and with a sense of relief, I said, "Hmm, maybe he just has something on his mind. The festival is almost over, and he may be preoccupied with what he has on his plate next week."

"Could be. We'll see. We're supposed to go out tonight, so I guess I'll find out later how things really are. In the meantime, I have too much to do to worry about it. Speaking of which, I wanted to let you know I'll be off-site for a little while today. Oscar's going to cover for me and handle any customers while I go to the supply house. Some of the large format paper I ordered is in, and I'll need it for a job on Monday."

"No worries. If Oscar's fine, I'm fine. And of course, if you need me to step in, just text me. That's what I'm here for."

"Thanks. We should be fine without bothering you. I'm sure you have your hands full helping Jack."

I nodded. "I plan on getting back to the security videos this afternoon. Oh, and guess who showed up last night after you guys left?"

"Who?"

"Walter!"

"No kidding?"

"Nope. Jack called him, and he took it upon himself to come."

"Normally, I'd tease you, but this is not a time to joke around, so I'll just say I'm glad Jack contacted him. I think it's good you're not there stewing by yourself."

"Yeah, I hate to admit it, but I slept better last night than I have all week."

Maggie looked at me sideways. "I'm not surprised." When I scowled at her, she winked at me and brought her camera up to quickly snap a photo of me before I could change my expression. "Perfect," she said. She hastily returned to the scene at the drawing room before I could give her a snappy comeback.

The rest of the morning alternated between fielding questions from patrons and roaming around to see what was happening with the artists. I was also on clean-up duty and walked from room to room to pick up any trash not put in the readily available, clearly marked, trash cans. I could never figure out why it was so difficult for people to throw out their trash, but over the years, I'd finally accepted it. Actually, no I hadn't. It still made me feel snarky.

I had just wiped down the area around the coffee urn, when I turned around and ran smack into Lena. "Oomph! Sorry!" I exclaimed, kneeling down to help pick up the books I had knocked out of her hands.

"My fault, I wasn't looking where I was going."

I handed the stack to her, and we walked out to the landing. "Are these for the sale table?"

"No, these are the freebies. I let kids root in the baskets and pick out a book to take with them after each reading circle. I trolled the flea market to look for some extra books to give away. Cool, huh?"

Our chat was halted when a familiar face approached. Lena started to move away, but I grabbed her sleeve to stop her. "Good morning, Ms. Bunkle. How are you?"

Ms. Bunkle, a formidable character and important patron of the arts, tapped her cane a few times as she replied, "How do you think? It's February, and it's cold. Don't you turn on the heat in this place?"

Lena and I gave each other a knowing look, and I said, "I'll check the thermostat right away, but in the meantime, maybe a nice hot cup of tea will help."

Lena gave her a wide smile. "Yes, that's the ticket. Have you been in our lounge yet?" She did a game-show arm swing at the cluster of tables.

Ms. Bunkle scowled and tapped her cane a little harder. "Of course not. I just got here. Are you girls daft?"

Lena chose to go toe to toe. "You know, Ms. Bunkle, sometimes I do feel a bit daft, but not today! Here, Alex, if you'll take these books, I'll take Ms. Bunkle to a table." She plunked the books into my arms and put her hand on Ms. Bunkle's elbow. "You didn't come here alone, did you?"

I followed one step behind and listened in.

"Alma brought me. She says she drives better than me, if you can believe that."

Lena admonished the absent Alma. "The nerve. I'm sure you're a wiz behind the wheel."

"You bet I am. I used to drag race when I was a teenager, you know."

"No, I had no idea!"

"Oh yes, we had an all-girl car club and were quite formidable."

"You still are," Lena gushed.

Ms. Bunkle approved of the compliment and said, "You're a dear. Now, I'm not getting any younger. Could you find a seat for me so I can sit down while I wait for Alma?"

Lena steered her toward a table for two. "How about here? You'll be able to see her when she's on the landing."

"Thank you. Hey, Tater-Tot!" she called to me. "Come keep me company while I wait."

I once asked Ms. Bunkle why she called me that, and she told me she assigned me the moniker because I'm short and a little rough around the edges, but also a bit tender on the inside.

Lena turned toward me with a wide smile. "Here, I'll take those," she said, reaching out to take back the armload of books.

I didn't really have time to linger but this was part of my job, so I cheerfully said, "It'd be my pleasure." Ms. Bunkle might be a little rough around the edges herself, but most of the time, I found her highly entertaining. Plus, she was a big supporter of the arts. I took the seat across from her, and she started right in.

"Sit up straight. If you don't, you'll end up like Alma, who's two inches shorter than she used to be. The last thing you need is to lose any height."

I sat up straighter in my chair. "You're right. I tend carry all my stress in my back."

Even while sitting, she tapped her cane. "Stress will kill you. You can't go around carrying the weight of the world around with you. Save the excess baggage for travel."

I smiled at her frank wisdom. "I need you to walk around with me and remind me of those wise words!"

"You just need perspective. So let me guess, Clive's murder is tying you in knots."

My eyes widened, and she added, "I read the paper, and I hear things. I have my finger on the pulse of everything in this town, and some board members told me you were asking questions about Clive. I also know you like digging around in a mystery. You probably read all the Nancy Drew books when you were young."

I swallowed, having flashbacks to high school

when I was under the eye of the principal. "Since it happened here at the festival, I've felt an obligation to help however I can. Mainly, I've been asking people about Clive. We know so little about his life outside of the Bennet House. But I'm afraid I'm not getting very far. No one seems to know much about him."

"You haven't been asking the right people," she said, matter-of-factly.

I perked up. "Who should I be talking to?"

"Me, you ninny."

I sputtered, "Well, I'd assume you crossed paths with Clive because of your involvement in the arts community, but did you know him personally?"

"I sure did. So did Alma. Speak of the devil, there she is." Ms. Bunkle waved her arm, and called out, "Alma! In here!"

I got up and pulled a chair over from a nearby table. "Good morning, Alma. Can I get you some hot tea?"

With her halo of white hair and soft blue eyes, she reminded me of a female version of Clarence from *It's a Wonderful Life*. And in stark contrast to Ms. Bunkle, Alma was gentle and soft-spoken.

"That would be lovely, dear, as long as it's no bother," she said, barely above a whisper.

"No bother at all, I'll be right back," I replied. When I returned and had put a cup of hot tea in front of each of them, I said, "Ms. Bunkle was just getting ready to tell me a little bit about Clive."

Alma's eyes turned sorrowful. "Sad business. Poor Clive."

"How did you two know him?"

Ms. Bunkle jumped in to take the lead. "We

volunteered together at the animal shelter. He'd spend time with the cats. Speaking of cats, is someone taking care of Clive's cat, Bella?" she asked, in a commanding tone.

"Don't worry. Maura, his ex-wife, is taking good care of her. So, you were saying he volunteered with you at the shelter?"

"Yes," Alma interjected, even though Ms. Bunkle scowled at her for doing so. "He loved the cats and would spend hours with them, giving each one special one-on-one time. He was so very kind to them."

"I don't care for cats," Ms. Bunkle said, shaking her head. "They're recalcitrant creatures. Plus, they poo in a box. Although, occasionally you come across one who acts like a dog, and they're all right in my book. I walk the dogs at the shelter. You can talk to dogs, and they respond in their own way, man's best friend and all. Alma here is equal opportunity…cats, dogs, birds, anything goes for her."

"Well, I don't really care for the snakes…" Alma replied, before taking a sip of her tea.

I needed to rein this in and get back to Clive, so it was my turn to interrupt. "So did you guys talk with Clive while at the shelter?"

Alma nodded. "Oh yes. We often did. He talked about how much he liked it here, both the town and his work at the Bennet House." She then tsk-tsked sadly and said, "The shelter staff adored him. It will be a real loss for them."

I looked at Ms. Bunkle to see if she agreed, and she nodded. When I looked a little perplexed, she said, "You know, Tater, sometimes people find it easier to talk to older people. They can be themselves because they don't feel judged. On more than one occasion, Clive spoke of his insecurities when dealing with people. He wanted to work on that, and we encouraged him to do so."

Alma nodded her head. "We sometimes had tea after volunteering. He was a good man, but in many ways, his own worst enemy."

I sat back and looked at them both in wonder. "Wow, I'm so glad I ran into you guys. It makes me feel much better knowing he had people outside of work."

"Can't judge a book…" Ms. Bunkle cautioned.

"No, you can't," I agreed.

She tilted her head in thought. "None of this helps with the inquiries, though. No one at the shelter would have harmed a hair on his head."

"But it does help give us an idea of who he was as a person. From piecing together what you've told me, and what his ex-wife told me, it just doesn't fit with his personality profile that he would have been involved in something unsavory."

"You got that right," she barked.

I looked from one to the other of these sage women. "I can't thank you enough."

Ms. Bunkle reverted to form. "You just trot yourself on out there and bring us a bag of those chocolate chip cookies, and we'll call it even."

I laughed. "Deal!"

After trotting out to buy them cookies, I made my excuses and was taking my leave when Ms. Bunkle caught hold of my wrist. She lowered her voice and said, "Alex, someone has committed murder. You be careful."

Chapter 16

I brought takeout from the food trucks back to the apartment. Since the table was still cleared off from the night before, Walter and I sat down to eat lunch like normal people, instead of standing at the counter like I usually do. I was trying to describe Ms. Bunkle to him, when my phone rang.

"Oh, good, it's Jack," I said. I answered and put him on speaker. "Hey Jack, I'm here with Walter eating lunch. You're on speaker. What's new?"

"Hey, Walter, what are you doing in town?" Jack innocently asked.

Walter chuckled. "Don't bother, I already told her you called me."

"Oops."

"Yeah, you big doofus," I chided, knowing he would hear the affection underneath. "So, back to the original question, what's new?"

"On the Marks front, Matt worked his magic, and the sequence on the slip of paper from the box is a Swiss bank account. We're going through some red tape to access who the account belongs to, and how much money is in there. Hopefully it won't take too much longer, but I won't hold my breath. The Swiss accounts are pretty tough to get information on."

"Interesting," I said. "I wonder if Gina knows about it."

"We'll see. I caught her before she left town and asked her to come back in for another interview."

"How did she respond? Amenable?"

"She was planning to leave this afternoon and, in no uncertain terms, let me know I've upset her plans."

Walter chimed in. "Well, she should want to help the investigation in any way she can."

I snorted and said, "You'd think."

Jack responded, "Contrary to Alex's opinion, I do think she wants justice for Eddie. She's just a prickly personality, and stress does funny things to people."

"I guess you've dealt with all kinds in your years in law enforcement," Walter surmised.

"Yup. It takes a lot to surprise me nowadays. So how about your end, Alex?" he asked.

I got up to clear the lunch plates and called over my shoulder, "I'm going to hit the videos again now, and will call you later with anything I've found. I'm hoping I'll see somebody with Clive, or someone going into the closet who shouldn't be. There has to be something, because we know that's where the weapon came from."

"Okay. Anything else?"

"I ran into Ms. Bunkle at the festival this morning," I replied, and then filled him in on my chat with her and Alma so he could talk to the people at the shelter if he wanted to.

Back at our work stations, Walter and I each tended to our own tasks, and our work was only interrupted by trips to the coffee machine.

At one such time, Walter was leaning against the kitchen counter, and asked, "Are you finding anything on those videos?"

I shoved my hair back from my forehead and perched my glasses on my head. "I'm on Sunday, and I'm chronicling the comings and goings in the lobby, but it's feeling like I'm getting nowhere. I mean, people are milling around, and a few have gone in and out of the closet, but it's not like a cartoon where the culprit tiptoes in while looking over their shoulder, emerging with a chisel in their hand and a dastardly look on their face."

Walter grinned. "No, I would guess it's not going to be so easy." He came around the counter to look over my shoulder. "This looks pretty organized. At least no customers entered the closet so far. That's something."

I scowled. "I was hoping to see someone from the public go in there! There is just no way I can believe it was one of the festival people."

"How far along are you in the day?"

"Only a few hours to go. Then I have Monday to get through."

He patted me on the shoulder. "There's still time to uncover your 'mystery' person," he said, using air quotes.

I reared back. "Are you patronizing me?"

"Of course not!"

"Then what is it?"

He looked me square in the eye. "I totally understand your need for it to be an outsider, but truth is, only a select number of people would even know to look for a chisel there. Other than the slim chance it could be someone that was at Ryan's demonstration, who then saw him put his tools away, I honestly don't think it was some random person off the street. Let the facts and data lead you to the truth. And if nothing else, you might narrow down the prospects, which will help guide Jack's inquiries. That's better than a wide field."

My eyes squinted involuntarily. "Ooooh, I hate it when you're right."

Walking back toward the office, he said over his shoulder, "I know."

"Big Mr. Know-it-all," I quipped under my breath, but then I sat bolt upright and exclaimed, "What an idiot!"

"What?" Walter called from the office.

I got up and stood in the doorway. "I could've looked at the last time Ryan used his tools and worked forward from there. He would have noticed if a tool was missing. So, nothing before his last demonstration would be apropos. Sheesh. I could have saved a lot of time. I'm going to check with him first, to make sure he used the chisel in all of his demonstrations, then I should be able to narrow this down."

"Good idea. Not a waste of time, though. You were still looking for any interactions with Clive, right? And having the backup of knowing who's been in and out of the closet isn't bad, either. One of them could have seen his tool bag and scoped out what was in it."

"You're right, but this could have sped up the process." I picked up my phone and called Ryan.

"Hi-dee-ho, Alex, what's up?"

"Hey, I'm working on the surveillance footage. Can you think back and tell me when your last demonstration was, and if you used the chisel during all of the demos?"

I could feel Ryan thinking on the other end of the phone, and when he responded, his voice was more serious. "Um, let's see...I did a demo late in the afternoon on Sunday, and early afternoon on Monday. Let me think…yeah, it was at three thirty p.m. on Sunday, and one p.m. on Monday."

"Did you use the chisel?"

"Yes. Definitely, yes. I was showing different stone-carving techniques. Actually, I didn't know it was missing until Jack showed it to me at the station. Does that help?"

"It sure does. Thanks."

"Good. We've been talking about going to the Lodge tonight. Will you be able to meet us there?"

I looked at my watch. "I think so. I should be done by this evening. Plus, Walter's here, so we might as well meet you guys and grab some dinner."

"Oh, cool. We'll see you later then. Say hi to Walter."

"Will do."

An hour later, I had compiled a list of people. Most were the same as at other times over the weekend: Hank, Mindy, Spencer, Declan, Annie, Penny, and Ryan. All had entered the closet at some point during the day. Clive lingered in the lobby a few times throughout the day to visit with patrons.

Since talking with Ms. Bunkle, I couldn't help noting how he was clearly at ease with the older visitors, while shying away a little from the younger or middle-aged ones. Anyway, I moved on to Monday's video and was cueing it up to Ryan's demo time when my phone rang; this time it was Maggie.

"Hey," I answered, a little distractedly.

"Hey, yourself. Did I catch you at a bad time?"

"No, no, sorry, just cueing up the next batch of surveillance videos." I reached the cue point and then slid off the stool to take the call in my bedroom. "What's up?"

"You would not believe what I just saw," she answered, her voice icy with anger.

"What?" I asked, sitting cross-legged on the bed.

Maggie exploded, "Declan, with another woman!"

"What do you mean? Where?"

"I saw him cozying up to another woman! I was driving back from the supply house and stopped at the café to get some soup to go." She then shifted to a more normal voice. "By the way, Claudia wants you to check at the end of the day to see how the bake sale goods are holding up."

"Yeah, all right. But what about Declan?" Sometimes keeping Maggie on point was a challenge.

"So, on my way out, I noticed Declan's car, and I was starting walk toward it to say hi, when I saw someone else in the car with him. Luckily, I stopped just as he leaned over to plant a kiss on her. What a jerk. Clearly, he's picked up some bimbo while here."

I refrained from pointing out that technically, he picked her up here, too, and instead cooed, "Oh no, I'm so sorry."

Maggie grunted. "At least I know why he was a little distant this morning."

"Look, I know you're upset, but you didn't know this guy prior to this week, so you don't know his usual MO."

"Oh, I know. I just don't like being played. After the initial shock, I'm not girly-upset anymore. I'm just mad."

"That's totally understandable."

"You can be damned sure, though, I'm not going to

give him the satisfaction of knowing it. I have enough experience with jackasses not to let any man get to me," she snapped. Then she whined, "I thought he really liked me though, and unlike the usual losers I date, he was smart, fun, and artistic. I don't hit the trifecta very often."

"I know. You were ready to take the next step with a long-distance relationship, which is saying a lot. But he doesn't deserve for you to give him one more thought. You go show him you have more important things to do than give him any more of your time. You had your fun, and now it's time to move on. You make the first strike."

"Yeah. That's right. He doesn't know I saw him. I'll play it cool this afternoon, and then dump him like a bad cold later."

"That's a good idea."

Maggie was on a roll. "I'll tell him my work needs all my attention right now, he's a nice guy and we've had some fun, but it's time for me to focus on a job I have next week. This is probably for the best. Frankly, the stupid whistle he does was starting to get on my nerves."

"There you go. You can cry about it later, and you know my shoulder is always here. But for now, don't let him know he got to you."

"Good advice."

"Why don't you come to the Lodge tonight? Ryan says some of the gang are going, and I haven't asked him yet, but I would imagine Walter and I will be there to grab some dinner."

"Okay. That sounds good. Thanks for letting me vent."

"Any time. Call me later if you need anything."

I sat on the bed a few minutes longer, thinking about how grateful I was not to be on the dating scene. Just thinking about it gave me the shivers. I had to applaud Maggie, though. She never allowed anyone to make a fool of her. I had a feeling Declan had met his match. If he thought she would blindly fawn all over him, he was sorely mistaken. That thought made me smile as I went back to the computer to continue with the videos.

The next time I looked up, it was after six p.m. I once again perused the list I had made for Monday, which was not much different than Sunday. A handful of patrons opened the door; only one lingered for a few seconds to eyeball what was in it, but it was while Ryan was doing his demonstration, so I chalked it up to curiosity, although I still made note of it.

Walter emerged from the office, stretching his arms over his head. "I've hit my limit for the day. How about you?"

"Yes. I'm just wrapping it up. Feel like going to the Thunderbird for dinner? Some of the gang will be there."

"Sounds good to me."

I freshened up and made a quick change from the flannel shirt I had on over my jeans to a turtleneck with a thick cable knit cardigan sweater. After adding one of JJ's stone pendant necklaces, I put up my hair in a messy bun. I didn't want to look like I was trying too hard, so I finished with just a quick swath of blush and a little mascara. I perched my glasses on my head and emerged from my room to find Walter lounging on the couch flipping through TV channels.

"Ready to go?" he asked.

It didn't escape me we lived in a world where all it took for men to look presentable was to shave once in a while and throw on a pair of khakis, while women were conditioned to jump through all kinds of hoops, and most of us had to exert a bit of effort or we felt like a total schlump.

But that wasn't Walter's fault, so I simply replied, "Just about. I want to put food down for Baxter, then I'm ready."

****

The Thunderbird was hopping, with hotel guests milling around the lobby, lounge, and restaurant.

"Alex! Over here!" Ryan called out to us.

We skirted around the clusters of bar tables to the edge of the lounge where the gang had congregated. Walter took a chair, and I slid myself and my tote bag, which I had forgotten to change out for a purse, onto the banquette. After shrugging out of my coat, I took the menu Spencer had passed down the table and mulled over the choices. Once we placed our order, I got up to chat with Annie and Jack and squatted between their chairs.

"I'm glad to see you taking a little time off," I said to Jack.

"Yeah. I've been burning the candle at both ends and felt like I needed a couple of hours off in order to keep focused."

"That's smart. So, how'd the follow-up with Gina go?"

"She claimed to know nothing about the bank account," he said, quietly.

"I figured as much. Could you read her at all?"

"Her cool exterior covers up a lot of emotions, but as we talked, she kept eyeing the piece of paper with the account number, and I could see the wheels turning about how to ask for it. So I preemptively told her once we know who the bank account belongs to, we would notify her, and if it was Eddie's, then the account information would go to her. She then casually asked if she could have the things Eddie bought."

"What'd you say?"

"I told her we weren't quite finished with everything, but I'd make arrangements to return his belongings when we are."

I got up from my squat and took the seat next to Annie that someone had just vacated. Leaning across her, I said to Jack, "I've actually got the blasted box in my bag. I meant to work on it this afternoon but wanted to get the Clive footage done first, which I did. I got through till the evening when we all left to go to the café."

Annie looked at me with interest and Jack asked, "Did you see anything important?"

"Nothing definitive in the data. I'll email it all to you tonight. Other than people mistaking the closet for the restroom, it was pretty much the same people going in and out all weekend. I notated who Clive talked with, etc." I turned to Annie with a grin. "I saw you in the afternoon on Monday, going in for some paper towels."

She rolled her eyes. "Clean up on aisle three, as they say…I knocked over my soda. Luckily it didn't land on the rug. I kept thinking Clive would have reamed me out if it had, and then later, after he was murdered, I felt awful for thinking that."

I patted her shoulder. "Clive was who he was."

Then giving her a smart aleck grin, added, "And you would have totally gotten a lecture if you had messed up the rug."

Annie was looking over my shoulder in sudden interest. "What's going on over there?" she whispered. I started to turn, and she hissed, "Don't look!"

"Well, how I am I supposed to know what's going on if I can't look?"

Jack interjected at this point, looking at us like we were a couple of idiots. "Okay, I'm outta here. I'm gonna go talk to Walter."

"Yeah, sure, honey," Annie said distractedly, before returning her focus on me. "All right, be discreet. Twelve o'clock behind you."

I casually turned, as if looking to see if my food had come, and surveyed the scene. Turning back to Annie, I said, "Who are you talking about?"

"Maggie and Declan. What's going on with them?"

I moved over to Jack's chair on the other side of Annie so I could watch the room without turning around and saw Maggie and Declan off to the side of the lounge. Declan looked a little like a deer caught in headlights. Maggie was clearly in charge.

"Ah," I said. "So, earlier today, Maggie was at the café picking up soup when she saw Declan in his car with another woman. She called me on the way back to the Bennet House to blow off some steam about it."

"Well, well. I wonder who it was? I always thought he was a player. I mean, seriously, he's a really good-looking guy, he's smart, and creative, but just hasn't found anyone to form a long-term relationship with? Un-uh, doesn't ring legit. Single 'cause he prefers to play the field? More likely. Didn't Preston say something along those lines?"

I thought back. "He said he hadn't had serious relationships because he's on the road too much, but he also hadn't left a string of angry women in his wake, so he felt he must handle things well."

Since Annie had swiveled toward me when I switched seats, she now looked over her shoulder, then turned back. "Double-dipping in the same week isn't really handling it well, if you ask me. But if anyone can put him in his place, it's Maggie. That girl doesn't take crap from anyone."

"I know. And from the looks of it, she's shutting him down right now. I suggested she come up with a reason to break it off, and not even let on she knows he was canoodling with another woman."

Annie giggled. "What a great word, 'canoodling.' "

My food had arrived at the other end of the table, so I pulled myself away and returned to my seat to dive in, eating with a laser-like focus. I was pushing the empty plate away from the edge of the table and was leaning back on the banquette in satisfaction when Maggie plunked herself down next to me.

"It's done," she declared, putting her hand up to get the attention of the waitress.

"Good for you," I said. "How'd it go down? Like you planned?"

Maggie gave her drink order to the waitress, then nodded her head. "Pretty much. I kept myself busy this afternoon and avoided talking to him, but tonight he tried to be all schmoozy, and touchy-feely," she said with disgust. "As you suggested, I pulled him aside and told him, 'Look, I've had work come in that I will need to focus on, and on top of closing out the festival, I'm just not going to have any free time to hang out.' "

"What did he say?"

"He blustered a bit and asked if he did something wrong, and I told him, 'Of course not. We were just having fun, right? And now, I've got to focus on my work.' I told him he was a great guy…gag…and I hope to run into him some time at another festival or show."

I looked at her youthful face, multiple ear piercings, and brightly colored hair, noting how her intensely sharp eyes overrode any notion she might be flighty. She had way more sense than I did at her age.

"I'm proud of you. You handled this like a champ," I said.

"It still stings. But, yeah, you reminded me I don't have to show what's in my head, and I could control the outcome. You would have laughed out loud when I shifted to be all buddy-buddy, saying I was so grateful to have met a new friend and finished with, 'Come on, I see Hank and Twila. Let's go get a drink!' "

"Oh, you are good," I intoned, clinking her glass. "Cheers."

The next couple of hours passed quickly. I made the rounds and enjoyed taking the time to sit down and catch up with everyone. This was really the last night the whole artist group would be gathered together. Tomorrow night, some would either call it an early night, or start packing up so they could make a quick exit to get on the road Sunday at the close of the festival.

Therefore, tonight there was an air of celebration to the gathering. Spencer was holding court telling stories and jokes, which caused frequent bursts of laughter. Ethan and Hannah were, true to form, engaging in quiet one-on-one conversations with almost everyone. Declan and Preston meandered around, never settling in one place for long, but both seemed to fit in well with this crowd. Declan looked a little deflated after Maggie blew him off, but I had feeling he would rebound just fine.

Ryan seemed to have found a new buddy in Preston, and along with Elliott, they had their heads together at one point debating which hockey team was best this year. Oscar had become a favorite over the week and seemed at home in the company of this new family of artists. He and Maggie had forged a bond from sharing the library.

I particularly enjoyed the time with Hank and Twila. I sat between them, and Hank draped his arm around my shoulder while we talked about the prospect of adding some of their glass works to the sculpture garden. It made me feel warm and fuzzy to know I would be seeing them in the coming months, and I was excited by the prospect of planning art glass placement in the gardens.

Eventually, it was time to head home. I noticed Maggie looked like she might have had one more cocktail than she should have. Her cheeks were flushed, and she was laughing a little too loudly. I stepped over to her and quietly said, "Why don't I drive you home?"

She looked at me and thought for a split-second before saying, "Yup, good idea." She sashayed toward the bar to put her glass down, and called over her shoulder, "But hey, I left my laptop at the Bennet House. Would it bum you out to swing by there, first?"

"No problem. Let me see if Jack will drop Walter off at the Workshop, and I'll grab my stuff and we can head out."

"I'll get your bag and coat for you," she replied.

I walked over to Jack and secured Walter's ride, then explained the plan to Walter. He had his own key fob to the building since he was now a silent partner of sorts in the Workshop, but I remembered at the last minute to slip my apartment key off my keychain. Handing it to him, I said, "I shouldn't be more than half an hour."

Maggie approached us. "Here's your stuff," she said, handing me my coat and bag. "And thanks, Jack, for taking Walter. Sorry for the hassle."

Maggie hadn't noticed my satchel was open on the banquette, so I set it down to stuff the contents back in and flipped the front flap to close it up. We waved to Dustin, who was manning the front desk, and exited the warm building into the cold night air, our steps making loud click-clacking sounds on the pavement as we hurried to the car. With the seat heaters warming our rear ends, we made the short trip to the Bennet House.

Chapter 17

Entering the back door of the building, Maggie spluttered, "Thank you again for doing this. I only had two drinks, but they were strong and went straight to my head."

"Really, it's no big deal. I want to run upstairs anyway, to take a tally of the bake sale stock. Heck, I have some cash on me. I think we should take advantage of the situation and get some cookies to eat on the road to your house!"

Maggie let out a tipsy giggle. "Great idea!" she gushed.

She reached under the display table to grab her laptop bag, and then we made a beeline for the staircase. We hadn't bothered to turn on any lights since the stairs and hallways glowed from the emergency exit signs, emitting just enough light to see. We easily made our way to the table and started pawing through the available selection.

"Thank goodness there's enough here. Now I don't feel guilty about our late-night snack," I said, digging in my bag for my wallet.

"No, let me," Maggie said, shoving my hand away. "It's the least I can do. What do you want?"

"Let's get both peanut butter and chocolate chip."

"Good thinking." Maggie slipped a twenty under one of the pie boxes, double the actual cost. When I looked at her in the dim light, she said, "It's for a good cause."

We wandered into the lounge, enjoying the dark solitude of the mansion. You could still feel the energy from all the people, sort of like being in a library or museum after closing. Maggie was sway-dancing to some melody in her head, and I walked over to the reading circle, where I could feel the happy vibe of kids eagerly listening to Lena read a story.

There was something cool about the atmosphere, so instead of leaving, we went back to the landing and plopped ourselves on the window seat while we dove into the bags of cookies. We talked about the festival for a few minutes, and then I returned to the topic of Maggie's personal life.

"You're handling this Declan thing really well. On top of the stress and anxiety of Clive's murder, and Ryan being a suspect, plus keeping the festival going at the same time, it could have made it even harder to handle."

Maggie mumbled through a mouthful of cookie, her tipsiness making her smack her lips more than usual, "Actually, it probably made it easier. I mean really, on top of the truly serious issues this week, getting upset over a relationship is at the bottom of the scale of importance."

"That's true, but still, it's a lot to handle."

She cocked her head while chewing, then added, "Granted, I was ticked. I even snapped some pics of him and the mystery woman. I thought about printing them out and making a collage to leave at his display table."

I raised my eyebrows at her, and she hastily added,

giggling, "I know, very high school. If it makes you feel any better, I only thought about it for a few minutes, and then I calmed down after talking to you. Wanna see the pics, though? They're very artistic in an almost noir way." She grinned.

I popped the rest of a cookie in my mouth and held out my hand. "Yeah, let me see."

She dug in her pocket and pulled out her phone. After swiping through her photo library, she settled on an image and handed it back to me. "Here, you can scroll through."

The first image showed the back of Declan's car. Being a photographer, Maggie often worked in black and white, even on her phone, so the image did have a film noir quality with the snowbank, the hot steam coming from the exhaust pipe, Declan's face in the side mirror, and the silhouette of the woman's head. I swiped to the next image, and this one showed Declan turning toward the woman. She had also turned, showing her profile. I leaned closer to get a better look, and I froze.

No, It can't be. My finger swiped to the next image.

I let out a hushed, "Oh, my, gawd. Maggie, do you know who I think this is?"

Maggie had gotten up to meander around and was sway-dancing again. "What?"

"Come here. I think I know who this is, and you are *not* going to believe it." I swiped back and forth through the three or four images while Maggie sat back down and leaned in to look.

"Who is it?" she asked.

"I'm almost certain this is Gina, the snow queen.

Eddie Marks's wife. What the *hell*?"

Maggie grabbed the phone from me, suddenly devoid of any tipsiness. "How would he know her? This is crazy. You know what this means?"

"Yes, I do." I frantically rooted around in my bag for my phone. "Send me those pics, okay? I have to call Jack."

"Okay, I'll text them to you."

I finally got my hands on my phone and tapped Jack's name in my favorite's list. After a few rings he picked up. "Jack, where are you?" I asked urgently.

"I'm over here at your place hanging out with Walter. What's wrong with your voice? You sound funny."

"It's a long story, but Maggie has photos of what looks like Eddie's wife, Gina, with Declan."

Jack perked up. "What? Where are you? At Maggie's?"

"We're still at the Bennet House. We got distracted by cookies. Anyway, if you stay put, I'll be home as soon as I drop her off. Maggie's texting the pics to me, and I'll shoot them over to you."

"Okay."

I was going to ask if he wanted me to bring him some cookies, but the back door of the mansion clanged open, then banged closed. I set my phone down by my bag and cocked my head at Maggie. "Who could that be?" I whispered.

She shrugged.

As we listened to the fall of footsteps, Maggie started to walk toward the stairs, but instinctively, I lunged to grab her arm. "Wait!" I hissed. "Something feels off. Why would someone be here at this hour?"

We waited for what felt like an eternity but was likely only a few seconds. Then we heard a light whistling, and the hair stood up on the back of my neck. It was Declan. His normally whimsical whistling suddenly sounded ominous.

Maggie and I froze.

"Oh Alex…Maggie…I know you're here. We need to talk," he said in a lilting tone.

We heard more footsteps as Declan progressed from the library toward the parlor. "Come on now, it's just me. Where are you?" The creepy sing-song quality of his voice scared the bejeezus out of us.

Maggie looked at me frantically and whispered, "Why does he sound like that? Why is he here?"

I looked into the dark lounge. "Come on," I barely whispered, pulling her over to the wall separating the lounge from the landing, where we would not be visible from the stairs.

"Maybe he won't come up here," Maggie breathed.

"My car is in the lot. He knows we're here."

"Come out, come out, wherever you are," Declan sang, as his footfalls slowly crossed the lobby to the drawing room. "Are you going to make me search for you?"

"Oh my gosh," Maggie whispered. "What does he want?"

"I don't know, but it can't be good." I patted my pockets. *Damn it.* I'd left my phone out on the landing. "Do you have your phone?" I asked Maggie, with hope in my voice.

"No, it's out there on the window seat. I'm assuming yours is out there, too?"

"Yup, and we're not going out there. From here we

can't be seen, which buys us some time."

Think Alex, think! I shouted in my head. I looked around the room trying to figure something out. My eyes landed on the child-sized beanbag chairs at the reading circle. I gave Maggie the hand sign to stay put, and I stepped away from the wall. She reached out to stop me, and I gave her more hand signs to be quiet and calm down. I took one step at a time in an effort to remain silent, then reached down and gently picked up one of the beanbag chairs, carrying it like it was a bomb ready to blow.

I retraced my steps, laid it by the door, then stood next to Maggie. I was breathing hard even though the bag only weighed a few pounds. I could hear my heart pounding in my ears and felt sure it was loud enough to reach Declan.

Maggie looked at me in bewilderment and whispered, "What are you going to do, sit down?"

"No, I have a lame plan. Do you have any brilliant ideas?" I whispered back.

"Other than panicking, no, no plan."

I looked over at the coffee counter for something to use as a weapon. Sugar packs and stirrers weren't going to cut it, and the urn itself was too cumbersome to do any good. My eyes scanned every nook and cranny of the room. Nothing. We were stuck.

Maggie's legs were shivering from fear, so I took hold of her arm and gently squeezed, trying to relay that everything was going to be okay. I didn't really believe everything was going to be okay, but deceiving oneself sometimes was not such a bad thing.

While we stood there, listening to Declan walk through the lower floor, hearing closet doors open and close, I started to put the pieces together. If Declan knew Gina, it meant Declan probably knew Eddie. If Declan was in a relationship with Gina, then it's entirely possible either Declan or Gina killed Eddie. Otherwise, why hide the affiliation?

Then the really horrible thought came to me. If Eddie was killed by Declan, it was likely that he and Declan met at the truck stop. And if this premise was true, could it mean Clive saw Eddie going toward Declan's car out of camera view while he was getting gas? Even if he never saw Eddie get in Declan's car, it created a convergence of events tying the two murders together. And if that was true, it meant Declan was a very dangerous man.

I was doing okay until that last thought came to mind, and then my own knees started to buckle. If Declan had killed both Eddie and Clive, he had little to lose. He would try to eliminate us to clear his path for escape. But why us, and why now? Did he see Maggie as she walked away after taking the pictures? That didn't make sense, he seemed fairly normal throughout the evening tonight. So what made him come after us?

Maybe if he went to the back of the mansion, I could sneak over and get my phone. I leaned forward to see if it was in the sight lines of the doorway and I noticed my bag, still open, with the contents spilling out from when I was digging around for my phone. Even in the dark, I could make out the corner of the wooden puzzle box jutting out of the open bag.

My bag had been sitting on the banquette at the Thunderbird, open, just as it was now. *Oh holy crap. The box. He wants the damned box! It's not about Maggie. He wants whatever is in the puzzle box!*

223

Now I knew we were in real trouble, and I tried to scope out Declan's progress downstairs. Eventually, he would make his way up here, and the clock was ticking.

A few seconds later, we heard him in the lobby. "Well, I was hoping you two would make your way downstairs, but I guess I'll have to come up there. Kind of silly if you think about it. You'd have had a chance to get away if you had come down. You might as well make things easier for yourselves, and come out from your hiding place. There's nowhere to go up there." He waited two ticks, then we heard the soft thud of his footfalls on the stairs. "Oh well, have it your way." While climbing the stairs, he resumed the creepy whistling.

I leaned close to Maggie's ear, "You stay here. Do *not* come out unless I'm in real trouble."

Maggie shook her head and mouthed, "No, don't go."

I grabbed her wrist and looked her square in the eyes. "Stay here."

When Declan's footsteps neared the top, I took a deep breath and crept to the other doorway at the opposite end of the room, farther away from Maggie, and walked through to the landing. Declan had just reached the top step. "There you are, you silly girl." He looked around and asked, "Where's your buddy?"

"She's not here. I'm here by myself."

Even in the dim light I could see Declan's body tense up with anger. "Don't play games with me. I followed you from the Lodge, where I saw both of you get in the car, so I know she's here."

"Well, you're wrong. She left through the front door after we got here to go meet Ryan."

Declan paused, trying to judge if I was telling the truth.

"Why don't you tell me what the problem is," I said. "What do you want? Why are you here?"

Now Declan relaxed, knowing he had the upper hand. "Oh, come now, Alex. Don't pretend you're dumb. It doesn't suit you. You know exactly what I want. I want the puzzle box. I saw it in your bag at the Lodge, and I need it back."

I had slowly started walking toward him, hoping I could defuse the situation, but now I knew it was game over.

"What's in the box, Declan? You must know from Gina that we found the slip of paper with the overseas bank account number, so what else is worth killing for?"

I was now close enough to him to see the look of malice on his face as he scoffed, "Like I'm going to tell you. I just need to finish this, retrieve the box from your bag, and get out of here. I'd hoped to catch you on your way out." He dropped his voice to a stage whisper and said, "You and Maggie would have just disappeared. *Poof!*" Then he returned to full voice. "But you took too long, and I couldn't risk drawing attention to myself sitting there in my car. So, I've had to alter my plan. Do you want to hear it?"

I shook my head no, but he continued anyway. "You'll have an unfortunate accident. You came back to pick something up, and since it's dark up here, you accidentally trip and fall down the stairs to your death. No one will be able to prove otherwise."

I felt like I could pass out from the sheer terror of hearing him calmly outline my death.

He tilted his head, saying, "Sort of poetic if you think about it…returning to the scene of the crime where Clive met his untimely demise."

Hearing him mention Clive made my heart wrench, and it gave me the will to not give up. "Why did you have to kill Clive? What did he have to do with this?" I asked, trying to keep him talking.

Declan swatted the air like a gnat was bothering him. "Clive suddenly decided to be a do-gooder. He pulled me aside at the end of the day and told me he saw me at the truck stop and had noticed someone who looked like Eddie walking toward me. He was reminding me because I said I didn't recognize him when you showed the photo around."

I shivered when I remembered how Clive had cocked his head when he looked at the photo that day, and then he looked at Declan for a beat before saying he hadn't seen him at the festival. I had witnessed the moment of recognition. Why didn't he say something in that moment? It would have saved his life!

Declan's menacing voice shoved these thoughts aside. "I mean, who knew Clive was so observant? I didn't even notice he was there. Anyway, he said he understood I might not want to get involved but urged me to relay what I knew to the police."

Clive had wanted to do something good but had misjudged the situation. "He was being honorable," I said.

"Stupid man," Declan continued, "and so gullible. All I had to do was treat him like I wanted to be his friend. I told him he was right, and I would talk to the police the next morning. I then suggested we meet back here after closing time and go out for a friendly beer.

He eagerly agreed. Eliminating him was as easy as taking candy from a child."

"That's just cruel and inhumane," I said, my disdain now overriding my terror.

He ignored my indignation. "And I thought it was a nice touch to leave Ryan's tool buried at the scene. A little game to provide some misdirection. Anyway, back to your unfortunate accident. Gina will swear I was with her at the time, the affair being an easy and totally believable explanation." He mocked a look of sheepish embarrassment. "My bad, I had an affair with my friend's wife. Oops. Yessir, she will corroborate I was in her motel room all night." He quickly transitioned back to malice, and raised his gloved hands. "Okay, it's time, Alex."

I turned to run, but he was too quick and reached out to grab my arm, yanking it so hard I yelped in pain. "Don't fight it, this will only hurt for a moment. And don't provoke me. I don't want to leave any unexplainable marks on your body, but if you make me mad, I *will* hurt you first."

He wrangled me toward the top of the stairs, and I writhed with every ounce of strength I had, trying to get out of his grasp. He had his forearm around my chest and neck and forced my steps from behind by raising each knee to shove my legs forward.

A flash of movement caught my eye. Maggie was peeking out from the doorway and I widened my eyes and shook my head to implore her not to come out. My hope was she would remain safe if she stayed hidden, and if my outcome was not good, she would be able to tell Jack what happened.

But I wasn't going to go down without a fight. In

my struggle, I had shifted his coat sleeve above his gloved hand, which revealed a patch of skin, so I took my shot, clamping my teeth down as hard as I could. My mouth filled with the metallic taste of blood, and the ensuing scream meant I had achieved my goal.

He dropped his arm and shouted, "You stupid bitch! How dare you!"

I stepped back, catching my breath as I wiped his blood from my mouth with the back of my hand. He started to come toward me again, and I had primed myself to fight when a frenzied blur ran past me.

Chapter 18

Maggie let out a guttural scream as she hurled herself at Declan. Using the child-sized beanbag chair as protection, she shoved with her full body weight and catapulted Declan down the stairs. There was a look of shock in his eyes as he started to fall, and then he went head over feet in a series of awkward somersaults, until he landed on the marble floor at the bottom of the stairs.

Maggie and I stood frozen in time, until the silence eventually broke our paralysis. We inched over to the top of the stairs and surveyed the scene at the bottom to make sure Declan wasn't coming for us again.

Declan wouldn't be coming for anyone. His body was splayed out, with a pool of blood growing around his head, the dark red contrasting starkly with the white marble floor. I don't know why, probably hysteria, but all I could think was Clive would have been livid about blood stains on the marble. But I also could feel his satisfaction that we had beat Declan.

The silence was broken by the back door crashing open and Jack's voice calling out to us. I don't know how he knew to come, but all that mattered was the cavalry had arrived.

Maggie and I stood at the top of the stairs, clutching each other, as I called out to Jack. He and Walter rushed into the lobby and stopped short at the sight of Declan. Jack instantly shifted into his role as chief of police, telling Walter to step aside as he pulled out his phone to call for an ambulance. While Jack documented the scene with the camera on his phone, Walter made a wide arc to avoid the crime scene and then sprinted up the stairs toward us.

Grabbing us both in a bear hug, he gasped, "Are you okay?" When we didn't answer, he pulled back, grabbing a hand from each of us, and tried again. "Alex, Maggie, are you okay? Are you injured?"

Maggie had a glazed look in her eyes, and I stammered, "Not injured…not okay…" I couldn't avert my eyes from the scene at the bottom of the stairs. "Oh my gosh, oh my gosh…"

Walter did a visual assessment, and finding no apparent injuries, shifted to damage control. "Come on, let's go sit down," he said, gently pulling us from the landing to the lounge. He took each of us by the shoulders and lowered us to the sofa and then rushed to turn on the lights and grab two bottles of water from the counter.

Maggie was still in a stupor, but I could hear voices coming from the lobby and looked up at Walter. "How did you know to come?"

"When you were talking to Jack, you didn't disconnect the call. He was talking, but you weren't answering, and he realized you had put the phone down before you guys finished talking. At first, he thought you were just ignoring him, then he heard you and Maggie whispering, then it went quiet. He hung on the line until he heard a man's voice, which we now know was Declan, and we hightailed it over. We kept the line open the whole way here and heard pretty much everything."

I looked through the archway at my bag sitting on the window seat and there was the phone, where I had set it down when we heard the back door open. I was still at a loss for words, and just uttered, "Oh."

Jack bolted into the lounge and rushed over to us. "Ambulance is on the way. Are either of you hurt?"

Walter answered for us. "They're okay, at least physically. I think they're both in shock."

Jack knelt on the floor and scrutinized our faces. "I'll have one of the medics come check them out. Alex, can you talk to me?"

My eyes drifted between he and Walter, and I mewed, "Is he dead?"

"No. His pulse is weak, but he's still breathing."

I started to shake uncontrollably and was unable to connect my brain to my mouth to speak.

Jack grabbed my hand and said, "Hold tight. I'll get someone up here." He looked at Walter, who needed no words to understand he was to stay with us. Jack jogged to the head of the stairs and called down for one of the paramedics. Moments later, the medic entered the room with his kit bag of medical supplies and Jack rushed back downstairs.

"Help her first," I declared, pointing to Maggie, who had remained mute, and staring, as if trapped in the nightmare of her mind.

The medic used a gentle voice as he walked Maggie through his examination. When he was through, he turned to us and said, "No apparent injuries, but she is in shock. Her BP is a little low, so I'm going to administer some oxygen. And we need to warm her up."

He pulled out a first-aid foil blanket, and with

231

Walter's help, wrapped it around her. He then pulled out a portable oxygen device and gently placed the cup around her nose and mouth.

"Now let's take a look at you," he said to me.

"I think I'm okay."

He ignored my statement as he repeated the steps he had taken with Maggie. As he peeled the blood pressure cuff off my arm, he reported, "You've clearly had a shock, but your vitals are good. You're going to be fine."

"What about Maggie?" Walter asked.

"I would like her to stay with me for a little while until she's stable," he said, "but I need to get her out of here."

I said, "The elevator is across the landing and down the hall. You'll come out near the kitchen."

As the medic guided her out of the room, Maggie turned back toward me. I wanted to cry seeing the scared look in her eyes.

"I'll be right behind you. Don't worry," I told her.

Once they were out of sight, I suddenly felt woozy and dropped my head between my knees. Walter silently laid a hand on my back. A few minutes later, I sat up and inhaled deeply.

"Holy cow," I said in bewilderment.

"Ditto," Walter replied. We sat for a few more minutes, and then he stood up and held out his hand. "Do you feel ready to go down?"

I nodded. "I'm not going to feel better until I get out of here."

We slowly walked to the landing, and averting my eyes from the scene at the bottom of the stairs, we proceeded to the elevator.

We arrived in the kitchen just as the medic was placing a cup of hot tea in front of Maggie. The back door banged open, and Jack entered in his most official manner. "They are moving Declan to the ambulance. Marcus, you're in the backup vehicle, right?"

"Yessir. We'll see how she rallies," he said, indicating Maggie, "and if she doesn't need to go to the hospital, is there someone who can take her home and stay with her?"

"I'll call Ryan," I offered, looking around for my phone, which was still upstairs. Jack handed me his, and after I gave a brief outline of what had happened, Ryan jumped into action.

Jack got out his notepad. "Alex, I know you are still reeling, but I need to get a basic statement about what happened, and then you can give a full report later."

"I understand," I said, "but I need the restroom first."

"Of course."

I went to the one near Penny's office and, without hesitation, leaned over the sink and took handful after handful of water to rinse my mouth. I still had the taste of Declan's blood, and I couldn't stand it for another minute. Penny had some essentials in the bathroom cabinet, and I pulled out the mouthwash and rinsed four or five times before shutting off the water. I silently stared at myself in the mirror, then I re-clipped my hair, straightened my clothing, and returned to the kitchen.

"Ready?" Jack asked.

"Yes."

I went step-by-step through the event from the moment we heard the back door open. When I got to the part about Maggie flying across the landing with the beanbag chair, she emitted what sounded like a strangled giggle. We all turned to look at her. Her eyes had a faraway look, but she spoke for the first time since Declan's fall.

"How absurd! What was I thinking?" she croaked.

Jack stepped in. "You were very brave, and you did what you had to do to save Alex, and yourself."

Now she started to giggle uncontrollably, verging on hysteria, which prompted Marcus to stand up and say, "Okay, I think I should take Maggie to the hospital. Did you say someone was coming to be with her?"

I answered, "Yes, Ryan's on his way. He should be here any minute."

Marcus started to unfold Maggie from the chair. "Have him meet us at the hospital."

I felt anxious, and suggested, "I should go with her."

Jack put up his hand, "She'll be fine with Ryan. I'll call and reroute him to the hospital. Go home, Alex. Once you've had a chance to recover a little, Walter can bring you down to the station."

Walter, always good in a crisis, knew I wouldn't want to talk on the way back to the Workshop, and we drove in silence. I put my head back and closed my eyes, only opening them when Walter turned off the car.

When we entered the apartment, Baxter jumped from the couch and ran over to us. I knelt down to hug his scruffy neck, and out of nowhere, the flood gates opened, and I cried like a little girl. Baxter was confused, but he sat patiently and occasionally licked the salty tears from my cheeks. Eventually, I got up and gave my nose a good blow.

"Okay, I'm better now," I said, definitively.

"I knew you would be. Why don't you go take a nice long shower, and I'll have a cup of tea for you when you come back out."

I stood under the hot shower, letting the water soothe my already sore muscles, until my fingers became pruny. Then I put on my thick pink bathrobe, put my hair up in a towel turban, and emerged from the bedroom to the scent of Earl Grey tea.

"Now that's what I call timing," I said, taking the mug of tea over to the couch.

Walter sat down next to me, looked me over, and asked, "Feeling any better?"

"Actually, I am. I think I'm ready to face whatever is coming."

"Good. I got a call from Ryan. Maggie's doing all right. The ER is sending her home with a sedative, and he'll stay with her tonight and then take her to the precinct in the morning to give her statement."

"Dang, it's a good thing Jack was on the line to hear some of what was going on. That will help make this a clear case of self-defense. Any word on Declan?"

"No, not yet."

I drained the rest of my tea, and took the mug to the kitchen. "I guess I better get dressed. Jack will be waiting."

I put on fresh clothing, choosing the softest and coziest pieces I had—thick black leggings, with a soft turtleneck and a gray Purana wrap sweatshirt with long sleeves over the hand with thumb holes. I put on a pair of gray cable knit leg warmers, laced up my gray and white sneakers, then dried my hair. For some reason, this time I avoided looking at myself in the mirror. I think if I saw my own reflection, the reality of what happened would come crashing down on me.

Walter had made two travel thermoses of coffee and handed me one. "I have a feeling you may want this."

****

What a difference a couple of hours made. This time, instead of riding in silence, we hashed over what might be happening at the station. It was after midnight, and the streets were empty, so our ride was a quick one. As we pulled in to the parking lot, the station was lit up like a Christmas tree, with light spilling onto the sidewalk from the plate glass windows.

Walter pulled the door open for me, and we waited at the reception counter until Gabe, who was on the phone, waved us through. "Jack's back there," he said, with his hand over the mouthpiece of the phone.

We followed the sound of voices and found Jack standing outside his office door, barking orders to Travis and Matt, who were across the room at their desks. "Put out an APB on her now. And Travis, go pick up Preston. We don't know if he was in on this, so when you get to the Lodge, tell whoever is manning the desk you need his room number, and that Preston is *not* to be alerted first."

Eventually, Jack noticed us and motioned for us to follow him into his office. "Take a seat. How are you holding up, Alex?"

"I'm all right. The shower helped. You need to formally interview me, right?

"I do. We'll take care of it now, before all hell breaks loose around here. I'm pulling Preston in for questioning, and it looks like Gina has left town, so we've got to get her back here." He looked at Walter. "Travis got your statement about what you heard on the phone while we were at the Bennet House, so you don't have to stick around if you'd rather go get some sleep."

Without reservation, he responded, "I'll be here until you're done with Alex. I'm assuming after the interview, she'll be able to go back and get some rest, right?

"Yes. And Alex, I'm guessing you'll want to be here when Maggie comes in the morning," he said, looking at me.

"Absolutely."

"All right then. Let's get this done, and then you can go get a few hours of sleep. Walter, make yourself comfortable. We'll be back in a bit."

Jack and I walked down to the interview room, where he turned on the recorder while we settled ourselves on opposite sides of the table.

"Saturday, February seventeenth, one twenty-six a.m. Present in the room, Jack Maddox, Chief of Police, and Alexandra Montgomery." He put a folder and notepad in front of him. "You are here, willingly, to give a statement of your involvement in both murder investigations, and about the events of Friday evening, February sixteenth, correct?"

I leaned forward, and said, "Yes."

"Thank you. Please take me through your involvement as a consultant in the investigation this past week, ending with last night, and what transpired at the Bennet House. I need a formal statement on all of it."

I spoke for what felt like an eternity, going all the

way back to the morning we investigated the death of Eddie Marks, through the events of today, well, yesterday now, and how I was able to connect the dots between Eddie-Gina, Eddie-Declan, Declan-Gina, and Declan-Clive.

Reliving the fear, I choked up when talking about my struggle with Declan as he tried to drag me to the stairs, and Maggie's heroic attack.

"At any rate, I am certain she saved my life, and ultimately, her own. If Declan had succeeded with me, he would have gone after her." I took a deep breath, and let it out. "So, that's it. Hopefully, you can corroborate you heard some of this, since you didn't disconnect the call after I set my phone down."

"Yes, Walter and I heard enough of it. Thank you for filling in the rest." Jack then turned off the recorder.

A wave of nausea hit me. "Damn it, Jack. If I had answered the phone when Clive called on Sunday night, none of this would have happened. It might have saved his life! I would have told him to call you and would have cautioned him not to meet Declan. Clive would be alive, Maggie wouldn't be carrying the burden of pushing Declan down the stairs, and we could have avoided all of this trauma. It's is all my fault!"

"Now hold on just a minute. This is not your fault. You are not responsible for Declan being a killer. You are also not responsible for Clive deciding to take this on himself instead of waiting to talk to you. From what Declan told you, Clive talked to him *before* he called you. The wheels were already in motion. You cannot shoulder the responsibility for other people's actions."

I just shook my head in despair.

Jack's voice dropped to a gentle, brotherly tone.

"Seriously, Alex, do not take this on as an extra burden. Think about it. Clive talked to Declan during festival hours. He could have called you any time after you showed him the photo. Or he could have called me. That would have prevented his death, because there would have been time to stop him from meeting Declan. And if Clive had at least left in his message he was going to meet Declan, we would have known immediately who to look for after the murder. You might not have been able to prevent his murder, but we could have brought Declan in right away."

"I know you're right, but I still feel horrible about not answering his call."

"It's natural to try and figure out how this could have been avoided and place blame, in this case, on yourself, but it's counterproductive. So please, don't go there."

I looked at him long and hard and realized he was right. I knew it would take some time to come to terms with it, but I put these thoughts away in my mental lockbox to think about later. "Have you gotten any word from the hospital on Declan? Is he going to live?"

"It was touch-and-go, but the consensus is he may pull through. He has some broken bones from the fall, and his brain got sloshed around pretty good when he hit the floor. They'll know more if he makes it through the night."

"I hope he pulls through, but only for Maggie's sake. Even though it was self-defense and she saved my life and her own, I'm not sure how she'll live with herself if he doesn't survive. Plus, she was dating the guy. Can you imagine having someone you were intimate with show you how evil they are? And I don't use that word lightly. I'm serious, Jack. Between his damned whistle and the sing-song voice, Declan was enjoying the cat and mouse game. And he had no qualms about killing. It's going to be a long time before I get his voice out of my head, so I would imagine for Maggie it will be one hundred times worse."

"I agree, and furthermore, I want him brought to justice. Death is an easy way out as far as I'm concerned. Plus, we need to get to the bottom of why all of this happened. We still don't know what this was all about."

"So what now?"

"Travis is going to pick up Preston. We need to see what his involvement is in this."

"Man, I hope he wasn't involved. I think my head will explode if they were in this together. It's bad enough Declan bamboozled us, but holy crap, if they both did, I would really question my ability to judge people."

"If he's clean, then maybe he can help us put the pieces together." He paused then added, "Speaking of pieces, I need the puzzle box. If Preston's in the clear, then I need him to get into the box for us. Maybe it holds some answers."

"I have it with me, so I'll get it for you. Did I hear you issuing an APB for Gina?"

"Yes, she left town last night, and we need her back here. If she was involved with Declan, she's bound to have information, and she's likely complicit."

I could have curled up right there on the table and gone to sleep, so I stood up, preparing to leave. "Anything else?"

"Just the grinding wheels. We're having Declan's

car towed here so we can do a proper search and print check. If we're lucky, we'll find Eddie's prints in it. Waiting on Gina. Talking to Preston. Waiting on Maggie." Looking at his watch, he said, "Since it's Saturday now, I'll just say it's going to be a long day. Go home, get a few hours of sleep, and I'll see you back here later in the morning."

We found Walter talking with Matt, managing to look at ease and in control, even in a police station. After handing off the puzzle box, I gathered my stuff, and we made our way back to the Workshop, where I crawled in bed, fully clothed, and fell into a turbulent sleep.

****

Saturday

In the morning, I looked at my reflection in the mirror and let out a gasp. There was nothing I could do about the deep pockets of fatigue under my eyes, so I pretended I hadn't noticed and got on with the more critical task in front of me. I needed to call Penny. I knew it was early, but this was an emergency.

"Hello," answered the groggy voice at the other end of the line.

"Hi, Penny, I'm sorry to wake you, but we have a situation." I gave her an outline of what had transpired the night before, and after the subsequent exclamations of disbelief, and a brief discussion, I continued with the agenda at hand. "So, we need to shift the opening of the festival today until the afternoon. Can you handle notifying everyone?"

"Absolutely. I'll get out a press release right now and get the volunteer crews to handle the park entries to hold people back. I'm assuming we need a clean-up crew in the building too. Oh my God, Alex. I'm talking about a clean-up crew like someone tracked mud, not to clean up after Declan, who happens to be a murderer who fell down the stairs and bled on the marble!"

"I know, believe me, I know. It's taking everything I have to keep my head from exploding. But the only way forward for me is to take care of business, so let me see if Jack is done with the crime scene, and yes, we need to have a service lined up ASAP. Otherwise, we won't be able to open, and the festival is almost over. If it was just me, I'd bag the whole thing, but if we can pull it off, then we won't let down the artists and the public."

"I know, you're right. I'll line up the cleaners. And we should hold a meeting with all the artists before opening."

"Yes, good thinking. Let's say twelve thirty, with the plan to open at one p.m. Does that sound about right?"

"It does," she replied.

"Okay, we'll stay in touch, and I'll let you know as soon as Jack clears the building." I paused after we had covered the business and said in a hushed tone, "Damn, Penny."

"I know. But like you said, we have a job to do. We can fall apart later. Too many people are relying on us right now."

I breathed in deeply. "Right. We can do this." Just as I disconnected the call, Walter emerged from the guest room, looking as fresh as if he had received a full eight hours of sleep. "Geez, how can you look so rested and, I might add, cleaned and pressed?"

Walter laughed. "Years of experience. So, who

were you on the phone with this early?"

"Penny. Getting our game plan in order."

"Ah, of course. Did you get any sleep?"

"I was out before my head hit the pillow, but my subconscious mind was working overtime, so I wouldn't say it was restful. Sleep is a luxury for later. In the meantime, keeping busy will get me through it."

"That's good. One day or, more accurately, one hour, at a time."

"I'm going to have a couple cups of coffee and get some food in me, then I'll be heading back to the precinct."

"I have a conference call this morning. Are you going to be okay going on your own?"

"Of course. You do what you need to do, and I'll be fine. Honestly."

Later, as I put on my coat and scarf, Walter walked up to me, placed his hands on my shoulders and planted a kiss on my forehead. His face was close to mine as he quietly said, "Hang in there today. Text me updates, and call at any time."

I leaned in for a hug, my voice muffled as I spoke into his chest. "I will." Pulling back, I looked at Baxter and said, "You be a good boy and keep Walter company." He wagged his tail in response.

****

The station was even busier than it had been the night before. Gabe just waved me through, and I found Jack, Travis, and Matt huddled around the white board, all talking at once. Jack had the marker and was drawing lines from one side of the board to the other to connect names and places, like a matching game. When I approached, they barely acknowledged my presence until the marker was capped and put down on the ledge.

Jack turned to me, and I asked, "Do you want to catch me up?"

"Just a sec," he said, then turned back to Matt and Travis to give them their next tasks. "With me, with me," he said to me, walking with a clipped stride toward his office.

At his desk, Jack shuffled some papers, then started the update. "Ryan is with Maggie, and they'll be here in a little while. Preston is in the interview room. I've been at him for hours and have really put him through the ringer, but I had to be sure he had nothing to do with this."

"What do you think?"

"He's been thrown for a loop. He had no idea Declan had been deceiving him with his Jekyll and Hyde personality. Unfortunately, he hasn't been able to help us figure out why Declan would kill Eddie and Clive."

"It's got to be the box. Is he going to get into it for us?"

"That's the next step. I actually let him get a little sleep on the cot we keep in the back room, and we just had some food brought in for him." Jack looked at his watch. "We'll take him the box in a few minutes."

"So what about Gina? Any word?"

"She was spotted at a restaurant on her way back to Ohio, and she's being brought back here. Should be here in another hour or so."

"I think you might get some answers now. I would lay good money she won't take the fall for Declan."

"You're right about that." Jack stated, while reaching into his drawer to retrieve the wooden box.

"Let's go have Preston get into this. That way I'll know what I'm dealing with when I talk to Gina." He looked up and added, "I'm assuming you want to come, too."

"You bet! But first, Penny wants to know if she can bring in a cleaning service at the Bennet House. Are you finished there?"

"Yes, tell her she can do whatever she needs."

I texted Penny, giving her the all clear, then we walked down the hall to the interview room.

Preston looked a little rough around the edges, with an early morning five o'clock shadow and bloodshot eyes. The cot Jack provided allowed him to lie down, but I would imagine sleep evaded him. He had just finished breakfast and was putting the trash in the can by the door when we walked in.

He rushed toward me and grabbed my hand. "Oh Alex, I am so sorry. You have to believe me when I say I had no idea. None! I just can't believe what Declan has done."

"I believe you. I saw firsthand what a sociopath he was, so I'm not surprised he could pull off a dual personality for years."

Preston rubbed his face with his hands. "All right, what can I do to help?"

Jack put the box on the table. "We got one compartment open, and we think there is another secret drawer. We need your help finding it. And please, do not touch anything you find. We may need to dust for prints."

Preston perked up. "Sure, I'm happy to help." He took it and ran his hands over the carved box. "This one is a little more complex, but no problem, I can do it."

He went through a series of maneuvers, his hands

245

moving pieces at lightning speed while shifting the angle of the box.

We heard a click, and Preston said, "Voilà!"

A drawer had popped open, and he handed it over to Jack. After putting on gloves, Jack took a small felt bag out of the compartment and placed it in front of him. The three of us looked at it in silence until he opened the bag and dumped the contents onto the table, at which point we all sucked in our breath.

"Whoa," Preston gasped.

Chapter 19

A handful of emeralds had tumbled onto the table. Even in the dimly lit interview room, the green reflected the light brilliantly. These were the most beautiful stones I had ever seen. I leaned over to pick one up but stopped myself and instead grabbed a pen to move them around.

"This one has a slightly bluish tint to it. The color saturation is incredible.

"Those are some big stones," Preston said. "They must be quite valuable."

Jack shoved back from the table and opened the interview room door. "Matt!" he barked. When Matt reached the doorway Jack said, "Get on the horn to the owner of Smythe Family Jewelry and see if someone can come down here to evaluate some gems. And we need to get these dusted for prints ASAP."

"Got it," Matt said, and turned to leave, not even stopping to look at what Jack was talking about.

I couldn't drag my eyes from the emeralds, and said, "Well, this certainly explains the 'why' of the investigation. It would seem Declan had a side business with Eddie and Gina Marks. Didn't Gina say Eddie was supposed to fly out of Philly for a business trip to Brussels?"

Preston spoke up. "I bet Declan made these boxes for Eddie to get the gems through security undetected!

There might even be some metal lining in those drawers to throw off the scanner."

I continued the train of thought. "So Eddie is going from Ohio to Philly, makes a little side trip here to pick up the box, puts the gems inside, along with the Swiss bank account number, in preparation for the flight to Brussels. Under normal circumstances, he delivers the gems, money is transferred to the account, he does a little legit business picking up a piece of art for a buyer, then flies back, and no one is the wiser."

Jack rubbed his chin. "That's believable. So do you think Declan had the gems and passed them to Eddie or was he just the delivery system?"

We both looked at Preston for an answer. "Wow, guys, I don't know what to say. I have no idea how he would have gotten the gems, unless someone brought them to him. Declan hasn't traveled out of the country as long as I've known him. When he went on the road, it was usually by car, and only occasionally by plane if more than a two-day drive. Of course I don't know if he flew out from another city."

"I guess it would depend on who is fencing them, and where the buyer and seller are. Hell, maybe Gina was in on it too," I said. "I can't wait to see what she has to say about this. Would this be why Eddie used a fake name at the motel?"

Jack stood up. "Possibly. His passport was in his own name, so maybe it was just so there would be no trace to Declan. So, first things first. Preston, you are free to leave. It's been a long night, and I appreciate your patience and your assistance. For the time being, I hope you understand I must caution you not to talk about this with anyone. You can go back to the hotel, but frankly, I would just stick to your room until the meeting Alex is holding before the festival opens. Can you do that for me?"

Preston put up his hands. "No argument from me. I just want to go back to the hotel, take a shower, and crawl in bed. I still need to come to terms with all of this and don't really want to talk to anyone anyway. Alex, I don't envy you having to explain things this afternoon."

"I think by then I'll have a clear outline of what happened, and I'll make sure everyone knows that you assisted in the investigation."

"Thank you."

After Jack walked Preston out, we sat in his office hashing over the chronology of what happened, the evidence against Declan, and what he was going to need to get out of Gina.

"What about Declan's car?" I asked.

"Matt went over it with a fine-tooth comb. He not only found Eddie's prints, he also found a receipt from the truck stop with his prints on it, time stamped right around when Clive would have been there. Also, Eddie's phone was in the glove box, with both his and Declan's prints on it."

"He must have taken it off Eddie after he hit him with the car, right?"

"Possibly. There are signs of impact on the front bumper. Trace evidence has been sent to the lab, and we're confident there will be proof Declan killed Eddie with his car."

I started ticking off the points. "So, we know Eddie got in Declan's car. We know all three were at the truck stop around the same time, and while we don't have it on video, it appears Clive saw Declan and then he saw Eddie walk over to meet him."

"Yup, it was just common curiosity. Seeing Declan there caught Clive's attention."

"And seeing him there is why Clive decided to call me. His mistake was saying something to Declan about it, first."

"He probably didn't realize the significance," Jack said, rubbing his eyes.

"But wait, Declan supposedly went back home on Sunday night. But he was here, meeting and then killing Eddie. So did he go back to the Lodge afterward or did he drive home?" I asked.

"I had already checked at the Lodge. He did not return to the hotel, so he must have driven home after he killed Eddie."

I thought back to the list I had made from the video of the comings and goings in the Bennet House lobby, and pulled the sheets out from my bag.

"We actually have some additional evidence. Declan was one of the regulars who was in and out of the closet during the festival." I shuffled through the pages until I found what I was looking for. "But on Monday, he and Clive had a little powwow late in the day in the lobby. Declan went into the closet afterward to get a box. Now, there's no proof he took the chisel when he went in there, but it adds a check mark in the evidence column." I handed the pages over to him.

"Yes. Had he not gone to the closet that day, it could have made things difficult. The weapon had to have been removed after Ryan's demonstration on Monday."

While we were talking, he got a call from the

hospital. Declan had made it through the night, which was the first hurdle to get through, and his status was now critical-but-stable condition.

A few minutes later, Maggie and Ryan arrived. She looked tired, but I was relieved to see her eyes had regained their focus. Ryan said he'd wait out in the reception area, and the three of us went to the interview room.

Jack assured Maggie she was not facing any charges. There was already clear evidence Declan was guilty of murder, and he clarified she was here willingly to give her statement.

I sat beside her while she relayed what transpired at the Bennet House in her own words. Her story lined up with my account of what happened, and when she finished, Jack sat back and took a soft tone. "May I ask you about your relationship with Declan?"

Maggie meekly said, "Yes."

"Looking back, did anything stand out to you as unusual? Did anything give you pause, but under the circumstances, you found other explanations for?"

Maggie leaned her forearms on the table. "I've been thinking about this ever since I woke up this morning. It's so hard to believe I wouldn't have seen some indication of his true personality. But the truth is, Declan showed me what he wanted me to see. He was very careful."

"I'm sure he was," Jack said.

"While at the festival, he played the smart, funny artist. He didn't talk much about his childhood or friends, but quite honestly…" Maggie now fidgeted with embarrassment. "We were a little busy flirting with each other, and then, um…" She couldn't finish the sentence, and put her head down on her arms and bleated, "Oh my gosh, how mortifying."

I put my hand out and lightly shook her arm. "Hey, come on now. There is nothing to be embarrassed about. The guy was a master manipulator, and he charmed the pants off you."

She turned her head toward me and then buried it again in her arms. "Aaughh!"

I shook with silent laughter. "Sorry, honestly, I didn't mean it that way."

She looked at me again, and finding the laughter infectious, joined me. "I was so stupid!"

Jack cleared his throat, knowing we were on the verge of stress-induced hysteria. "Um, okay, we've established there was nothing to indicate who he was outside of the persona he presented."

Maggie sobered and pushed herself upright. "Right. Although, it was a risky move to be seen with—what's her name? Gina?"

"I agree," I stated. "What would make them be so reckless?" I thought for a moment then said, "How does it line up with the timing of you pulling Gina in about the Swiss bank account?"

Jack flipped back through his notes. "She came back in the same afternoon."

I started to see a scene playing out in my head. "Okay, so you tell her you need to talk to her further about some new evidence. She freaks out and calls Declan. They're trying to figure out what evidence it would be—the gems or the bank account? And they needed to come up with a story to cover themselves. He figured they'd be anonymous there in the Café parking lot."

"Could be," Jack said. "Anyway, thank you, Maggie for coming in." He concluded the interview and turned off the recorder before saying, "I'm hoping we'll find out the extent of Gina's involvement, soon. I have an idea how to get her to talk."

We heard a light knock on the door, and Gabe stuck his head in. "Gina Marks is here. Shall I put her next door in interview two?"

"Yes. Offer her something to drink. Make her feel comfortable, and I'll be in shortly. I want her to stew a little while."

"Yessir," Gabe answered with a grin, as he quietly shut the door.

Jack looked from Maggie over to me. "Okay, do either of you have anything else to add?" We both shook our heads.

"Maggie, you are free to go, and if I need to talk to you again, I'll let you know. In the meantime, as I told Preston, lie low for now. Don't talk to anyone except Ryan…and maybe stick with him until Alex's meeting in a few hours with all the artists."

I guessed Jack added the last bit not for her safety, but for her sanity.

"Absolutely," she said. "I'm so embarrassed I really don't want to see anyone else."

I walked Maggie and Ryan out to the parking lot, where we talked things over, and Jack went back to his office to formulate his game plan for the interview with Gina. Coming back through the reception area, I stopped at the coffee table and assessed the risks. As expected from my past experiences, there was a sticky film on the plastic table cloth from spilled coffee and sugar mingling, and the old clumpy powdered creamer

253

made me cringe, but the coffee itself looked less like motor oil than usual.

I looked over at Gabe and held up the carafe. "Who made it today?"

"I did. We decided Jack should no longer be on coffee duty."

I filled two cups and walked them back to Jack's office, where we sat and sipped while he outlined his plan of attack for Gina's interview.

While I was outside, Jack received another call from the hospital. Declan had regained consciousness, but Jack was going to hold this tidbit back from Gina. Travis was on his way to the hospital to get Declan's statement. David, from Smythe Jewelry, had arrived during Maggie's interview, and he'd just completed a quick, rough-estimate appraisal of the emeralds.

Jack tapped the piece of paper on his desk and looked at me with a gleam in his eyes. "Believe it or not, that little handful of emeralds is worth in the neighborhood of a half million dollars. And we lifted Eddie's prints from one of them."

"Woo-wee." I whistled. "That's a pretty strong motive."

"It sure is," he declared.

After what he deemed was the appropriate amount of time, he loaded up a box with all the evidence, and we walked down the hall. I wasn't allowed to sit in, of course, but he granted permission for me to watch.

Jack was a master. He read Gina her rights, and before giving her the opportunity to respond, he told her Declan was not conscious, and things weren't looking good—a slight misdirection—so he needed her help to close the case against him. She seemed to relax a little at this news and agreed to talk to him without an attorney present.

He laid out his evidence. Declan was seen meeting Eddie at the truck stop and was driving the car when Eddie was killed. Gina gave an Emmy-winning performance of looking shocked. He then outlined the evidence from the search of the car, the surveillance footage, the chisel used in Clive's murder, and relayed Declan's confession to me and Maggie the night before. In total, Jack was able to connect the dots that Declan was responsible for both Eddie's and Clive's murder.

Again, Gina face registered shock and dismay. I really wished I had some popcorn. Her performance was excellent. I couldn't help but chuckle, though, when her eyes widened like saucers as he dumped the emeralds on to the table and told her the appraised value of half million dollars. Her shock fell just short of convincing.

Hearing Declan might not come out of the coma, Gina felt safe in laying all the blame at his feet. She blustered and stammered, "Declan and Eddie had a side business of moving gems around the country and abroad. I knew about it, but I had no part in it."

"How did it work?" Jack asked.

"Declan made the boxes to sidestep security, and Eddie did the transporting while he was doing legitimate art buying."

Jack put the photos of her in Declan's car in front of her. "When did your relationship with Declan begin?"

She physically jerked when she saw the photos. "Where did you get these?" But then she expressed remorse, acting the victim. "Oh, it doesn't matter. I feel like such a fool. I allowed myself to be drawn into it about a year ago. I shouldn't have fallen for his phony charm."

"Did Eddie know?"

"No. I know he didn't."

"So what do you think happened? Why would Declan kill him?"

"Right before this trip, Eddie said he thought it was time to get out of the business. He felt the risks were too high, they had made their money, and it was time to get out before they got caught."

"Did he tell Declan this?"

Now she threw Declan under the bus. "Yes. Declan challenged Eddie on the decision and said he didn't want to stop the cash flow he'd been enjoying. Declan told me what happened here. He said they were arguing, and Eddie was mad and got out of Declan's car to walk back to the truck stop, where he had left his own car. Declan hit him in a fit of anger. Afterwards, he felt awful, but it was too late. Eddie was dead."

"I see."

"He said it was an accident, he didn't mean to kill him. But then, Declan called me about having to silence Clive." Her face now registered an appropriate amount of fear and disgust, and she said, "It was a horrific thing Declan did, but I had no choice but to go along and keep quiet, because he told me he would say I was in on the whole thing. And he actually threatened me."

"So what did he want you to do?" Jack asked, playing along with her story.

"Declan told me he had given Eddie the box, but he didn't think Eddie had transferred the gems to the box yet, so he wanted me to check into the same room at the motel and search the places he would normally hide them, like the air vent, under an edge of carpet, or taped behind the headboard. When I came up empty, I told Declan he must have transferred them to the box, and now the box was with the other evidence at the station."

"Did this concern him?"

"No. He said he made the compartments so tricky to get into you'd never find them, so he bided his time until you returned it to me. But then, you called me to come in again. So I met Declan in order to come up with a story for anything you might have found." She pointed to the photos. "That was when these pictures were taken."

She paused to shift in her chair and smooth her hair. "I knew he played around. I also knew he was loyal to me over anyone, so I didn't really care, but I always cautioned him not to get involved with a girl when on a job, but he just didn't listen, and here we are."

"Did you know he was going after Maggie and Alex?"

"No. All I can guess is he saw the box was in the possession of those two women, and he went after them in order to get it back."

Jack tilted his head. "You could have come to me about all of this. It was too late for Eddie, but it might have saved Clive's life and avoided the trauma Alex and Maggie went through."

She leaned forward and gushed, "As I told you, he threatened me. It wasn't safe to do so. I'm horrified to know I was sleeping with a monster. And now I'm learning he not only killed my Eddie, but also that poor man, Clive. I just don't know what to say. It was all

Declan." She sat back, satisfied with her performance.

I had to admit, she was good. She often maintained eye contact when others might look to the side. But I did note some other characteristics that indicated someone was lying. Her body language and vocal register gave her away a few times when she became overly animated or theatrical. That went against her normal character.

Jack discreetly looked down at his phone, then returned his attention to Gina and said, "Thank you for explaining some things. It's a great help." He stood up and removed his cuffs from his belt. "However, Gina Marks, you are under arrest for conspiracy to commit murder, impeding an investigation, and a host of other crimes the DA will lay out for you. Please stand and put your hands behind your back."

"What? What are you talking about? I just told you Declan is responsible for all of this!"

"Oh, you'll be happy to know I just received a text from my deputy, who is at the hospital. Declan has regained consciousness. But you might not be thrilled to hear that he just ratted you out as being a co-conspirator in all of it."

"He's lying!" she shouted.

"Doubtful. He says he has plenty of proof. We already have his phone, and he kept all the texts and voicemail communication between the two of you. He probably assumed he might need them one day."

Gina's features twisted in anger, as she shouted, "That son of a bitch! I swear, I'll kill him if I get my hands on him."

"Now, now, let's not add another charge to the list. I've already read you your rights, but I'm going to urge you to call your lawyer now," Jack said, as he cuffed her hands and marched her out of the room.

I didn't want to run into Gina, so I waited a few minutes before peeking my head out into the hall. Seeing the all clear, I tiptoed back to Jack's office, where I waited until he returned.

He sat heavily in his chair, then gave me an ear-to-ear grin. "Did you enjoy the show?"

"Holy cow, Jack. You rocked it. How the heck did you know Travis would be able to come through before you had finished with her?"

Jack spoke with a lazy drawl. "Oh, I could have kept her talking for a while. And Travis and I had a plan. He told Declan he was under arrest for the murders, and then said Gina was, at that very minute, blaming him for everything. He turned on her in a heartbeat. He said if he was going down, he wasn't going down alone, and gave Travis enough so he could text me the go ahead. The full questioning will happen later, but we have enough to charge and hold them both. I'm sure her cadre of attorneys will be here soon."

"Man, I'm impressed," I marveled, reaching out to give him a high-five.

He chuckled. "Me too. We got lucky. Actually, we are lucky he confessed to you about Clive's murder. And Gina confirmed Eddie's murder. And we haven't even gotten to the gem smuggling, which is a whole different batch of charges with all kinds of complexities because of the international connection."

"Even so, job well done."

He grinned. "I could say the same to you."

Chapter 20

At the Bennet House, Penny had done a good job of keeping the public at bay. There was a volunteer stationed at the entrance to the parking lot, and after she found my name on the clipboard, I was allowed entry. I swept in through the back door after the obligatory foot stomp to release the packed snow from my boots and went past Penny's office to the front lobby. I stood in silence for a moment. The contradiction between the spotlessly clean marble floor and the horrific scene from the night before was tangible.

In the assembly room, Penny was putting a coffee urn and some snacks on a folding table. The chairs were still facing the podium, just as we had left them after the introductory meeting. How strange, to be back in the room where our only concern had been how quickly we could get out of Clive's meeting.

I was first bombarded with hugs and questions from my gang of friends who had been on this journey with me, and then I took a few minutes to chat with everyone else as they arrived. Eventually, I walked to the podium and looked at the room full of friends, both new and old, and felt grateful as I spoke.

"Thank you for coming. I have a quick statement, and then I'm happy to answer whatever questions I can." I cleared my throat before continuing. "This morning, Declan Chapman was charged with two counts of murder…"

I relayed the facts Jack had laid out for me before I left the station and fielded a few questions from the shocked group before wrapping it up. "We have the public arriving shortly, so just a few more notes. Chief Maddox has asked us to refrain from gossiping with the public until he releases his statement to the press this afternoon."

I surveyed the room, and said, "I want to thank you all. It's been quite a week, but we've gotten through it thus far, and we'll continue to get through it together. I definitely could not have handled it without the incredible help from Penny, who's doing a brilliant job handling the business of the Bennet House."

I paused for the round of applause for Penny, who stood shyly at the back of the room. "Penny will relay information about a memorial for Clive. And as Lena said to me recently, Clive knows how hard we worked to find his killer, and we should all take comfort in that. I know I do."

Later, after everyone dispersed, I ran into Penny and Ryan in the kitchen and I took a seat at the table in sudden exhaustion.

"I am beat!" I proclaimed.

"I bet you are. I'm tired, and I didn't go through what you did last night. Why don't you take off and get some rest," Penny suggested. "I can handle things this afternoon."

"I'm not going to leave you holding the bag. You've already done way more than your share."

"I'll help out," Ryan offered. "Maggie doesn't need to be here either, so if she wants to head home, I can cover her station, Elliott can cover mine, and then I can help Penny at the close of the day."

I looked from one to the other, too tired to argue. The adrenaline had finally run out, and I was spent. Plus, my muscles were sore from the struggle with Declan. "I think I might have to take you up on that. I have run out of steam."

I trudged out to my car, drove back to the Workshop on autopilot, and dragged myself up the stairs to my apartment. Walter saw my face and said, "Uh-oh, time for you to get in bed, huh?"

"Yup," I answered, dropping my bag next to the couch. I waved over my shoulder and said, "Make yourself at home, I'll just catch a little nap and see ya in a bit."

****

Sunday

When I woke up, the sun was streaming through the windows. I had a vague memory of leaving the bedroom when I smelled a pizza Walter had ordered for delivery, but the rest was a dark abyss. I lay for a minute, assessing how tired I felt and was surprised to find I was ready to get up and going.

When I emerged, dressed for the day, Walter assessed me briefly before breaking into a wide smile. "Morning! You look like a new person."

"I feel like a new person! Wow, I really zonked out, didn't I? Sorry to have been such bad company."

"No worries. Baxter and I had a great time watching the hockey game. I'm assuming you're heading over to the festival. What's the plan after that?"

"The gang will probably go to the Lodge after the close of the festival at five p.m. What time do you have to leave?"

"I have a meeting in DC tomorrow morning, so if I leave by seven tonight, I'll still get a decent night's sleep."

"Cool. I'll be back later this afternoon."

"I'll see you over there. I'd like to wander around to look at everything, and maybe even shop."

"Of course! You've only seen the inside of the Bennet House during the aftermath with Declan." I shook off a passing cloud and said, "Yes, please come by, you'll have a good time!"

****

There was a spring in my step as I entered the back door of the mansion. I thoroughly enjoyed the day, wandering through each of the rooms, feeling free to embrace all the creativity around me.

I stopped to talk to Annie, whose face registered concern until she saw I had recovered enough to be functioning okay. In the library, Preston and Maggie were making a good effort at normalcy. Patrons were admiring Preston's work, and I noticed he had removed all trace of Declan. Good for him. I was confident he was going to be just fine.

Maggie looked rested and even sported a new pink streak in her hair. I went over and gave her a sideways hug and we gave each other a knowing look; we would talk over our ordeal another time, once we had our own private recovery.

I was on my way to the parlor when my phone rang. Seeing it was Jack, I slipped back toward the office as I answered, "Hey, how are things there?"

"Moving at a rapid pace. Both Declan and Gina are battling it out to try and make a deal."

"I'm assuming no deal for Declan, right?"

"Nope. Two murders and attempted murder, along with gem smuggling, means he won't be offered a deal of any significance."

"Good. I'm glad there's no wiggle room."

"And I have to tell you, it looks like your hunch was right. Declan snuck out over the balcony of his room to go meet Clive. Travis found a couple of deep boot prints under the fresh snow under his balcony, and his prints are on the outside of the slider where he slid the door back open from the outside. He had removed his gloves because of the blood from stabbing Clive."

"Unbelievable."

"And then he went to the bar later, as if nothing had happened, which was what the keycard showed."

"Wow, that's cold."

"Sure is. He hasn't told us where he dumped his clothing, but we'll find it, and I'm sure it will have both his and Clive's DNA on it. As to the smuggling, it will take some time to sort things out with the Feds. Now, how are you doing? Are you coping okay?"

"I'm actually all right. I know I'll have some issues to deal with, but I'm okay."

"Just take things one day at a time. And listen, things were chaotic enough I probably didn't say thank you for all the help. You really worked a lot of angles on this one, and I appreciate it."

"I think we were a pretty darned good team."

"We were. We are. But let's just hope we don't have to do it again any time soon, right?

"Right!"

"Go relax and have some fun tonight."

"Will do. Thanks Jack."

After I ended the call, I found myself welling up,

and I couldn't control it, so I popped into the restroom by the office. I stood at the sink, staring at my reflection in the mirror, and mentally talked myself through the moment. This was normal. I'd been through a lot, and a sudden swell of emotion was to be expected. The emotions escalated, then eventually subsided, and I took a deep breath, dried my eyes, and continued on my way.

****

At the end of the day, even the out-of-towners lingered and decided to congregate at the Lodge for a proper send off. As evening approached, I got a final big bear hug from Hank before he and Twila hit the road.

"I wish you guys didn't have to go. I'll miss you," I lamented.

"Aw, don't you worry, little bird. We'll be back in no time to go over which glass pieces you will want in the new sculpture garden," he said with encouragement.

"I can't wait."

I watched them as they walked out, hand in hand, and my heart swelled with fondness.

Preston and I carved out a few minutes to talk privately before he left. "Are you hanging in there?" I asked.

"I am, thanks in no small part to this amazing group of people," he said. "I think it will really hit when I get back home."

"I know you haven't had time to consider too much, but what will you do about the business?"

"Well, thankfully, we kept everything separate, so I can continue on my own, financially. And I can take my time and figure out my next step."

"Well, if there's ever anything you need, we are here for you."

"Thanks, Alex," he said.

Maggie walked up to us and linked his arm. "Okay, I'm ready if you are."

"Are you taking off?" I asked her.

"I am. I'm still pretty beat and am going to call it an early night. Preston kindly offered to walk me to my car on his way out."

I wondered how long it would take for Maggie to feel safe again, but I shoved those concerns aside and said, "I have a feeling I won't be far behind. Get some rest and I'll see ya in the morning."

Walter had come up behind me. "Time for me to go, too."

"I'm really glad you came," I said.

"Me too." He pulled me in for a quick hug.

"Text me when you get to D.C. tonight, yes?"

"You bet. Now go back in and have some fun."

I watched him pull out of the lot and disappear down the road before turning to go back inside.

Epilogue

Monday

It was good to be back on a normal schedule. The Workshop was buzzing with the artists back in their studios, and our classes had resumed. I reveled in the hustle and bustle of working at the front desk, fielding phone calls, and chatting with people as they came and went.

I walked the halls throughout the morning, peeking through the windows in the doors; Annie was back at her easel with her magnifying visor perched on her nose; Maggie was framing one of her large format pieces for the job she was working on; Ari was mixing colors on her palette; and Shelby held court with the quilting class. JJ and Bitsy were in their studio, animatedly talking and laughing. Hannah and Ethan were quietly and calmly working at their pottery wheels. Ryan was back chiseling on the sculpture I had seen during the search of his studio, and Spencer was scrutinizing a prop composition, getting ready to take the photo for his next painting. All was right with the world.

Later, I jogged upstairs to grab a cup of coffee. While there, I decided to do some quick housekeeping and stepped in to strip the sheets from the guest bed. Walter, of course, had done it already and left everything tucked into a pillow case at the bottom of the bed, with the quilt neatly smoothed back into place. But there was an extra surprise waiting for me. A gift bag was sitting on the bedside table, and my brow scrunched as I sat on the bed, wondering what this was all about.

Baxter, who had jumped on the bed to sit with me, watched as I moved the tissue paper aside and pulled out a beautiful wood box. *What in the world?* I thought to myself. I unfolded the piece of notepaper on top of the box and recognized Walter's handwriting. I read aloud, "Another little puzzle for you to work out."

I looked at Baxter. "Are you kidding me? Another damned puzzle box?" I said, with exasperation.

I turned the box this way and that. However, as it turned out, this one wasn't complicated. There was a small panel button on the side, and when I pushed it, a drawer popped open. Inside was one of those little Valentine candy hearts stamped with "Be Mine." I held it in my hand and sat there for a moment mulling this over, then I popped the candy in my mouth and set the box aside.

I called Baxter while putting on my coat, and we went down the stairs and out the front doors into the bright sunlight. A fresh snow had fallen the night before, and the scene was postcard perfect. While we walked, I pulled out my cell phone and tapped Walter's number. "Hey, it's me…"

A word about the author...

Sydney Abrams' arts and crafts mystery series is steeped in a life's experience in the arts coupled with a love for mystery books. She was immersed in both these worlds from childhood, and that influence stayed with her as an adult. Sydney has created artwork for auctions and commissions and has been part of an art group of professional and amateur artists for twenty years. Literature and the arts go hand in hand, but these worlds collided when Sydney realized that her art group offered up the perfect cast of characters for a cozy mystery.

A Deadly Craft is the second book in her Arts and Crafts Mystery series.

To learn more about Sydney, please visit
https://www.sydneyabrams.com/

Thank you for purchasing
this publication of The Wild Rose Press, Inc.

For questions or more information
contact us at
info@thewildrosepress.com.

The Wild Rose Press, Inc.
www.thewildrosepress.com